$\mathcal{P}$RIDE AND $\mathcal{P}$REJUDICE $\mathcal{S}$EQUELS

(Three Jane Austen Inspired Novellas)

CHERYL BOLEN

Some of the praise for Cheryl Bolen's writing:

"One of the best authors in the Regency romance field today." – *Huntress Reviews*

"Bolen's writing has a certain elegance that lends itself to the era and creates the perfect atmosphere for her enchanting romances." – *RT Book Reviews*

The Counterfeit Countess (Brazen Brides, Book 1)
Daphne du Maurier award finalist for Best Historical Mystery

"This story is full of romance and suspense. . . No one can resist a novel written by Cheryl Bolen. Her writing talents charm all readers. Highly recommended reading! 5 stars!" – *Huntress Reviews*

"Bolen pens a sparkling tale, and readers will adore her feisty heroine, the arrogant, honorable Warwick and a wonderful cast of supporting characters." – *RT Book Reviews*

One Golden Ring (Brazen Brides, Book 2)
"*One Golden Ring*...has got to be the most PERFECT Regency Romance I've read this year." – *Huntress Reviews*

Holt Medallion winner for Best Historical, 2006

Lady By Chance (House of Haverstock, Book 1)
Cheryl Bolen has done it again with another sparkling Regency romance. . .Highly recommended – *Happily Ever After*

The Bride Wore Blue (Brides of Bath, Book 1)
Cheryl Bolen returns to the Regency England she knows so well. . .If you love a steamy Regency with a fast pace, be sure to pick up *The Bride Wore Blue*. – *Happily Ever After*

With His Ring (Brides of Bath, Book 2)
"Cheryl Bolen does it again! There is laughter, and the interaction of the characters pulls you right into the book. I look forward to the next in this series." – *RT Book Reviews*

The Bride's Secret (Brides of Bath, Book 3)
(originally titled *A Fallen Woman*)
"*W*hat we all want from a love story...Don't miss it!"
– *In Print*

To Take This Lord (Brides of Bath, Book 4)
(originally titled *An Improper Proposal*)
"Bolen does a wonderful job building simmering sexual tension between her opinionated, outspoken heroine and deliciously tortured, conflicted hero." – *Booklist of the American Library Association*

My Lord Wicked
Winner, International Digital Award for Best Historical Novel of 2011.

With His Lady's Assistance (Regent Mysteries, Book 1)
"A delightful Regency romance with a clever and personable heroine matched with a humble, but intelligent hero. The mystery is nicely done, the romance is enchanting and the secondary characters are enjoyable." – *RT Book Reviews*

Finalist for International Digital Award for Best Historical Novel of 2011.

A Duke Deceived
"*A Duke Deceived* is a gem. If you're a Georgette Heyer fan, if you enjoy the Regency period, if you like a genuinely sensuous love story, pick up this first novel by Cheryl Bolen."
– *Happily Ever After*

Books by Cheryl Bolen

Regency Romance

Brazen Brides Series
   Counterfeit Countess (Book 1)
   His Golden Ring (Book 2)
   Oh What A (Wedding) Night (Book 3)
   Marriage of Inconvenience (Book 4)

House of Haverstock Series
   Lady by Chance (Book 1)
   Duchess by Mistake (Book2)
   Countess by Coincidence (Book 3)

The Brides of Bath Series:
   The Bride Wore Blue (Book 1)
   With His Ring (Book 2)
   The Bride's Secret (Book 3)
   To Take This Lord (Book 4)
   Love in the Library (Book 5)
   A Christmas in Bath (Book 6)

The Regent Mysteries Series:
   With His Lady's Assistance (Book 1)
   A Most Discreet Inquiry (Book 2)
   The Theft Before Christmas (Book 3)
   An Egyptian Affair (Book 4)

The Earl's Bargain
My Lord Wicked
His Lordship's Vow
A Duke Deceived

Novellas:
Christmas Brides (3 Regency Novellas)

Inspirational Regency Romance
Marriage of Inconvenience

Romantic Suspense
Texas Heroines in Peril Series:
Protecting Britannia
Capitol Offense
A Cry in the Night
Murder at Veranda House

Falling for Frederick

American Historical Romance
*A Summer to Remember (*3 American Historical Romances)

World War II Romance
It Had to be You

Pride and Prejudice Sequels

Miss Darcy's New Companion

(Jane Austen Sequels, Book 1)

CHERYL BOLEN

$\mathcal{P}$rologue

"Were you, my dearest, satisfied with Miss Wetherspoon?" Elizabeth Darcy asked her bridegroom as he came strolling into her study at Pemberley. He and the prospective companion for Miss Georgiana Darcy had been closeted in his library for almost an hour. This convinced Elizabeth that Miss Wetherspoon must be a most determined talker, for though the Darcys had been married but two days, Elizabeth perfectly understood her husband's deficit of language.

He came to stand beside the desk where his bride was penning a letter and brushed a kiss upon her cheek. Her pen stilled, her lashes lowered. All her coherent thoughts departed whenever her dear Darcy demonstrated his tender affections. She gloried in the knowledge that their love had transformed her formerly stiff Mr. Darcy.

"I took the liberty of engaging the lady for Georgiana's companion," said he.

Elizabeth whirled to face him. "I pray you did not make so hasty a decision just because we are scheduled to be in Dover by week's end. I am perfectly willing to put off our wedding trip until you are perfectly satisfied with a candidate to replace Mrs. Annesley. Italy will be there whenever it is convenient for us to see it." Elizabeth kept to herself her opinion that no one would be capable of filling the exceedingly competent Mrs.

Annesley's shoes.

"I flatter myself that the young woman will do very well."

A slowly unfurling smile brightened Elizabeth's face. "How very agreeable! See, my darling, just yesterday you were sunk in despair because Mrs. Annesley must leave your service."

He grimaced. "Wretched timing, her sister dying and leaving all those motherless nieces and nephews to Mrs. Annesley's care."

"But all's well that ends well. Was Miss Wetherspoon as genteel as my Aunt Gardner recommends?"

He nodded. "Her manners could not be improved upon, and she appears to be possessed of uncommon understanding."

"Which, I will own, is a bit astonishing, given that her father is said to be a fool."

"Actually, Mr. Wetherspoon—who is sometimes most cruelly referred to as Mr. Wether*fool*—was a noted scholar at Oxford. His misfortunes derive from his propensity to invest in unsound schemes which promise unreasonably large dividends."

Her Aunt Gardner had acquainted Elizabeth with the failure of Mr. Wetherspoon's sugar plantation which resulted in the loss of their home in Bloomsbury, a loss that left homeless his ten unmarried children of varying ages. Aunt Gardner had explained that as the second eldest of the children (though, at five and twenty, she was no longer a child), Miss Lucy Wetherspoon was accustomed to looking after the needs of her younger siblings, and she was in possession of more sense than her father.

It then occurred to Elizabeth to inquire upon the lady's appearance. "I suppose that since she is unwed at five and twenty, she must be exceedingly plain."

Dear Mr. Darcy hesitated a moment before answering. "I daresay my judgment is faulty, but I believe her to be tolerably good looking. In fact, I wondered what could account for her failure to attract a husband."

As critical as her husband was, Elizabeth determined that Miss Wetherspoon must be very handsome to produce such a description. "Do you know, I recall my aunt mentioning Miss Wetherspoon's misfortune in matrimony. She was jilted."

"Then perhaps she is not a competent judge of character."

Elizabeth thought of women like her dear friend Charlotte who had not the luxury of wedding where love blossomed but wedding where a lone proposal was extended. Many a woman viewed a loveless marriage as superior to the life of an old maid. How grateful she was that she'd had the courage to court spinsterhood rather than leap at her first proposal of marriage. "We need only hope she can protect dearest Georgiana from fortune hunters." She set down her pen. "Do you know, my dearest love, that since Charlotte has expressed an interest in seeing Pemberley, I believe I'll have her come for a brief stay whilst we are from England. I can persuade her that I need her assurances Miss Darcy is in good hands with Miss Wetherspoon, but in reality I shall spare you the necessity of playing host to Charlotte's odious husband."

Darcy regarded his wife with devilishly sparkling eyes. "How well my wife understands me. An excellent plan! I have also taken the liberty of requesting Lord Fane to look in upon Georgiana. Be assured I will not give Miss Wetherspoon sole responsibility over my sister while we are out of the country. Lord Fane said that upon his return from London next month, he will call on her nearly every day during our absence."

She eyed him from beneath lowered brows. "I declare, Mr. Darcy, you mean for Georgiana to capture his heart!"

"I have always thought they would suit well."

"Then he's younger than you?"

"No. He's four years older than I. He's two and thirty."

"You do not think she would prefer someone closer to her own age? Two and thirty is twice her age!"

"It's good for the wife to look up to her husband."

Elizabeth took that for an invitation to move from her chair and fit herself to her husband—which necessitated her gazing up into his most beloved face. "Indeed it is, my love."

$\mathcal{C}$hapter 1

One month later

"I fear, my dear Miss Darcy, that despite your many attributes you will be a sad wallflower when you come out if you cannot manage to liberate your tongue. Depend upon it, young gentlemen are sure to mistake your silence for disinterest."

Miss Lucy Wetherspoon felt badly that she had criticized the dear young lady, but Mr. Darcy had made it clear when he engaged Lucy that he expected her to groom his young sister for a successful come-out. Sadly, success was measured by the ability to capture a husband.

Lucy meant no flattery when she remarked upon her charge's abundant attributes. While the lady was not a beauty, she was tolerably good looking. Compensating for Miss Darcy's lack of beauty was her unerring eye for fashionable clothing that accentuated her green eyes, fair hair, and slender figure. No one could rival the beauty of her singing. Moreover, Miss Darcy was possessed of an exceedingly sweet temperament. Few would ever presume that so modest a person could accompany a fortune of thirty thousand pounds.

The afternoon light that streamed in from the tall windows in the drawing room fell on Miss Darcy's flaxen hair, with silvery strands glancing off her smart coiffure. Lucy could not help but be struck by how so lovely a chamber could render everything in it lovely. Miss Darcy's elegant muslin dress of pale green draped beautifully along the slight curve of her youthful figure as well as over the golden damask of the settee upon which she sat. Lucy picked up her sketch book and immediately began to try to capture the lady. What a pretty watercolour this would make!

"I have little need to talk when you, my dear Miss Wetherspoon, can give voice to my opinions with far more precision and clarity than ever I could."

Oh, dear. Lucy *was* possessed of a lamentable habit of incessant babbling. She really ought to allow Miss Darcy the opportunity not only to form her opinions but also to impart those opinions. "Forgive my unmannered domination of conversation. It *is,* however, my profound belief that men would not wish to unite themselves with empty-headed females so I would encourage *you* to contribute to what is being said."

"You must allow that I am learning a great deal how to think merely by absorbing your own sage observations."

"I should be horrified if I am guilty of imposing my opinions on an unformed mind—not that yours is unformed," Lucy readily amended. "It is just that you've not been enough in the world."

"Permit me to say that my own judgment is not so deficient that I cannot acknowledge the merits of your thoughts."

"Merits of my thoughts?" Lucy questioned. "Pray, enlighten me."

"I have profited ever so much from you. From you I have learned how the City of London is governed. You have also explained about the offices of Parliament. I must own, I never quite understood what duties were carried out by the Lord Chancellor. I have also learned about plantations in the West Indies, and about all the most fashionable painters. I wonder how it is you know so very much?"

Lucy shrugged. "When one has ten siblings, there is great variety of experiences to share."

"You're fortunate to have so large a family."

And how Lucy missed them! When the house on Milsop Street had been lost, the ten unmarried siblings had scattered like leaves in autumn's wind. The three oldest boys were now in His Majesty's Royal Navy; Sarah and Margaret had gone into service like her, only as governesses rather than companions; and the four youngest had been shipped off to various aunts and uncles, with Papa promising to unite the family once again when "My ship comes in, laddies and lasses."

Lucy directed her smiling countenance upon Miss Darcy. "And you are blessed to have so devoted a brother."

It pleased Lucy to see Georgiana Darcy smile. When she smiled as she was doing now, Miss Darcy could almost be a beauty. The girl had the misfortune to be as reserved as her brother. Even though Lucy had spoken to Mr. Darcy only at the initial interview and on the day of his departure, a more solemn or quiet man Lucy was sure she had never met.

"I believe it would please my brother if I did not have a season in London at all."

"No matter how much your brother enjoys being at Pemberley—and I fully comprehend

Pemberley's claims on anyone's admiration—he will not begrudge you two months in the Capital."

"Oh, it's not his love of Pemberley which contributes to my belief. It's his long-held view that I should marry Lord Fane."

Lucy's eyes widened. "Surely your brother—who obviously has wed a woman he loves most violently—does not expect you to marry at his whim?"

"No, he would never do that. It's just that he poorly conceals his aspirations for me. He's repeated to me on many occasions how fondly my parents wished to see me marry the Earl of Fane."

Lucy set down her sketch pad and regarded her young companion. "And your opinion of Lord Fane?"

"He is all that is admirable, but I cannot say that he has ever demonstrated any kind of preference for me."

"That can certainly be attributed to your youth. How perverse it would be for a man to crave a union with a child!"

Miss Darcy pouted. "I am no longer a child."

"No, you are not. You will make some man a very fine wife in the very near future." Lucy's brows lifted. "Would marriage to this Lord Fane please you?"

"At present, it's impossible to say."

The door to the drawing room drew open and Tibbs made a show of clearing his throat. "Lord Fane to see Miss Darcy."

* * *

Alexander Farrington, the Earl of Fane, was beastly glad to be back in Derbyshire after several months in London. How clean the air was here! How gratifying it was to ride his horse over hills and vales that had belonged to Farringtons for the past five centuries. How satisfying it was to sleep in the same bed in which the last four Earls of Fane had been born.

A pity the roof leaked. And an even greater pity it was that he lacked the funds necessary to replace Bodworth's ancient roof.

His mother, who had happily given up life at Bodworth House to reside in more modest circumstances in the Capital, could understand neither his love of the country nor his aversion to marrying an heiress—and she never ceased imparting those opinions to him. "If you love Bodworth House so well, you must resolve to wed an heiress," she told him with the same regularity she lambasted country life. "And Miss Georgiana Darcy would well satisfy all your requirements. Even were she not possessed of a thirty-thousand-pound dowry, she would make an agreeable wife. She comes from good stock. I know no man who was ever more amiable than her father. You could do much worse."

Perhaps it was time to capitulate to marrying an heiress. Not that he had ever desired to do anything so mercenary. But at two and thirty and having been a great deal in Society, he had begun to despair of ever making a love match. He had never once even fancied himself in love. Yet it was time he marry, time he see to securing the succession, and since he had failed to find a lady upon whom he could bestow his affections, he would be a very great fool not to seek an heiress for his countess.

Those were his thoughts as he rode over the three miles that separated Bodworth from Pemberley. He had not seen Miss Darcy since she had left the schoolroom—which was only during the past year. Darcy had employed an army of masters to teach her every accomplishment before he would be willing to launch the poor girl into a Society that was certain to prey upon her.

He tried to recall what Miss Darcy had looked like, but his only impression was of frailty and fairness and an unprepossessing personality that was perfectly fitted to such an appearance. Her aunt, Lady Catherine de Bourgh, who admittedly had tried to foist her own homely daughter upon Fane, had said her niece had turned out to be *wholly without beauty*. "By Jove, Lord Fane, the chit is as tall as you!" Lady Catherine had said. Even given that his height was not great, Fane credited Miss Darcy with uncommon height for a girl.

Once he was admitted to Pemberley and presented himself to the Darcy's butler, he found himself following that same butler up a curving staircase to the drawing room. From that chamber he heard two sweet feminine voices. *The companion!* He should be thankful not to be alone with Miss Darcy, who was but half his age. The older woman was insurance against long pauses in conversation.

As soon as he stepped into the huge, sunny drawing room, he recognized Georgiana Darcy. She was very fair, very tall, and very young.

But he noticed her for only a second.

Like a beast who forgets the fallen berries for meaty fare, his gaze abandoned Miss Darcy to take in the loveliness of her companion. To be sure, this plainly dressed companion was in a subservient position, but that in no way detracted from her extraordinary beauty.

She was a small thing, though not especially youthful. She had to be at least five and twenty. Most astonishingly, how could a woman of such loveliness not have snared a husband in a quarter of a century? She must be deficient not only in birth but also in understanding. That must be the explanation! She had to be exceedingly simple minded.

Lustrous dark hair drew away from the porcelain perfection of a flawless face from which peered enormous smoky brown eyes. It was difficult to judge her figure for it was covered in a bombazine of dark blue with a high collar.

Her dress was in opposition to Miss Darcy's, which dipped low in the front, in accordance with current fashion. Miss Darcy's breasts—or lack of—were sadly unfitted for such a display.

He must not look too long at the companion, lest she think him ill mannered. He went first to Miss Darcy and offered her a bow. "How good it is to see Miss Darcy all grown up."

She managed a thin smile, but she looked nervous, and her voice trembled. "How good of you to come, my lord." Then quickly swinging her gaze to the companion, she added, "May I present to you Miss Wetherspoon?"

He moved to the gilt chair where Miss Wetherspoon sat, and he bowed before her.

Unlike Miss Darcy, she offered him her gloved hand, and he made a display of kissing it. *So she has been in Society.*

"Mr. Darcy said he had asked you to call on us when you returned from London," Miss Wetherspoon said. "How very good it is of you to come. Tell me, my lord, are you happy to be back in Derbyshire?"

"I'm always happiest in Derbyshire." His comment met with silence. It was obvious to him the more outgoing Miss Wetherspoon awaited a response from Miss Darcy, but when that response was not forthcoming, she prompted, "Is that not your brother's very sentiments, Miss Darcy?"

So Georgiana Darcy was possessed of no more conversational skills than her brother. Not that there was anything objectionable in Darcy. Given years of acquaintance, he improved to a more satisfying degree than aged cheese.

Miss Darcy nodded. "Indeed."

Miss Darcy's responses were to be limited to single words. Thank God for the companion!

He continued to stand there, awkwardly awaiting an invitation to be seated.

"Perhaps, Miss Darcy, you'd like to ask your guest to sit?" Miss Wetherspoon suggested.

Miss Darcy turned scarlet. "Oh, forgive me, my lord! I am unaccustomed to serving as a hostess."

He directed a smile upon her. "Which is perfectly understandable. I daresay this is your first experience of being the Lady of the House."

"Indeed." Her nervous gaze darted to the sofa. "Pray, my lord, won't you sit upon the sofa?"

He sat facing the two ladies, Miss Darcy opposite, Miss Wetherspoon to his left. "Have you heard from your brother since he departed?"

"No."

Miss Wetherspoon whirled at her charge. "I think, my dear, his lordship was inquiring if you'd had news of your brother since he left."

Obviously, the companion's understanding was greater than that of the young lady of presumably superior rank—eliminating stupidity as the reason for Miss Wetherspoon's spinsterhood.

"Oh, dear me. I did not hear from my brother, but his wife dispatched a letter from Gibraltar."

"And their voyage was agreeable?" he asked.

The tender-hearted Miss Darcy's face crumpled. "Alas, no. My brother was frightfully ill, but dear Lizzy assures me that once he stood on firm ground, his complaints were thoroughly resolved."

Another silence stretched before them.

"Can we offer you tea, my lord?" the companion asked.

"Thank you, Miss Wetherspoon, but I'm not thirsty at present."

Once more, a silence stole over the chamber. He could tell from the lively flash in Miss Wetherspoon's fine eyes that were it up to her, there would never be a lag in conversation, but she was struggling to keep her place.

"And your brother?" Miss Darcy finally asked. Only then did her face grow expressive. "How is he?"

Fane's brows lowered. "To which brother would you be referring?"

"Forgive me. I refer to Robert." She coloured. "I mean, Captain Farrington."

Some dozen years younger than Fane, Robert had spent much time with Georgiana Darcy when they were children. "He enjoys the military life very well."

"Do you not worry about him?" Miss Darcy asked, her face once again crumpling.

He bloody well did! "I do most grievously."

"I remember him in my prayers every night and when I go to church on Sunday, too."

He would wager that Robert's presence would have succeeded in loosening the lady's tongue. He gave her a grateful nod. "As do I."

It was too much for Miss Wetherspoon to remain complacent. "How I pray this wretched war would end!"

He happily eyed her. "I couldn't agree with you more."

Another silence loomed.

"So, Miss Darcy," said he, "have you set a date for your presentation?"

"Not an exact date, no. We will once my brother and his wife return from their wedding trip."

"Then there will be balls and assemblies at Almack's." He directed his attention to Miss Wetherspoon. "Have you been to Almack's?" As soon as he said the words, he wished to detract them.

"I have not had that pleasure, my lord. I am bereft not only of rank but also of acquaintance with persons who move in those circles."

"Then it is a very great loss for the young men who attend those gatherings."

She favored him with a smile. "I am flattered by your words—especially since I am no longer young."

"Both of you ladies seem very young to me." He drew his breath. "I came to see if I can persuade the two of you to ride with me. I will own, I have sorely missed riding over these Derbyshire hills."

"Miss Wetherspoon doesn't ride."

He directed his attention to that lady. "How can that be?"

"I have lived my entire life in London, my lord."

How was it he had never met her? Despite the drabness of her clothing, she was definitely a gentleman's daughter. Would she not at some point have been sure to cross the same paths as he? One possessed of such perfection of appearance would be the toast of the town. Yet, he would most certainly have remembered had he ever met her.

"Actually, my lord," Miss Darcy amended, "I have just begun teaching Miss Wetherspoon how to ride as she is teaching me how to speak Italian."

The Beauty addressed him with a good-natured laugh. "I must own, my lord, that Miss Darcy is progressing far better in her endeavors than I." She flashed him a smile that revealed stunning white teeth that were as perfect as her milky skin.

"I am impressed that you speak Italian." He wondered if perhaps her mother might be Italian, but he would not ask so indelicate a question.

"Oh, Miss Wetherspoon speaks six languages!"

The companion shrugged. "If one counts Latin—which you will own, I have little opportunity to speak."

How astonishing! "You are fluent in Latin?" he asked, incredulous. He had never met a woman who was possessed of such a skill.

She watched him with lively eyes as she shrugged. "*Sine scientia ars nihil est.*"

"*Without knowledge, skill is nothing,*" he murmured. "How is it you learned Latin?"

"Papa is possessed of the bizarre notion that his daughters should be educated in the same manner as his sons."

"Do not tell me you studied Pythagorean theorem!" he inquired, astonishment in his voice.

She gave an impish smile while nodding her head. "Another useless accomplishment of Mr. Benjamin Wetherspoon's daughters. Tell me, Lord Fane, to your knowledge has Euclidean geometry ever been introduced into a drawing room?"

How refreshing to meet with a woman with such a sense of humor, and who also was exceedingly learned. He chuckled. "A wise observation, to be sure, Miss Wetherspoon."

"I declare," Miss Darcy said, "you must be conversing in Greek!"

"You're very close, my dear Miss Darcy," said he before redirecting his attentions upon the linguistic, mathematical scholar. "For what purpose could your father have wished his daughters to acquire such knowledge?"

"He said such a distinction would make his daughters more eligible to attract husbands." She gave a little self-conscious laugh. "Unfortunately, Papa was—as has often been his lot—wrong. We are sad failures. Only one of his daughters has achieved such an ambition, and it grieves me to say her husband is not so very great a conquest." She laughed. It was not a self-conscious laugh over her failure. It was more like she found such failures of great amusement.

Her comment about being a failure made him feel awkward, as if he should assure her of the erroneous nature of her statement. But a woman still unmarried at her age *was* a failure.

For once, Miss Darcy rescued him from the uncomfortable silence. "Miss Wetherspoon is also fluent in French, Spanish, and German."

"Then I am possessed of great admiration for Mr. Wetherspoon. Fluency in any language is always commendable." He eyed Miss Darcy. "And you? Which languages do you speak?"

"At present, only English and French, but Miss Wetherspoon says I have an aptitude for Italian." She turned to her companion. "And I am happy to say that Miss Wetherspoon's aptitude for riding improves daily—though she has much fear to conquer."

"You are afraid of horses?" he asked, clearly dismayed. All his sisters rode as well as he.

"You might say frightfully so," Miss Wetherspoon said with a nervous laugh.

His eyes narrowed with concern. "What is there about so docile a beast to give fright? Darcy's stables are the best in Britain."

"You, my lord, might refer to those huge beasts as docile, but I assure you they fairly terrify me. It's a very great drop from the top of one of Mr. Darcy's horses to the hard earth beneath their hooves."

Even though her riding skills were sure to be woefully inferior, he found himself looking forward to riding with the novice.

His eyes met hers. "I give you my word, Miss Wetherspoon, you'll never fall as long as I am riding beside you."

He found himself pleased that he had come to Pemberley that afternoon.

$\mathcal{C}$hapter 2

How fortunate was Miss Darcy to attract a suitor like Lord Fane. Though he was not a particularly handsome man, there was something in his appearance which Lucy was obliged to admit she found appealing.

Lord Fane was not nearly so tall as Mr. Darcy. He was probably no more than five-feet- eleven— which was a great deal taller than Lucy. Despite deficiencies in height, everything about him bespoke power and masculinity. She did not think she had ever seen a more well-formed man. He was in possession of wide shoulders, trim waist, and muscled legs.

It was difficult to judge his age. Perhaps he was thirty, give or take a year. Or two. He must have been riding much of late for his skin was tanned, and his stylishly-cut light brown hair bore golden threads. There was nothing objectionable in his pleasant face, and when he smiled he seemed handsome, but perhaps that was owing to the excellence of his white teeth.

Though he dressed in well-tailored clothing, his breeches were faded, and the elbows of his woolen frock coat showed signs of having been worn these past few years. Was that because he was no slave to fashion, or because funds were low? The latter would certainly explain Lord Fane's enticement to come to Pemberley.

Such a thought made Lucy feel traitorous toward sweet Miss Darcy, but Lucy's mind was merely traversing in the same direction as others' would. Being an heiress was a difficult lot, to be sure. How would an heiress ever know her prospective husband loved her or her money?

What a heavy burden was placed upon the shoulders of the rich. Lucy should be happy she was bereft of fortune. If she ever attracted a husband, she would know he loved her for herself.

Then she grew melancholy. *I shall never wed.* She lacked the attractions—namely, birth and pecuniary considerations—to secure the affections of men who appealed to her. Now, at five and twenty, she had been firmly and irrevocably pushed to the back of the Old Maid Shelf. As she eyed the exceedingly appealing Lord Fane, she lamented most grievously that it would never be in her power to attract a fine man such as he.

After Miss Darcy changed clothing, she and Lucy met Lord Fane at the rear of Pemberley where he and a groom waited with three saddled horses. Had there been any way to avoid coming, Lucy would have. Not just because of her extraordinary fear of horses, but even more so because of her humiliation over her garment. While Miss Darcy looked fetching in a riding habit of scarlet velvet, Lucy continued the afternoon in her serviceable bombazine.

She had never claimed to be fashionable. But she was proud.

Lord Fane, with cordiality, greeted Miss Darcy first. Then his gaze traveled to Lucy. And stopped. During those seconds his lazy amber eyes skimmed over the length of her she knew he must be thinking how utterly unfashionable was she.

She had never felt more humiliated.

"I have been assured," he told her, his hand stroking the deep, chocolate-coloured hide of the beautiful beast, "that the horse you'll ride today is the most gentle horse in the kingdom."

Miss Darcy tossed a glance at her companion. "That is true, Miss Wetherspoon. My brother looked long and hard to procure the perfect mount for his young godson."

Though Lucy did not doubt the veracity of Georgiana Darcy's statement, she was not assured. Her thoughts quickly flicked to the generous Mr. Darcy, who had gone to so much effort to procure a special mount for his godchild.

The groom assisted Miss Darcy in mounting her spirited horse, while Lord Fane stepped up to Lucy. "Permit me to help you." Then his big hands encircled her waist, and he easily lifted her toward the saddle.

His very touch had the effect of accelerating her heartbeat. No man had ever before touched her so intimately. Not even Lawrence.

After she was mounted on the beast, nervously gripping the pommel, he stood beside her horse, stroking it again and sweet talking to it as if it were a lover. Not that she could understand one word out of five he uttered.

Then he directed his attention upon Lucy. "Will you be all right while I mount my horse?"

"Can you assure me this one's not going anywhere?" she challenged. While her voice rang with levity, she was terrified at the thought of the horse going into a rage and rocketing away.

"He won't move until your heels connect with his sides, but if it will make you feel less frightened, I shall have the groom help with your reins until I finish mounting."

"It *will* make me feel less frightened." What a spineless ninny he must think her!

Once they started to ride across the velvety green lawn of Pemberley's park, he attempted to offer comforting words. "I should like to assure you, Miss Wetherspoon, that in my entire life I have never seen anyone thrown from a horse noted for its gentleness. I daresay, like a leopard's spots do not change, neither will the agreeable habits of a mild beast."

"That is true," Miss Darcy agreed.

"It is very kind of both of you to try to ease my fears, but it is a mistake to believe an animal—or person—cannot change for the worse. Take Mr. Throckmorton, who lived near us in Bloomsbury. He was affectionate to his children, indulgent to his wife, and generous to his church. Never did we see him that he did not extend cordial greetings and display amiable smiles. " Lucy's voice still rang with levity when she delivered the surprise ending: "Then thirty years into his harmonious marriage, he murdered his wife as she slept."

"Oh, how horrid!" Miss Darcy shrieked, her face collapsing, her hands clutching at her chest.

Lord Fane gave a deep chuckle, then he eyed her with a serious expression. "If it is any consolation, Miss Wetherspoon, I give you my word that whilst I am at your side, no harm will ever come to you."

Smiling with amusement, she looked askance at her male companion. "Then you must vow never to return to Bodworth, my lord."

His refusal to comment confirmed that her aggressive manner of speaking to a peer of the realm was not acceptable. What a pity that Lucy had never been one to do what was expected of her.

When they reached the copse, they turned westerly and began to ride toward the rise of a hill. To her dismay, Lord Fane began to chuckle. Since he was Miss Darcy's suitor, Lucy thought it should be Miss Darcy, not herself, who should comment upon his mirth, but the young lady was much too inhibited in his company to speak freely.

Finally, Lucy turned to the earl. "I beg that you impart to us what you find so humorous."

"I believe, Miss Wetherspoon, you have just explained why you have never married."

It took her a moment to realize the direction of his thoughts. "I assure you, my lord," she snapped with outrage, "My fear of horses does not extend to men. I don't abhor all men because of Mr. Throckmorton's heinous act."

"But your story does make one think," Miss Darcy said in a woeful voice.

What an imbecile Lord Fane must think Lucy! As they rode on in silence, his lordship never more than an arm's length from her, she mulled over his comment. She began to be flattered that her marital state had occupied his thoughts at all. And if he were looking for a reason why a woman of her age had never wed, that too was flattering. She knew without conceit that she was considered to possess a pleasing appearance. Lord Fane must have noticed that as well. Which was also flattering.

Were she blessed with Miss Darcy's birth and fortune, Lucy thought with a pride she was powerless to suppress, she could have had the opportunity to be wooed by a man like the Earl of

Fane.

But the only men who ever wooed her were not ones she would have. Except for Lawrence. And that ended disastrously.

Her days of being wooed were over. She was consigned now and until the end of her days to being the drably dressed paid companion to wealthy young ladies.

As they came to the lake, Miss Darcy's gray mount was stopped close to water's edge. "I wanted you to see our lake, Miss Wetherspoon. It's a great favorite, and the fishing is said to be uncommonly good."

The lake was vast, with trees at the opposite shore, hills rising above the tree line. At its narrowest point, a formal, Romanesque bridge of creamy coloured plaster spanned the lake.

"Mr. Darcy is kind enough to allow me to use it whenever I like." He gave a little snort. "When I was a lad, this belonged to our family. My father sold it to the late Mr. Darcy."

An edge of disappointment crept into his voice. Had his father been one of those men who gambled away his family's fortunes at the clubs on St. James?

Perhaps Miss Wetherspoon and Lord Fane *did* have something in common. Her Papa had not lost his fortune at the gaming tables, but her father gambled his volatile fortunes upon unsound speculations on the Exchange and on islands decimated by hurricanes. The results of the two types of gambling were the same.

Since Miss Darcy was once again reduced to silence, Lucy responded to the earl. "Then you are blessed to receive both the enjoyment of the lake and the money it contributed to your family's coffers." Her gaze slowly fanned across the lake and the stunning land surrounding it. "It's a beautiful spot."

"Should you like to dismount and cross the bridge on foot?" he asked. "Perhaps sit at the bench to fully absorb the beauty of Capability's design?"

Indeed she would, but it was not *her* wishes which needed to be consulted, but Miss Darcy's. Her gaze flicked to the younger lady. "What would you prefer, Miss Darcy?"

"I have seen the lake hundreds of times. I encourage you to enjoy the tranquil setting for a few moments while I take a gallant gallop across the vale."

"You two go on," Lucy said. She was anxious to dismount but afraid of doing so.

Lord Fane leapt from his horse as easily as getting up from a chair. "Allow me to assist you, Miss Wetherspoon."

The next thing she knew, those sturdy, muscled arms reached for her, and those large, manly hands cinched around her waist as he lifted her from the horse. Then he turned to Miss Darcy. "If it is not objectionable to you, I'll stay here with Miss Wetherspoon. My poor beast has already been pushed to his limits earlier today."

Miss Darcy flashed a quick smile, nodded, then burst forth like the shot of a musket ball.

Lord Fane did Lucy the kindness of offering his crooked arm. "Shall we cross the lake?"

She took his offered arm, and they began to lazily stroll toward the grand bridge balustered with elegant ivory stonework. To break the lengthy silence, she finally said, "So this landscape was designed by Lancelot "Capability" Brown?"

"You know his work?"

"Who doesn't?" *Uh, oh.* She really must learn to speak to a peer with more cognizance of the respect due to one of his rank. "Forgive me," she quickly added. "I believe my knowledge of his lovely gardens comes only from prints I've seen. I have not had the good fortune—until today—to actually have the opportunity to inspect one of his legendary landscapes first hand." She looked up into his face. "Did your father commission him?"

"Actually, it was my grandfather. He was responsible also for Adam's new facade on Bodworth. It was one of the Scotsman's earliest commissions. Have you seen Bodworth?"

"No, but I am a great admirer—again, principally through prints—of Robert Adam's houses."

Lord Fane shrugged. "Then you will be disappointed with our interiors. They reek of the Jacobean. Mr. Adam's work encompassed only the exterior of Bodworth."

She was hoping for an invitation, but even one as undisciplined as she knew that good manners prevented her from expressing her desires on that score.

"It would contribute greatly to my felicity if you and Miss Darcy would call upon me at Bodworth."

Her eyes danced. "It would much more enthusiastically contribute to *my* felicity were I to gratify my curiosity to see Bodworth."

"Then I hope you can come tomorrow. I shall speak to Miss Darcy on the subject."

Miss Darcy was far too sweet natured to disappoint his lordship—and she was far too frightened of him to refuse! "As lovely as Pemberley is," Lucy said, "I should think Miss

Darcy would enjoy a change of habitat. She sees so little of the rest of the world."

"That's why a season in town would be good for her."

How noble of him to suggest something that would put what was sure to be the kingdom's most sought-after heiress in the path of many other men of rank. Other men in pursuit of fortune would have tried to snatch Miss Darcy before she ever got the opportunity to go to London.

"Indeed it would. For many reasons. I hope that before she gives her hand to one man, she has the opportunity to know many. I believe the likelihood of erring decreases when the field of candidates increases. It all comes down to mathematical probability. One out of one: large probability of error. One of twenty, likelihood of error much lower."

His step slowed, his eyes widened. It was all Fane could do not to stop dead in his stride along the bridge his grandfather had commissioned. Never in his two and thirty years had Fane heard a *female* discuss mathematical probability. Yet Miss Wetherspoon's analogy made perfect sense.

Finally, he found his tongue. "I would never have applied mathematical probability to courtship, but it demonstrates sound reasoning."

She nodded with the confidence of . . . a peer of the realm! Women had a tendency to be awed in his presence—as if he were in some royal realm by virtue of his rank. Very few women had ever been less affected in his presence than was Miss Wetherspoon. It was really astonishing, considering the disadvantage of her circumstances. It had always been his experience that the lowlier one was born, the more apt that person was to lose her tongue in the presence of nobility.

He came to a stop when they reached the crest of the bridge. "When we were children, we would stand here and skim stones across the water." Why in the bloody hell was he telling her this? What could it possibly matter to her?

And why in the blazes was he standing here with an undoubtedly penniless woman when he should have been making himself agreeable to one of the richest women in the kingdom? He should have left this exquisite creature here and gone off with Miss Darcy.

But Alexander Farrington, the Earl of Fane, had never been one to perform tedious duties when pleasure was to be indulged. And standing upon Capability Brown's bridge with the lovely Miss Wetherspoon offered him a great deal more pleasure than riding with Miss Darcy, who was too tall, too skinny, and too bloody young! He was quite sure Miss Darcy looked upon him in the same way one looked upon an aged uncle.

Still, he knew where his duty lie, and it wasn't on this bridge. As enjoyable as it was being so close to The Beauty.

They stood there gazing at the tranquil lake for some little time, neither uncomfortable with the absence of speech when so many other pleasant sounds filled their senses. The sweet trill of birds rang from trees rippling in the breeze, and water softly lapped at the lake's shore.

Finally, his curiosity to know more about the intriguing Miss Wetherspoon won. "Tell me, do you often get the opportunity to demonstrate your skill with all those languages you understand?"

"Not nearly often enough. I seldom get to speak Italian, since I know not a single person of Italian birth. However, it is most helpful for reading Dante. It is so beautiful to recite Dante in Italian. Have you ever read him in Italian?"

He shook his head. "My proficiency in Italian is purely conversational, owing to some time I spent there when I reached my majority."

"And when was that?"

Such a personal question coming from anyone else would have seemed ill mannered, but from Miss Wetherspoon, it was in perfect harmony with her outgoing personality. "Eleven years ago." His own good manners demanded that he not ask her age. Suffice it to say, she was in her mid-twenties. And should have married long ago.

Surely men must have made complete cakes of themselves over her. Why had she not wed one of them? Was marriage—even without love—not to be preferred over being a paid companion to a rich girl?

"And do you converse in German?" he asked.

"Actually, yes. My father—dear dear man though he is—has an unfortunate need to emulate nobles, even royals. Therefore, he says if our Royal Family is proficient in German, then the children of Mr. Benjamin Wetherspoon must also be proficient in German. It was French at the dinner table and German in the drawing room. I daresay I've never played whist in English!"

He pictured a large, ill-dressed family sitting around a drawing room conversing in German. "I've not played whist in German, but I have played *vingt-un.*"

She directed a mock glare at him. "But not in your drawing room, I'll wager!" Her hand flew to her mouth, her brows lowered, and her smooth ivory cheeks reddened. "I beg your forgiveness. Ladies are not supposed to say they wager, are they?"

He tossed his head back, laughing. "I know many, many ladies of noble birth who have no compunction about wagering anywhere they can."

"You are too kind." Her gaze flicked to her shoes poking out from beneath that horrid dress. "Shall we see if we can find Miss Darcy?"

They strolled back to where their horses were tethered, neither of them saying a word. He helped her mount, and a few minutes later, they caught up with Miss Darcy. The three of them rode along in relative silence, three abreast.

"Miss Darcy, I forgot to tell you my brother Hugh plans to join me here at Bodworth."

"How delightful! When does he arrive?"

"I expect him late this afternoon, if the roads are good."

"Since it hasn't been raining, I should think they would be," Miss Darcy said. Like so many women, she was much more comfortable with his untitled brothers than she was with him. Even talking about his brothers relaxed this young lady.

After a few more moments of silence, Miss Wetherspoon spoke. "I am fortunate, my lord, in my intercourse with Miss Darcy to understand her in much the same way as I understand my sisters. Because of that, and because she is by nature shy, I know I speak for her when I say she would be obliged if you and your brother would dine with us tonight."

"Indeed I would, my lord! It's been an age since I've seen Hugh," Miss Darcy said.

"I am gratified over the invitation and delighted

to accept."

Chapter 3

"Whatever would I do without you, Miss Wetherspoon? I am so unaccustomed to the role of hostess, Lord Fane must think my manners deplorable."

"Do not chastise yourself. Lord Fane is most certainly acquainted with your fine attributes— and he cannot be such a goose that he does not give allowances for your youth and inexperience."

"I am gratified that you thought to ask them to dinner. As good company as you are, I shall be happy to enlarge the circle in our dinner room. Do you think Hugh will make it to Derbyshire in time to dine with us at Pemberley?"

So she and the younger brother were intimate enough friends to use Christian names. "As you noted, the weather's been good. The roads must also be good."

"I shall wear my new ivory gown." Miss Darcy flew to her linen press and withdrew an elegant dress of very fine muslin that was so thin as to be almost transparent. Its bodice was embroidered with snowy white scrolls. "Is it not lovely?"

"It may be the loveliest dress I've ever beheld," Lucy said with complete truth. "Will this be the first time you've worn it?"

Miss Darcy nodded. "What will you wear?"

Lucy sighed. "Alas, what you see is one of only two dresses which I possess."

"We must rectify that!" The younger lady's eyes flashed as her gaze swept over Lucy. "You are as slender as I. If we have Marie hem my dresses, they should fit you most tolerably."

"As grateful as I should be, I cannot ruin one of your lovely dresses."

"Oh, you wouldn't be ruining one of my *new* dresses. I propose to bestow upon you my dresses from last year since I've lately gotten several new ones. I had already determined to give them away since I seem to have grown too tall for them."

The very notion of dressing in one of Miss Darcy's beautiful dresses—castoff or not—elevated Lucy's spirits most profoundly. No gift had ever brought so much happiness. "Are you quite certain you will not wish to wear them again?"

"Oh yes! I pray I do not grow any taller. Do you think I am finished growing? I fear I'll end up as tall as my brother."

Lucy's brows lowered in contemplation. "It is most likely you're finished growing since you're almost seventeen. I have never known of a girl becoming taller after that age—though one of Papa's friends who has made the study of the human body his life's work says he has recorded instances of females growing up to the age of three and twenty."

Miss Darcy's face fell. "I shall most determinedly commit suicide if I end up as tall as my brother."

"Do not worry. I am almost certain you have now reached your full height, and it's a most becoming height. Have you not observed how well a taller woman wears a dress?"

"I pray you are right—and thankfully you usually are." Georgiana Darcy turned back to the clothes press. "Here, allow me to show you which ones I will no longer need." She selected five dresses—each one beautiful—and handed them to Lucy. The least attractive of them, a promenade dress in which gray fabric was paired with green, was still far lovelier than anything Lucy had ever possessed.

Her eye alighted upon an exquisite one suitable for a dinner gathering or an assembly (for Lucy Wetherspoon never aspired to attend fancy dress balls). It was also of a very fine, snow white muslin accented with lavender trim and a lavender satin sash. She immediately knew that she would be the happiest girl in the kingdom if she were permitted to wear it to tonight's dinner.

Her first thoughts had been of how heartily she wished for Lord Fane to see her dressed so beautifully. She tried to squelch such thoughts. Lord Fane was courting Georgiana Darcy. Lord Fane would never look favorably upon an alliance with a daughter of Benjamin Wetherspoon. If only Lord Fane did not treat that daughter with such courteous affection.

Lucy was unable to suppress a gasp. "I have never owned anything so beautiful." She peered up at Miss Darcy with shimmering eyes. "It is excessively generous of you, and I am most sincerely grateful."

"I declare, this is more fun than getting a new dress! I cannot wait to see you tonight."

"Tonight?"

"Indeed. I know you're not confident with your sewing skills—having been educated more like a boy—so I shall have Marie take your measure and make the dress yours this afternoon. Mark my words, Miss Wetherspoon, his lordship will not be able to remove his eyes from your loveliness."

"You mustn't say that!" With her brows lowered, Lucy regarded the younger lady. "Can't you see Lord Fane is interested in being your suitor?"

"All that I see is the way he looks at you. I believe he has great admiration for you."

"What a silly notion! No nobleman would ever be attracted to me."

"And I credited you with being intelligent! Noblemen can be enamored of anyone they choose."

Lucy's brows lowered. "But not necessarily with honorable intentions."

Miss Darcy crossed the chamber and set a gentle hand on Lucy's forearm. "I know you would never be anything less than a lady, my dear Lucy. May I call you that? We've become like sisters."

"I should be honored."

"And I should like you to address me as Georgiana."

Lucy had not articulated even to herself her feelings for Georgiana, but now she realized in this instance the younger woman's understanding was superior to her own. They *had* become like sisters. While spending nearly every waking moment together for the past month, they had grown close in the same way Lucy was close to her sisters Mary Ann and Sarah. Remarkably, the interests of wealthy young ladies was much the same as the interests of not-so-wealthy young ladies. They adored perusing the newest fashions in Ackermann's every month. They enjoyed walking through parkland on a fine day. They read with interest of the *haute ton*. And they dreamed of being swept off their feet by the perfect mate.

In addition to sharing so many interests, Lucy admired Georgiana for her sweet nature. The girl always treated Lucy as one would a dear friend. Never had she made Lucy feel as if she were a servant, though that is exactly what she was.

For the next few hours, Lucy was repeatedly obliged to disrobe whilst Georgiana's ever-competent French maid had her try on the newly-modified dress for various fittings. "I shall need to reduce the length of Miss Darcy's dress by more than six inches to fit Mademoiselle," Marie commented after she took Lucy's measure.

Once the dress was hemmed, the maid determined the gown's bodice would need to be adjusted. Lucy blushed when Marie said, "Mademoiselle's bosom it is a great deal larger than Miss Darcy's."

"It is vastly unfair," Georgiana complained, stomping her foot in mock agitation. "You are already the prettiest lady of my acquaintance, and now all the gentlemen will see how perfect your figure is too. I daresay no man will ever notice me if you're in the same chamber."

"That is certainly not true! If you'd like, though, I will revert to my blue bombazine."

"Forgive me, my dear Lucy. I was only teasing. I have never enjoyed anything as much as watching your transformation and knowing I had some little part in it."

Once the talented French seamstress had completed her handiwork, Lucy tried on the dress one final time. When Lucy peered into the looking glass and saw how indecently low the dress was in the front, she blushed anew. "Do you not think my dress is too revealing for the purposes of modesty?"

Georgiana set hands to her hips and glared at Lucy. "I most certainly do not! You have seen the pictures in Ackermann's. You have seen Mr. Cruikshank's drawings of London's nobility at a variety of events. It is the fashion to display a lady's creamy chest and the promise of breasts, and it's thought to render a lady more elegant when the full effect of a graceful neck can be displayed."

Lucy bowed her head. "I defer to your superior judgment." But, oh how mortified she would be if Lord Fane's gaze dropped to the swell of her so-called womanly attributes. Perhaps she should wear a shawl. Sadly, the only shawl in her possession was knitted long ago of red wool which had faded with years of usage. To wear it over Miss Darcy's dress—for Lucy still could not believe herself to be the owner of such beautiful clothing—would be like allowing a small child to scribble upon a Turner landscape.

Perhaps Lucy could borrow one of Georgiana's lovely Kashmir shawls. "I have often wondered whilst we dined if you get terribly cold in those beautifully scant dresses."

"One gets used to it," Miss Darcy said.

"Perhaps, then, you would allow me to borrow your ivory shawl tonight? Whilst I become accustomed to dressing in such a manner."

Georgiana Darcy giggled.

* * *

Even though it was dark in the carriage, Fane was aware his brother was regarding him with interest. "I say, Fane, have you decided to finally take Mama's advice and marry an heiress? That's the only thing I can think of to explain your interest in dining at Pemberley tonight—when Darcy's off on the Continent."

"I am considering it, but it is much too early to say. Currently, I believe Miss Darcy regards me as ancient, and she appears to be terrified of me."

Hugh began to guffaw, and when he recovered, he tried to reassure his brother. "Like her brother, Georgiana Darcy is very reticent."

"I'll vow she's not so shy when in Robert's presence."

Hugh nodded. "They *have* always been close friends, but a woman with a fortune cannot throw her fortune away on a third son. Is it true she's got thirty thousand?"

"That's my understanding."

"Then I don't think you could ever do better. Think, my dear fellow, of the improvements you'll be able to make to Bodworth House! This is very good news indeed."

Fane held up a flattened palm. "Whoa! There is no news. Marriage to Miss Darcy is just something I'm exploring."

Hugh shrugged. "Why not go ahead and allow yourself to commit to it? It's not as if you've got to be in love with the girl. The Earl of Fane will never lack for interested lovers."

"That's the pity of this business. I'd thought to marry for love and then to practice fidelity—which I realize is a rather novel concept in the British aristocracy."

"Indeed it is. Papa will roll over in his grave if you don't take a mistress."

Fane frowned. He had always disapproved of his father's many marital infidelities.

"It is difficult to imagine your falling in love with Miss Darcy. She's awfully young. And she's also a bit plain."

"When I started on this prospective journey, I told myself that a love match was not to be in my future. If falling in love has eluded me for two and thirty years, it's never going to happen."

"Come, Fane! You've not fancied yourself in love at least once?"

"Not once."

"What about Mrs. Johnson?"

His former mistress. "She was possessed of many good qualities, but I must own she was not a woman one introduces in polite society; so, no, I was not in love with her."

The coach slowed at Pemberley's gatehouse, then proceeded on to the main house. Fane wished his own Bodworth was half as well maintained as Darcy's lovely home. He wished his father had not squandered away so much of the family's fortunes, leaving Fane a mass of debts which had taken years for his son to clear.

"So I expect Darcy's left his sister in Mrs. Annesley's excellent care."

"Mrs. Annesley has left Pemberley, owing I believe to a family emergency. She's not expected to return."

"Then Darcy has engaged the services of another competent older woman?"

At the thought of Miss Darcy's lovely companion, something inside of Fane softened, and he found himself anxious to see her again. Was she really as lovely as he remembered? Would the poor woman dine in that hideous dress she'd worn earlier? "I would estimate the woman is but eight or nine years older than Miss Darcy."

"I would have thought Darcy would have someone older."

"Miss Wetherspoon, I believe, will be a good influence on Miss Darcy. She's . . . well, you shall have to judge for yourself. She's terribly clever. Speaks six languages—including Latin!"

"She sounds like a remarkable young woman. Does she. . . look like a dragon?"

Fane's pulse accelerated as he pictured her. "You shall have to judge for yourself. I thought her most handsome." *Beautiful.* Now Fane found himself hoping she *would* wear that ugly blue dress. He didn't want Hugh to notice her beauty. Of course, any man who was not blind would notice it.

Hugh would be very well suited to marry a woman like Miss Wetherspoon; as the heir with too scant a purse to maintain the properties he had inherited, Fane could never consider aligning himself with a penniless woman who was not even aristocratic.

Inside Pemberley, the butler showed the brothers into the drawing room, and a moment later the two ladies entered the chamber. He saw Miss Darcy first and crossed the chamber to sketch a bow and greet her cordially.

He was vaguely aware that Miss Wetherspoon was not wearing that ugly blue dress, but she was hidden behind Miss Darcy. Once Miss Darcy moved to Hugh (and greeted him much more enthusiastically than she had Fane), he saw the lovely Miss Wetherspoon.

And nearly lost his breath.

In all his years of visually examining perhaps hundreds of lovely debutants at Almack's, he'd never beheld her equal. Good lord, she could be a duchess! Certainly, an eligible duke seeing her would not hesitate to offer marriage, for the desire to possess something so exquisite was very strong.

His gaze—unmindful of good manners—pored over her from that lovely face, along the elegant neck, to the swelling bosom that dipped beneath the bodice of her fashionable gown. The lady's figure was as perfect as her face.

"Miss Wetherspoon," he finally managed, "how very lovely you look tonight." She looked like one born to wealth and privilege. No doubt, the sweet-natured Miss Darcy had a hand in this transformation.

"Thank you, my lord."

Fane turned his attention to his brother in an effort to gauge Hugh's reaction to the Incomparable.

Exactly as Fane had done, Hugh abandoned good manners to sweep his admiring gaze from the tip of Miss Wetherspoon's dark brown hair down the length of her pretty figure. "What a delight to meet you, Miss Wetherspoon. Is it true you converse in six languages?"

Miss Wetherspoon tossed her head back and laughed. "I'm flattered that his lordship remembered, but I must own I have little opportunity to converse in Latin. The other five, I try to practice with native speakers at every opportunity. It was ever so much fun this afternoon to speak in *Français* to Miss Darcy's French maid."

The butler re-entered the chamber to announce that dinner would be served.

"Shall we continue this conversation in the dinner room?" Miss Darcy suggested.

As they went downstairs to the dinner chamber, Fane cautioned himself to devote more attention to the hostess. Nothing good could come of this infatuation with her paid companion.

I must consider Bodworth's needs, he told himself with every step he took. He owed it to his descendants to be a responsible steward of the four-hundred-year-old architectural gem that had been in the Farrington family since the day its first brick was laid. If he did not act soon, much of Bodworth would be lost to future generations of Farringtons.

He fleetingly wished he was not a firstborn. His fortunate brothers could very well marry any woman. Though they would be wise to marry women who brought generous dowries.

He vowed to address most of his dinner comments to Miss Darcy. He had been much too neglectful of The Heiress.

When they reached the large dinner room, he drew a deep breath. *I must not allow myself to converse with The Beauty.*

$\mathcal{C}$hapter 4

Like everything at Pemberley, the scarlet dinner room was elegant. What first caught Fane's eye upon entering the chamber was the profusion of expensive wax candles. He would guess there were nearly two hundred blazing. Three massive silver candelabra brightened the table, and above that, two huge crystal chandeliers glittered with rings of blazing candles. How fortunate was Darcy to be able to display his home to such stunning advantage. Ah, to have pockets as deep as Darcy's!

When Fane had come to understand the dire need to reduce household spending at Bodworth, he had sat down with his wise housekeeper to devise strict measures for economy. She had educated him about the high cost of candles and suggested many ways to reduce the number— even to using the more inexpensive tallows in the servants' chambers. He no longer dined in the dinner room when it was just he or a small family circle. They could eat at a smaller table in the morning room, where there were no chandeliers.

Miss Darcy, as their hostess, sat at the head of the table, and as the highest-ranking guest, Fane not only was the first to enter the dining chamber, he was also designated to sit to her right. He was pleased to see that since there were only four of them, the place settings were all at the one end—

the one nearest the marble chimneypiece, where a fire blazed on this chilly night.

Cutting down on the number of fires was another of the cost-saving measures implemented at Bodworth. Thank God for Mrs. Neely's common sense.

He was possessed of a most lamentable thirst to be near The Beauty, but he meant to suppress that gnawing need. He did not know which seat Miss Wetherspoon could take that would lessen her ability to distract him. Were she across from him, it would be difficult not to stare at her loveliness, but were she to sit next to him, it would be uncommonly rude of him not to direct at least some comments to her.

She sat next to his brother, across from Fane. He attempted to school himself *not* to peer at her.

He purposely gazed at the vibrant red silk draperies—such a contrast to the sun-faded draperies throughout Bodworth—and was forced to remember his pressing need to marry an heiress and restore Bodworth to its former glory, to make it shine like Pemberley.

As a footman spooned soup into their bowls, Fane's gaze flicked to the bottles of burgundy on the table. How in the devil had Darcy managed to procure those? Of course, anything was possible when one was possessed of a large fortune.

"May I pour you a glass of wine, Miss Darcy?" he asked, directing his full attention upon her. *Thirty thousand pounds*, he kept reminding himself.

"Yes, thank you, my lord."

Since Miss Wetherspoon sat next to Hugh, his brother could not repeat the same question fast enough to Miss Wetherspoon. In fact, Hugh fairly made a cake of himself over her as the evening progressed.

"How is it you have learned so many languages?" Hugh asked her, in French. *"You truly were educated the same as your brothers? How many siblings have you? How do you like Derbyshire?"*

It was most difficult for Fane to give Miss Darcy the attention he needed to give her for Miss Darcy appeared as fascinated over Miss Wetherspoon as Hugh was. Fane wished like the devil the clever companion was not so beastly amusing. It wasn't as if she needed another attribute. He need only look at Hugh to see the kind of admiration she already elicited.

Fane was becoming so out of charity with his brother that he wished him to Coventry.

And when Hugh's simmering gaze dropped to Miss Wetherspoon's bosom, Fane nearly came out of his chair, hands coiled into fists.

"I understand, Miss Darcy," Fane said, "that you spent some time in London last year."

"Yes."

Those bloody monosyllables again! "Now that you've had the opportunity to live for a time in the Capital, I must ask if you prefer London or Pemberley."

Miss Darcy did not respond for a moment. "London, I believe."

Miss Wetherspoon, apparently sensing Fane's discomfort over their hostess's dearth of conversation, prompted the young lady. "I daresay that when one has spent almost her entire life in the same unvarying place, it can grow tedious—especially in contrast with London which is so vast and offers such a variety of attractions."

"Very well said." Hugh could not remove his adoring gave from Miss Wetherspoon. "Have you spent much time in London?"

"My whole life. I am ever so much enjoying the natural beauty of Derbyshire and its fresh air and clean skies."

"You will never guess, Hugh," Miss Darcy said, "that Miss Wetherspoon had never before been on a horse."

Hugh whirled at The Beauty. "Never?"

"Not until I came to Pemberley, and I shan't ever ride again unless I have your brother at my side. He has promised to protect me from harm." Miss Wetherspoon's huge, flashing brown eyes met his, and a smile lifted the corners of her perfect mouth.

Fane felt as if he'd grown a foot taller.

"How gallant of my brother." Hugh glared at Fane.

"I meant to tell you how much I admire the way you sit a horse," Fane said to Miss Darcy. "You look as if you were born in a saddle."

"Thank you."

"By the way, Miss Darcy, did you know my brother is standing for Parliament?" Fane asked.

Her admiring gaze flicked to Hugh. "How very exciting! You must tell us all about it."

Hugh shrugged. "Fortunately, my brother controls the Halifax borough, so my campaign is expected to be successful."

Miss Wetherspoon concurred with Georgiana Darcy. "That *is* very exciting. This is the first time I've ever been acquainted with a Member of Parliament." Ever cognizant of drawing out her reticent companion, Miss Wetherspoon's gaze swung to the head of the table.

"Me too!" Miss Darcy said.

"Tell me," Miss Wetherspoon asked Hugh, "are you a Tory?"

Fane cut in before his brother had the opportunity to respond. "You say that because we are aristocrats, no doubt. There *are* aristocrats who are Whigs."

"Yes, there are," she said. "I have a great respect for Lord John Russell."

Hugh looked at her with admiration—not that he'd yet looked at her with anything that was not completely worshipful. "It is most definitely fortunate for the House of Commons that Lord John was not the firstborn. I shall look forward to serving with him."

Miss Wetherspoon sighed. "I do so regret that women are no longer permitted in the galleries. I should love to hear his speeches. My father attends regularly, and finds much to admire in him."

Her father sounded like a remarkable man. "Was your father equally impressed by Pitt's oratorical powers—before the man died?" Fane asked.

"Who was not? But actually my late mother was much more complimentary—as some twenty years ago women were permitted in the galleries. You may have surmised that my father is a Whig through and through, so I daresay he is hard pressed to praise a Tory. Even one with the oratorical powers of Mr. Pitt."

Hugh addressed her. "Then your father must have been very fond of Charles James Fox."

"Indeed he was. For so very many reasons. They were actually boyhood friends since they attended Westminster School together."

Then her father was definitely on the fringes of the upper class. "I understand Charles James Fox was fluent in even more languages than you, Miss Wetherspoon."

"That's correct," she answered. "I believe he spoke—and read—at least ten languages." She directed her attention to the head of the table. "I expect, Miss Darcy, you're not old enough to have any memory of Mr. Fox."

"No," the other lady answered, "but from your conversation I have deduced that he must have been a well-known Whig."

Miss Wetherspoon nodded. "My mother would often watch the proceedings in the House of Commons and was fascinated over him."

"He was quite the orator. I had the good fortune to be able to hear him speak on several occasions." Fane turned to the head of the table to explain to his youthful hostess. "Mr. Fox was the youngest man to ever serve in the House of Commons, and from the beginning of his career there, he blazed a brilliant trail."

"Of course, King George despised him," Hugh added.

"Oh dear," Miss Darcy said with trepidation in her voice. "I don't know if I would have liked him, then. Was he anti aristocrats too?"

"Not at all. He was the grandson of the Duke of Richmond," Fane explained, "and the son of the Baron Holland."

Miss Darcy's affectionate gaze moved to Hugh. "So, like you and Lord John Russell, he was a younger son!"

Hugh nodded. "Would that I could ever distinguish myself in a manner half as distinguished as Fox."

Miss Darcy sighed. "I look forward to reading about your addresses in the House of Commons, Mr. Farrington."

"It will be a long while before I make my maiden address."

"Now, Georgiana," Miss Wetherspoon said, "you and I shall have to pay particularly close attention to Parliamentary news in the newspapers. We are most fortunate that your brother subscribes to both the Tory and Whig newspapers so we can better develop more informed opinions."

"I have never been acquainted with *females* who formed opinions on such matters." Miss Darcy's eyes widened.

"Whilst I live with you, you will most definitely be exposed to everything which gentlemen are exposed to."

Fane's amused gaze connected with The Beauty's. "I cannot believe, coming from the family you come from, that you are not already well informed on Parliamentary matters."

She favored him with a radiant smile. "I do not know if I would say I was well informed, but I *am* keenly interested in the daily proceedings of Parliament and attempt to stay abreast of the news."

The woman had more poise and intelligence than any woman he'd ever encountered. Why was it most women trembled in his presence, but she regarded him as would one of equal—or possibly even superior—birth?

He had to own that Miss Wetherspoon was a remarkable woman in every way. A pity she was poor. And an even greater pity that he seemed incapable of purging the lovely lady from his thoughts.

A footman came and removed the sides, then replaced them with turbot, buttered crab, French beans, and as many other dishes as fit on the opposite side of the table. Needing to divert his thoughts from the woman across the table, he speedily stabbed at the turbot and transferred it to his porcelain plate.

"Lord Fane," Miss Wetherspoon said, "do you serve in the House of Lords? I can't recall ever reading about any speeches of yours."

"I do serve, but I don't take a particularly active role. I have yet to make *my* maiden speech."

Miss Darcy's eyes rounded. "Did you ever meet Lord Byron?"

"Several times."

"Is he as handsome as reported?" Miss Darcy asked. A pity the animation in her face was not for him. Not being able to easily capture lady's affections was refreshing to Fane for its novelty. Fane had always held vast appeal to women, but he never flattered himself that their attraction was for anything other than his title.

He shrugged his shoulders and laughed at Miss Darcy's query. "I am incapable of being able to determine whether a man is handsome."

Miss Wetherspoon joined in his laughter.

Once more Miss Darcy directed her attention at his brother. "Have you news of Robert?"

"I have not received a letter from him in an age." Hugh peered at him. "Have you, Fane?"

"He's lamentably remiss about corresponding with *male* family members."

"Then our sisters have more frequent communication with him?"

"Indeed. Isabelle wrote to tell me that she thought Robert was falling in love with a Spanish noblewoman." Without moving his head a centimeter, Fane's gaze flicked to Miss Darcy to observe her reaction.

The smile present on her face seconds earlier vanished as her face fell. A pity the girl fancied his youngest brother. And an even greater pity that she fancied Hugh far more than she did Fane. *Thirty thousand pounds.*

He must endeavor to make himself more accessible to her. He turned his attention to the head of the table. "So, Miss Darcy, are you fond of Byron's poetry?"

"Yes."

Monosyllables again. He cleared his throat. "And have you a favorite poem of his?"

She did not reply for a moment. "I would have to say *Childe Harold's Pilgrimage,* since reading that is what made me love him so."

Hugh turned to The Beauty. "Why is it women always fancy themselves in love with that man? Does he not possess some kind of deformity?"

She nodded. "A club foot, I believe." Her gaze lifted to Fane. "Though I've never had the opportunity, like you, to see him in the flesh." Then, turning back to Hugh, she continued. "I think many women are attracted to fame, and I also believe that an imperfect man brings out certain nurturing instincts in women."

Miss Wetherspoon possessed the same kind of common sense as his competent housekeeper. Poor Miss Darcy. So close an association with a woman who, by her many accomplishments, intelligence, and stunning beauty, displayed the unfortunate Miss Darcy to inferior advantage.

What a paradox that he considered a young woman of large fortune unfortunate.

"I have observed that a wounded soldier—particularly if he is possessed of tolerable appearance—does tend to capture a woman's fancy. Why do you think that is, Miss Wetherspoon?" Hugh asked.

For once, the wise Miss Wetherspoon was stumped. "I will own, I have observed—even felt those same powerful emotions—but I am at a loss to define them."

Fane was so besottedly stupid over The Beauty that he suddenly felt jealousy toward crippled soldiers. *Good lord, what has come over me?*

He must not permit himself to think any more about Miss Wetherspoon. *Thirty thousand pounds.*

Miss Darcy directed her attention once more to Hugh. "Will any of your sisters be visiting Bodworth in the near future?"

"Fane would know better than I." Hugh lifted his brows in query.

"Not until next month."

"Miss Darcy," said Miss Wetherspoon, "you must tell his lordship about the letter you received from your brother's bride just this afternoon."

"They arrived in Naples, and dear Lizzie could not suppress her enthusiasm. One of the first things she and my brother did was climb to the top of Vesuvius."

He was grateful to Miss Wetherspoon for promoting conversation between him and the heiress. "Have you a desire to travel to the Continent?" he asked Miss Darcy.

The lady sighed. "I used to want to visit Paris, but that's not possible now. I believe I should adore Italy, too, but I don't know if I could tolerate the heat in summer."

Miss Wetherspoon nodded. "I have heard that

during the summer Englishmen traveling in Italy sleep in the daytime and ride in their carriages at night."

Fane nodded. "When the sun is beating down, the heat within the carriage can be most oppressive."

"You have been there, have you not?" Miss Darcy asked Fane. What an enormous breakthrough! She had spoken a half a dozen words to him.

"When I first left university. It's been a great many years now. Sir William Hamilton was ambassador in Naples whilst I was there."

"What a charmed life you've led, my lord," Miss Wetherspoon responded in her melodious voice. "Not only meeting Charles James Fox and Lord Byron but also the ravishing Lady Hamilton."

He remembered how stunning Lady Hamilton had been, though she been well past her first flush of youth. That had been nearly the same time as when she had captured Lord Nelson's heart. "Alas, I never actually met Mr. Fox. I merely had the opportunity to sit in the gallery and listen to him."

"Oh, but to have heard him!" Miss Wetherspoon's almond-shaped eyes were ablaze with excitement. "How fortunate you are."

"I am far more interested in the ravishing Lady Hamilton," Hugh said with a chuckle.

"It's best to avoid any talk of *ravishing* in the presence of two maidens," cautioned Fane, a grin upon his face. He lifted the bottle of burgundy. "More wine, Miss Darcy?"

She shook her head. "My brother says I must limit my consumption to just one glass until I become more accustomed to drinking spirits."

Fane nodded. Despite his resolve to address most comments to Miss Darcy, he was compelled by good manners to extend the same courtesy to her beautiful companion. "And you, Miss Wetherspoon?"

The Beauty tossed her head back in laughter. "As all of you have no doubt been able to observe, I am *not* a novice to adult dinner tables." She held out her glass, and Fane promptly refilled it.

It was almost inconceivable that one possessed of Miss Wetherspoon's abundant attributes had failed to marry. How could that be? Even given that her family was prohibited from moving within the *haute ton*, as the daughter of a gentleman, she had to have been exposed to any number of men, men who would make cakes of themselves over her in much the same way as his brother was doing tonight.

How fortunate Hugh was *not* to have been the firstborn, like Fane. He didn't have the worry of preserving Bodworth House for future generations. He didn't have the weight on his shoulders of generations who had responsibly built and maintained the magnificent old pile.

Within the bounds of sound reason, Hugh could marry anyone he wished. Even Miss Wetherspoon.

Why did the thought of his brother marrying The Beauty make Fane feel as if he'd just been struck by a cannon ball?

After the cloth was removed and the sweetmeats laid and after the ladies went to the drawing room whilst the two brothers imbibed the customary glass of port, the four of them gathered in the drawing room for whist.

"Will you do me the goodness of being my

partner?" Fane asked Miss Darcy.

She offered him a shy smile and a nod. He held out her chair, and she elegantly lowered herself into it. From the corner of his eye, he watched with envy as Hugh did the same for Miss Wetherspoon.

"I must warn you, Mr. Farrington, that we will face fierce competition," The Beauty said. "Miss Darcy is uncommonly skilled at whist."

"You shall put me to the blush," the younger lady responded. "Though I must own it is most satisfying to discover *one* skill in which I am not unfavorably compared to my dear Lucy."

"Your Christian name is Lucy?" Fane asked.

"Yes." She then directed her attention to Miss Darcy. "You mustn't say your skills are inferior to mine. Do not forget how wonderfully accomplished you are in music." Miss Wetherspoon's gaze lifted to Fane. "She not only plays several instruments to perfection, but she sings like an angel in a heavenly choir."

Miss Wetherspoon was more eager than he to promote a flirtation between himself and Miss Darcy.

He eyed Miss Darcy. "I shall eagerly look forward to hearing you."

"I hope I do not disappoint after Lucy's generous superlatives. It is a great deal to live up to."

"You could never disappoint," Miss Wetherspoon said.

During the next hour, he attempted to train his eye on either his hand or his partner, but he kept finding himself watching the rise and fall of The Beauty's womanly chest with each breath she drew. Then his gaze would lift to take in the perfection of her face, the piercing of the dimples in her cheeks, the length of her dark lashes.

Thirty thousand pounds, he reminded himself with ever-increasing regularity.

Then he would feel most grievously guilty. There was nothing whatsoever objectionable in Miss Darcy. Her appearance was tolerable. Her play at whist demonstrated a well-formed mind. Her manners as well as her eye for dressing most becomingly were unparalleled.

And there was the *thirty thousand pounds* which should render her highly sought after once she was launched into Society. He should count himself fortunate to be at the front of the queue, owing to her brother's marriage, which delayed her presentation. He should count himself fortunate if the wealthy young lady would consent to become the next Countess of Fane.

Then why in the devil did he feel as if he'd been forced to sell his favorite mount?

How proud he would have been—before his father lost the family fortune—to make someone as lovely and intelligent as Miss Wetherspoon his countess.

Attempts to steer his thoughts away from The Beauty sadly failed. That she sat next to him, their legs nearly touching, distracted him most profoundly. He could smell her sweet rose scent and observe the manner in which her slender fingers held the cards most elegantly. How would it feel to have those same hands stroke his face? How would it feel to clasp them in his? He drew a deep breath as he tortured himself imaging what it would be like to hold her in his arms.

I must abolish such traitorous thoughts. His gaze arrowed to Miss Darcy. "I see that Miss

Wetherspoon did not exaggerate your skill in the least. Now I shall even more eagerly look forward to the satisfaction of hearing you sing *like an angel in a heavenly choir.*"

"Miss Darcy is far too modest," The Beauty said. "She is the most accomplished lady I've ever known."

Miss Wetherspoon could not be faulted for the manner in which she sought to encourage a match between himself and the younger lady. More's the pity.

His thoughts returned to whist, and he smiled as he thought of Miss Wetherspoon playing the game in German. Even though he and Miss Darcy held a commanding lead, he became melancholy. He was perplexed at the source of his moroseness.

And then it walloped him with the force of a runaway coach-and-four. After failing to do so for two and thirty years, Alexander Farrington, the Earl of Fane, rather fancied that he *was* finally falling in love. With the wrong woman.

Since the first moment he'd set eyes upon Lucy Wetherspoon, he had been incapable of thinking of anything else. Every moment in her presence found him wanting to extend the time they were together. Would a lifetime be enough? It was as if he lived to hear her speak, to behold her exceptional beauty. Even the very sound of her voice was like an aphrodisiac to him.

But loving Miss Wetherspoon would never do. A marriage to the lovely lady—no matter how potently he might wish to unite himself with her—could never be.

$\mathcal{C}$hapter 5

As excessively fond as Lucy was of Georgiana, she was in no humor to make herself agreeable to the young woman on the following morning. Her ill humor owed its origins to her absence of sleep. Throughout the wretched night, she thought of Lord Fane. Every word, every look he had directed to her was endlessly recalled. Her many efforts to repress such thoughts were as successful as the likelihood of Benjamin Wether*fool's* daughter capturing a marriage proposal from an earl.

Even her lovely bedchamber was gloomy today, dominated by the unrelenting gray skies which filled the chamber's many tall, silken-draped casements. It was a good thing Marie had not refitted the other four of Miss Darcy's dresses yet. Dressing in a familiar manner ought to remind Lucy not to aim above her station. She set about dressing herself in her comfortable old blue bombazine.

Because it was so dreary a day and apt to rain, the likelihood of Lord Fane coming was greatly reduced. She needed him to see her in the bombazine; she needed to remind herself of her ineligibility.

She went to the little French desk in her chamber. How difficult it would now be to ever return to Milsop Street after living amidst such splendor. This was the first time in her life she'd ever had a bedchamber of her own. Or a desk of her own. Or even a bed of her own. She ought to write a cheerful letter to her sister Mary Ann, who could then forward it to their other sisters. Should she mention Lord Fane? How impressed her sisters would be to think of her sitting at the same dinner table with an earl!

But, upon remembering her dearest Papa's aspirations for her—his prettiest daughter—she thought better of it. Papa would be sure to boast, and knowing Papa's stretching of the truth, within a week, all of London would believe Miss Lucy Wetherspoon was betrothed to Lord Fane.

The very thought of being betrothed to a man such as he caused her heartbeat to accelerate. During her sleepless night she had attempted to analyze why she experienced so violent an attraction to him. It wasn't just that he was a peer of the realm. She was convinced that were he not a peer, he would still cause her pulse to race every time his honeyed eyes lingered on her.

Though he was not handsome, he exuded a masculinity that vastly appealed to her. But it wasn't just his physical attributes that she admired. He was perhaps only the second man she had ever known who was as intelligent as her father. She had been able to glean a knowledge of his interests in books, and they were remarkably compatible with her own.

She was also deeply touched over his exceeding courtesy to her. How many peers of the realm would make themselves so very agreeable to a lowly paid companion dressed in bombazine?

More than anything else throughout the night, she kept recalling his words when he'd said, *Whilst I am at your side, no harm will ever come to you.*

Her eyes filled with tears.

It was Miss Darcy—not Lucy—who would be the recipient of his lordship's tender care.

She dabbed a handkerchief to her eyes and picked up her pen. As she always did, she began with today's date. *The twenty-second!*

Oh, dear, at the memory of what was to occur on the twenty-second, she tossed down her pen and fairly flew to Georgiana's room, which was some little distance down the same corridor from Lucy's bedchamber.

She threw open the door to Miss Darcy's chambers. Dressed in an elegant light blue morning dress, Georgiana was seated before her *escritoire*, pen in hand.

"Did you remember who's to arrive this afternoon?"

Georgiana's face fell. "Oh, dear. I *had* forgotten."

"What is the name of Mrs. Darcy's dear friend?"

"Charlotte Collins. It's her husband who is said to be the disagreeable one."

Lucy rolled her eyes. "Dinner will be interminable."

"Perhaps not." Her pale eyes flashing mischievously, Miss Darcy picked up her pen again. "I shall send a note around to Lord Fane to invite him and his brother to return for dinner tonight. I am told Mr. Collins is in awe of nobility. Perhaps he will not be as determined a talker in his lordship's presence."

In spite of Lucy's morose mood, a comical thought struck her. "So you see, my dear Georgiana, there is one advantage to wearing an ugly dress such as this. I shall be spared from Mr.

Collins' regard."

Georgiana giggled. "Though it is against my nature to exercise any kind of authority, I shall *not* permit you to wear that dress again!"

"I declare, you are coming to wear the mantle of authority well. You have aged three years in a single month! Next, *you* will be dominating dinner conversations."

"My brother is eight and twenty and still quiet." Georgiana effected a mock glare at Lucy. "Marie said she will be finished with the last dress by late this afternoon. I shall expect you to wear it at dinner."

"Please, I beg that you allow me to continue in my bombazine until I've made a suitable impression on Mr. Collins."

Miss Darcy's giggles renewed. "I am not a fool! I see what you're about. You mean for me to have to carry on the conversation with the clergyman."

Lucy wondered if the noticeable change in Georgiana Darcy's formerly reticent personality was owing to her own influence. To be sure, Lucy was lamentably outspoken. A month earlier, Miss Darcy would never have freely offered her opinion.

Lucy's thoughts returned to the prospective visit of Mr. and Mrs. Collins. "Do you not find a toad-eating, rank-worshipping cleric at odds with Christian principles?"

"My, but you remembered every word of warning issued by my dear sister!" Then Georgiana nodded. "But, yes, you are, as always, right."

"Not always."

"What? Miss Lucy Wetherspoon is fallible?"

"I have been known to miscalculate the worthiness of more than one person." *Namely,*

Lawrence.

A half hour later, Tibbs knocked upon Georgiana's door. "A Mr. and Mrs. Collins await you in the drawing room, and Mrs. Reynolds wishes to know in which chamber you want their valises put."

"Oh, dear. Extend to Mrs. Reynolds my apologies for not apprising her that the Collinses were expected. They're only to be here two nights. Have her put them in the Yellow Room."

* * *

Given that Mrs. Darcy had asked her sister-in-law to give the Collinses—who had never before been to Pemberley—a personal tour, Lucy availed herself of the opportunity of further acquainting herself with what was undoubtedly one of the finest country houses in England. In the month since she'd arrived at Pemberley, she'd only had access to a half a dozen rooms.

She was stunned to learn there were over one hundred chambers in the u-shaped house. Only about a third of them were shown. "Some of the chambers are inhabited by servants," Miss Darcy told them, "and the ones in the north wing have not been used for more than a century."

There were almost a dozen staircases and more than a dozen chimneys.

Mr. Collins was unable to refrain from comparing it to the home of his patron, Lady Catherine de Bourgh—a name he would repeat with a frequency equal to involuntarily swallowing. "Bless my soul!" said he. "This surpasses the magnificence of Rosings. Rosings," he announced, his shimmering gaze meeting Georgiana's, "as you know, being her niece, is the stately home belonging to Lady Catherine de

Bourgh. You may have recalled that she is my most gracious benefactor. Rosings numbers five and seventy chambers and more chimneys than are ever used. Do you, my dear, remember the how many chimneys Lady Catherine has told us are at Rosings?"

Before his unfortunate wife could respond, he continued speaking to Miss Darcy. "Mrs. Collins and I have had the most welcome good fortune to be asked by my benevolent patroness to dine at Rosings sometimes as often as twice a week."

"I believe there are nine chimneys at Rosings," Charlotte Collins answered, flicking a smile at Lucy, the insignificant *servant* dressed in bombazine who had been ignored by Mr. Collins since the moment she had been introduced as Miss Darcy's companion.

When they reached the portrait gallery, Mr. Collins' enthusiasm knew no bounds. He had the opportunity to view a great many of Lady Catherine's ancestors, for Lady Catherine was the aunt of Miss Darcy and her brother. "Will you look at this, Mrs. Collins! 'Tis the portrait of Lady Catherine's mother. Can you see the resemblance?" He stood back in earnest contemplation of the greatness portrayed by the brush of Mr. Gainsborough. "Can you not observe the same aristocratic nose? Such a handsome woman! I do declare, she possesses a countenance equal to that of the noblewoman who is so very dear to our hearts, Mrs. Collins!"

"Such a lovely painting," Mrs. Collins commented. "I do believe Mr. Gainsborough is my favorite of all the British artists."

How smoothly Mrs. Collins had avoided praising the noblewoman her husband worshipped. Lucy had decided she quite admired Charlotte Collins, though she failed to understand what circumstances could have prompted her to unite herself with a man incapable of promoting domestic felicity. Perhaps Mrs. Darcy had enlightened Georgiana on why her friend had been compelled to wed the pretentious clergyman.

After Georgiana explained the various portraits, Mr. Collins studied them for the next half hour, frequently exclaiming over a newly discovered feature on a Darcy ancestor. "I do declare, I see my benefactress's brow! Do you not observe that, Mrs. Collins?" Or, "See that noble chin on Lady Catherine's papa?"

Since poor Georgiana was far too courteous to hurry along the gushing Mr. Collins, Lucy was determined to intervene.

She was spared when Charlotte Collins coaxed her husband. "As delightful as these portraits are to you, my dear Mr. Collins, you must consider Miss Darcy's sensibilities. I am sure the young lady has observed them nearly every day of her life." Mrs. Collin's gaze flicked to Georgiana. "Where do we go next, Miss Darcy?"

Georgiana offered the woman a grateful smile. "We have seen all there is of interest. Let us return to the drawing room for tea."

After they each returned to their respective places in the drawing room, Tibbs brought Miss Darcy a note. She carefully opened it, then looked up at the Collinses, who sat on a settee across from her. "We have the honor of having been invited to dinner tonight at the home of Lord Fane."

Unmasked glee brightened Mr. Collins' face. "Does his lordship know that you have guests?"

"Indeed he does. I had taken the liberty of inviting him and his brother to Pemberley tonight because I thought having them would enliven our dinner table—not that it would not have been exceedingly pleasant with just the four of us."

If possible, the glee on Mr. Collins' round face increased.

"However," Georgiana continued, "Lord Fane claims that since he and his brother dined here last night, he wishes to reciprocate by having the four of us to Bodworth."

The exuberant clergyman turned to his mate. "Did you hear that, Mrs. Collins?"

"Yes, Mr. Collins. I heard."

Were Lucy ever to have the misfortune of uniting herself with anyone as obnoxious as Mr. Collins, she would be incapable of issuing so courteous a response to him. Lucy would likely have replied with something of the nature "You are not the only one in this chamber in possession of ears."

"I daresay Miss Darcy has told his lordship of my connections to the nobility," a gloating Mr. Collins said.

After the tea tray was brought and the tea consumed, Miss Darcy turned to Lucy. "It has only just occurred to me, my dear Miss Wetherspoon, that since the day you arrived you have had scarcely a moment to yourself. Now that Lizzie has invited her dearest friend to come to me, I won't need your constant attentions. Please, feel free to do whatever pleases you during the duration of the Collins' stay."

Before Lucy could respond, Mr. Collins addressed Georgiana. "It is clearly evident that so benevolent a nature—one I have been the recipient of any number of times from Lady Catherine de Bourgh—is inherent in your distinguished family."

"Truth be told, Mr. Collins," said Georgiana, her eyes uncharacteristically narrowed, "I am out of charity with my Aunt Catherine."

Mr. Collins' eyes widened. "How can that be?"

"Has my aunt not told you she has vowed not to step foot at Pemberley because my brother wed a woman of whom she disapproved."

The expression on his face collapsed. He resembled a cowering hound. "Indeed. But you must consider it from that dear, altruistic woman's perspective. She had most fervently wished the connection with your brother for her beloved daughter."

Miss Darcy directed a haughty glare at the man.

Lucy was most sincerely enjoying the transformation that was coming over Georgiana as she transitioned from shy girl into wise woman.

"Nevertheless," Georgiana said, "it grieves me for anyone to disapprove of dear Lizzie. I could not be more fond of her were she truly my sister."

Mrs. Collins smiled. "I feel the same about Lizzie, and I am acquainted with her feelings toward you, Miss Darcy. Save for her sister Jane Bingley, she loves you far more than any of her other sisters."

"I am most sincerely appreciative to know that." Georgiana's gaze went from Charlotte Collins to her husband. "You must know my brother adores his wife, and she returns his ardor most perfectly. Their marriage has dramatically advanced their felicity."

He sighed. "I do understand that your brother's

affections were deeply engaged. It must have been the source of deep grief for his family to accept a connection that was so far beneath him."

"How can you say that, Mr. Collins?" Georgiana demanded.

Lucy felt as if she were at one of those plays in which she was obliged to swing her gaze from the audience of hissers and shouters to the actors upon the stage.

Miss Darcy continued addressing Mr. Collins. "Is not Lizzie's father a cousin to you and the gentleman from whom you have significant expectations?"

His cowering returned as he sheepishly nodded.

Georgiana glared at him. "I do not mean to be inhospitable to a guest in my own house, but it seems to me that if you malign the Bennett family, you malign yourself."

"I believe I said the very same, Mr. Collins," his wife said.

It was the first bit of defiant spark Lucy had been able to observe in the compliant Charlotte Collins. Lucy had never been sorrier for a gently born woman. She had been sorrier for wretchedly poor women who struggled for their very existence. However, she was not wholly convinced that were she given the choice, she would have chosen life foraging for food to a safe life in Mr. Collins' parsonage.

Lucy stood. "It's very kind of you, Georgiana, to allow me such freedom this afternoon. I believe I shall take advantage of a walk in your park before rain comes. A solitary stroll may help to clear my head."

"I am ever so afraid it may rain," Georgiana said.

"Then I'd best hurry."

* * *

Once she donned her old red cape and reached the park, she realized it was merely a dreary day. It would not rain after all. She had become unerringly adept at using her senses to detect the atmospheric changes that signaled rain.

Even if the sun was absent, Lucy was delighted to have the opportunity to be alone in the verdant setting. She was obliged to Georgiana not only for allowing her this free time but also for her good manners that would prevent her from ever asking why Lucy needed to clear her head.

If only Lucy were capable of sorting out these astonishing emotions Lord Fane seemed to induce in her. Perhaps she would feign sickness that night so she would not have to dine with him. Perhaps if she did not have to see him she could successfully purge him from her thoughts. Perhaps she needed to find a position in another household, a household where she would never have to see Lord Fane and never again be subjected to his mortifyingly appealing presence.

She was walking rather aimlessly, her thoughts whirling with these perplexing emotions, when she realized she had reached the lake. And there on the banks sat his lordship, fishing pole in hand.

If she turned away quickly enough, he might not see her.

But before she could do so, he called out to her. "Good day to you, Miss Wetherspoon. Have you come to fish?"

How ill mannered she would appear if she did not move toward the earl. "I have never in my life participated in any aspect of angling, my lord, and do not wish to do so now."

He continued to look up at her, a grin on his face. "Allow me to guess. Because you have spent your entire life in London, you have not had the opportunity to fish? Or to ride horses?"

She strode toward him. "Yes, but I daresay there are many things a city-bred lass like me has done that country misses have not." Now why was she speaking to him? And moving toward him? Had she not just decided that she needed to avoid the occasion of being with him?

"I beg that you enlighten me."

Her posture stiff, she regarded him. "Riding in a hack. Purchasing hot chestnuts from a street hawker. Or breathing the noxious airs that sometimes obliterate vision. Oh, the delights awaiting one in the Capital!"

The latter elicited a laugh from each of them.

"Won't you come and sit by me and allow me to teach you how to fish?"

"I could not possibly deprive you of your solitary enjoyment, my lord."

His gaze went somber, and she felt his lazy perusal of her from her eyes down along the soft folds of her abhorrent dress. Formerly, she had felt humiliated when he took in her shabby gown. Today, she felt embarrassed for a different reason. His simmering gaze made her feel as if she were standing in front of him wearing nothing at all.

"Where is the fetching dress you wore last night?"

"I am more comfortable in these clothes, my lord."

"It is quite remarkable that no matter what you wear, you're still lovely." He came to his feet and moved to her. "How ill mannered of me not to stand in your presence."

"An earl does not have to stand in my presence. I am considered without consequence."

His eyes softened. "Never say that, Lucy. You're the most remarkable woman I've ever met."

He had called her by her first name! No man had ever done that before. Not even Lawrence. "That is very kind of you, my lord, though I daresay I'm unworthy of such praise."

"Will you not at least keep me company whilst I fish?"

She had the oddest feeling their roles were reversed, that he, a peer of the realm, was begging her. "I have an abhorrence of worms, and I understand one must use worms as bait when one fishes."

His face brightened. "While that is often true, it is my pleasure to inform you that today I am using minnows for bait. Please, won't you come sit with me?"

She knew she should refuse, but one's heart does always abide by the wisdom of one's brain.

Once she plopped down on the bank beside him, conversation came easily. She almost forgot her perplexing infatuation with him. Almost. His amiability and inherent intelligence produced a man she could not help but to admire. The likes of him she had never before met.

"Why is it," asked he, "you have vast knowledge of Latin but not of Greek? Did your father not believe his sons needed to know Greek?"

Her lashes lowered, and she did not respond for a moment. "Is it a lie to omit telling the complete truth?"

He began to laugh. He laughed so heartily that he was obliged to put down his pole. Then he faced her. "I think I am coming to understand you perfectly, Miss Wetherspoon. You *do* read Greek, but you don't want anyone to know."

She morosely nodded. "Can you blame me? What woman would wish to own up to anything that is so much the domain of the male mind?"

He eyed her in a most affectionate manner. "No one would ever think you anything but feminine."

Then he did the most frightful thing.

His upper torso came closer to her, his eyelids looked as if they stayed open only by the greatest effort, and his face came within an inch of hers. Then he settled his lips over hers.

Lucy felt as if she had fallen from a great height, yet she was anchored to the spot, unable to move, unable to speak, and unable to break away from him as his arms came fully around her, and the intensity of the kiss deepened.

Though she had never before been kissed, she rather felt as if kissing Lord Fane was her destiny, that it was as natural as breathing.

But no sooner had her arms lifted to encircle him than she came to her senses and was cognizant of her impropriety. She yanked herself from his embrace, stumbled to her feet, and rushed away.

Chapter 6

Alexander Farrington, the Earl of Fane, had made a fine mess of things. How could what had in some ways been the best day of his life (owing to THE kiss) turn into the worst? How vilely he must have offended dear Miss Wetherspoon. First, he had taken the liberty of calling her *Lucy*. Then he had subjected her to his kisses. Because she had not initially pushed him away and because her initial response was somewhat obliging, he permitted himself to deepen the kiss. (And even the memory of it caused his breath to grow short!)

That must have been when she determined his interests toward her were dishonorable. He treated her no better than a . . . doxy. Nothing could have been in greater opposition to his true feelings. No doxy had ever elicited in him the profound hunger that Lucy did. He was pathetically besotted over her.

Because of her, he had not slept. Long after he and Hugh had come home the previous night, long after he'd gone to bed, Fane had thought of nothing but her. He recalled every word she had said. He remembered every facet of that lovely face. He even fancied he could smell her light floral scent.

At first he had told himself that he was merely drawn to her beauty. It was impossible to actually fall in love with a woman one had just met. Then he recalled his married sister telling him—as head of the household and Distributor of the Dowries— that she had known the instant she'd set eyes upon Frederick Beauclerk that he was the only man she could ever marry. Beauclerk had echoed Isabelle's very words when he'd asked Fane for his sister's hand. He, too, swore he had fallen in love at first sight. Surprisingly, Isabelle and Beauclerk enjoyed the greatest domestic felicity imaginable. Perhaps it *was* possible to fall in love at first sight.

After Lucy had left him at the lake, he'd started after her, wanting to beg forgiveness for his unconscionable act.

He could tell she was crying, and he felt beastly for having given her offense. Surely she didn't think he meant to compromise her good name! He wanted to explain that he held her in the highest possible regard, that he would never do anything to efface her from the esteem in which he held her.

But the sniffling Miss Wetherspoon had begged him to leave her alone.

He hadn't the heart to force himself on her a second time. He helplessly stood there on land the Farringtons had lost and watched as he lost the most perfect being.

Throughout the remainder of the afternoon, he consoled himself that he would do whatever was in his power that night when she came to dinner to repair his tarnished image in Miss Wetherspoon's eyes.

He immediately pictured her in the lovely frock she had worn the previous night. He grew anxious to behold her again, anxious to bridge the rift between them.

And that was when he realized he wanted to

marry Miss Wetherspoon! His heart would never permit him to offer marriage to an heiress he did not love. It would not have been fair to either of them.

But was he willing to put his own happiness above Bodworth? Four hundred years worth of ancestors had built the old pile of which he was exceedingly fond, and he owed it to the descendants of the next four hundred years to do everything in his power to maintain Bodworth for those future generations.

At what cost? He prided himself on the frugality that had, over the course of several years, wiped out the mountain of debts his father had saddled him with upon his demise. By Jove! If Fane could win Lucy's heart, he would not care if he ever went to Tattersall's again. Or bought another Canaletto. If it came to it, he'd be willing to sell off the Holbein or Gainsborough if it meant he could marry Lucy.

Feeling like a man released from indenture, he eagerly anticipated seeing Lucy that night. In fact, he would contrive to have her sit beside him.

And even though he knew Miss Darcy was not enamored of him in the least, he was obliged to make it clear to her that he did not intend to offer marriage.

He was determined to show Bodworth at its best that night to dear Miss Wetherspoon. God willing, she would become its next mistress.

* * *

But when night came, his hopes were cruelly denied. Miss Wetherspoon did not come. She had begged off by saying she had the headache, but he knew her true reason for not coming. She did not want to be with him. Not after the afternoon's stolen kiss.

All his eagerness to see her at Bodworth crushed under the heavy weight of disappointment. How interminable the night would be without her.

He felt so bloody bad it was difficult for him to be civil. Thank God for Hugh. His brother attempted to direct the dinner table conversation in the complete absence of Fane's participation. Even his normally talkative brother, however, was challenged to wedge in the occasional comment between long soliloquies from Mr. Collins.

Within five minutes of stepping into Bodworth, Mr. Collins imparted to whoever was forced to listen, all the pertinent facts of his (what must be exceedingly boring) life.

One would have thought when dinner was served, the pompous clergyman would have nothing left to say. But Fane had obviously miscalculated the man's determination to acquaint his fellow diners with his close relationship to the nobility.

Fane had never cared for Lady Catherine de Bourgh (who was forever throwing her daughter at him, even more so since Darcy had become betrothed), but Mr. Collins's admiration of the noblewoman more than compensated for others' limited regard for the outspoken matriarch who liked to dominate conversations in much the same way as did Mr. Collins.

Fane was only too happy that he had Miss Darcy on one side and Hugh on the other so that Mr. Collins would be somewhat prohibited from engaging Fane with the eye contact necessary for prolonged address.

"You are unmarried, my lord?" Mr. Collins

asked him over the turtle soup.

"I have never had that pleasure."

Mr. Collins began to shake his head. "Lady Catherine de Bourgh—my benevolent patroness, you will recall—has often expounded most eloquently upon a man's needs to be married." His smug gaze moved to his silent wife. "It was on Lady Catherine's coaxing that I decided to take a wife, and it was my very good fortune that I became known in the home of Sir William Lucas." It seemed almost that Mr. Collins's puffed up when before he continued, "My esteemed father-in-law, Sir William, has not only been knighted, but he has had the great honor of having been presented at court. So you see, we Collinses have much in common with your lordship, I daresay."

Good lord, Fane hoped to God he was not in any way similar to Miss Darcy's houseguest.

His brother did him the goodness of contributing to the conversation. "How is it that you are acquainted with Miss Darcy?" Hugh asked the clergyman.

"Oh, we had not previously met, but the new Mrs. Darcy is my wife's dearest friend—as well as being my own cousin and the daughter of the gentleman from whom I have expectations of a significant inheritance—and Mrs. Darcy begged Mrs. Collins and I to come and see that Miss Darcy was well in her absence." Not to be deterred from dominating the conversation, he added, "My dear Mrs. Collins had never before seen Pemberley and was most anxious to see it." He directed his attention at Miss Darcy. "We had been told it was one of the finest country houses in England."

"And do you find that its merit was exaggerated?" Miss Darcy courteously asked.

"Oh, dear me, no! It is even finer than Rosings." Then Mr. Collins's attention was directed to the head of the table where Fane sat. "Have you had the pleasure of seeing Rosings?"

"I have not."

Mr. Collins shrugged. "I daresay it's not as grand as Bodworth House, but it is definitely one of the finer stately homes in the kingdom. Is it not, Mrs. Collins?"

"I am sure it is," that unfortunate woman answered.

"Mrs. Collins and I have been distinguished by Lady Catherine, who invites us to dine with her sometimes as many times as twice in the same week—that is, if there are no other diversions for her and her daughter."

Fane was bloody glad for the diversion of the footmen laying the second course and the subsequent passing of the dishes resulting from the change. He allowed himself to hope Mr. Collins' affection for food was as great as his affection for Lady Catherine—which seemed likely, given that he tended to corpulence. Surely the portly fellow would amuse himself with heaping helpings on his plate. But the determined man was not to be silenced. His soliloquy never ceased.

"I could not help noting, your lordship, that the sconces on your wall here in the dinner room greatly resemble those in my humble little parsonage, which I flatter myself is as fine as any country parsonage in the kingdom. Do you not agree, Mrs. Collins?"

"It is a lovely home we have there, to be sure."

Mrs. Collins earned Fane's most sincere pity.

Next, Mr. Collins praised Fane upon the excellence of the meal. "I daresay your lordship must employ a French chef for Lady Catherine de Bourgh tells me that is the practice adopted in most homes of the nobility."

"I do not have a French chef, merely a very competent cook who's been in the Farrington family since I was a lad." Fane wondered how the dinner talk might have been different with the erudite Miss Wetherspoon's sparkling conversation. Oh, how he lamented her absence! In so very many ways.

Throughout the second course, he pretended keen interest in his food to prevent himself from connecting his gaze to The Soliloquist's. This practice enabled him to completely ignore the clergyman's rambling observations.

And left him free to direct all his thoughts on that most perfect being whose presence he'd been denied. Had his rash actions lost her forever? What could he do to assure her of his sincere affection? Of course, he was prepared to offer for her.

The very thought of marrying Lucy and making a home with her here at Bodworth gave him the sensation that his heart was swelling with love, a love that spread to everything. Save Mr. Collins.

Oh how he wished to be rid of the man! Poor Miss Darcy had his profound sympathies for having to be all that was polite to her houseguest.

Finally, Fane cut into Mr. Collins's lengthy praise of something to do with Lady Catherine. "How long will you be at Pemberley?" he asked.

"Alas just the two nights. Lady Catherine assures me that she cannot face a Monday without one of my enlightening Sunday homilies. I pray that you do not find me conceited, my lord. Mrs. Collins will assure you that I am only the conduit of the great Lady Catherine's words. Is that not right, Mrs. Collins?"

"Indeed, Mr. Collins. You are an excellent conduit of Lady Catherine's unending advice." There was only a slight hint of levity in her voice, but her conceited husband was too puffed up with his own perceived importance to notice it.

Mrs. Collins certainly possessed Fane's sympathies, but now he had more respect for her.

Unaware that his wife might not hold the great Lady Catherine de Bourgh in the same high degree of affection as he, Mr. Collins continued, "Yes, my dear, Lady Catherine *is* exceedingly generous with her advice." Returning his gaze to the head of the table, he added, "It was upon the dear lady's recommendation that Mrs. Collins added peas to her garden. I daresay Lady Catherine is as well acquainted with our local soil and weather conditions as is any farmer in the shire. We always defer to Lady Catherine's superior judgment, do we not, Mrs. Collins?"

It would have been impossible to appear more bored than the unfortunate Mrs. Collins, who spoke without the slightest inflection in her voice. "Indeed we do."

What a pity it was that everyone bound in matrimony was not as gleeful as his sister Isabelle and Beauclerk. And, of course, the little he'd seen of Darcy with his bride, Fane had been struck over how well suited they were and what felicity their union had brought to the quiet Darcy.

It suddenly seemed to Fane that he'd never wanted anything more than he wished to have Miss Wetherspoon—dear Lucy—for his bride. Would she even consider him? Did she loathe him after his actions of that afternoon?

He vowed to do everything in his power to win her affections.

"If Lady Catherine were here, your lordship," Mr. Collins said, "she would urge you to take a wife. Surely it's time for you to establish the succession." His gaze flicked to Hugh. "I daresay if your brother does not hurry and wed, it may be up to you to keep the Farringtons at Bodworth." Then directing his gaze at Miss Darcy, Mr. Collins said, "Though I see no reason for his lordship to remain unmarried when a young lady of Miss Darcy's many outstanding qualities is now ready to be presented. Mark my words, my lord, Miss Darcy will be married before the year is out. You must make haste." With that comment and a self-satisfied look upon his grinning face, Mr. Collins dug into the mound of roast beef on his plate.

What a quandary Fane was in. He did not want Miss Darcy to suffer under the delusion that he meant to offer marriage, but neither did he want to humiliate her in the presence of others by denials of her eligibility. "Indeed, I am sure you are right, Mr. Collins. Miss Darcy will surely be wed before she sees her first Season through."

Fane's thoughts wandered with the same repetitive images of Lucy Wetherspoon. How he yearned to see her, to be with her, to hear the lovely trill of her laughter. And, oh how he hungered to take her in his arms! He hoped to God *she* was married—to him—before Miss Darcy ever had a season.

In his entire two and thirty years, Fane had never sat through a meal under such conditions of complete wretchedness. He could not be rid of his onerous company soon enough.

* * *

Lucy was equally as wretched as his lordship, though she would never have believed that he could possibly possess tender feelings for her. What could she offer a man like him? Why, Lord Fane should easily be able to capture the heart of any heiress in the kingdom. Even Miss Darcy—once that young lady shed her uneasiness in his presence.

What woman would not fall in love with him? He was in possession of every attribute a man could offer—save for what she suspected to be a lack of fortune. His undeniable masculinity was most certainly appealing. He exuded a sense of authority that was almost at odds with his constant displays of compassion. His knowledge surpassed that of other men, yet he did not flaunt his superiority over those other men.

The attribute that most would say was the man's greatest asset—his title—Lucy considered the biggest hindrance. She was unfit to be a countess—so unfit that it was ridiculous to even contemplate such a farcical notion.

Why could he not have been a second born? Or third or fourth? The title holder could not throw away his eligibility on someone as insignificant as a paid lady's companion who dressed in unstylish, dated bombazine.

Then her thoughts would be jolted by the memory of The Kiss. How surprised she had been when he had moved so close to her, how powerless she had been to withdraw from him, how amazingly pleasurable it was to allow him possession of her lips.

Then, as if struck by lightning, it occurred to her that an earl would never have honorable intentions toward the penniless daughter of

Benjamin Wether*fool*. Because she was poor and of no consequence, Lord Fane most likely thought to make her a mistress!

That was when she bolted away from the heavenly feel of being encircled within his arms.

She knew she could not go to Bodworth for dinner. It would be entirely too painful after what had occurred between them that afternoon to have to sit so near him and know she could never be his.

For once his lips had touched hers, Lucy knew without a shred a doubt that she had fallen in love with the Earl of Fane.

Not only did she decide she could not be in his presence again, but she also decided she must leave Pemberley. At first she told herself that she owed it to Mr. Darcy to stay with Georgiana until he returned to England. He had done her the goodness of having faith in her abilities to be a proper companion for his much-loved sister.

But she had to leave Pemberley and its close association with the man with whom she had fallen so violently in love. She determined that she must feign a mysterious ailment that would necessitate her removal from Pemberley, and she would merely switch places with Mary Ann, her sister who was closest to Lucy in temperament.

Surely Mr. Darcy would understand. If he had approved of her, he was sure to also be pleased with Mary Ann. She felt beastly to forfeit Mr. Darcy's confidence in her, but she could not bear to be close to Lord Fane and know she could never again feel herself within those sturdy arms of his.

Even as she lay in bed in her darkened room that night, she still felt that breathlessness Lord Fane's touch had given her; she could still feel the agonizing pleasure of his possession.

It was as if her very heart were being crushed into a fine powder to be carried away on the next wind. And leave a void in her chest that would never again be filled.

$\mathcal{C}$hapter 7

The following morning as Mr. and Mrs. Collins made their way down Pemberley's grand staircase, they happened upon a middle-aged woman dressed in neat clothing that indicated her place as an upper servant of high authority. "Good morning, Mr. and Mrs. Collins," she greeted.

The male half of the pair came to a stop and regarded the woman. "I daresay you must be the capable woman who keeps Pemberley's place as one of the finest homes in England."

Her head inclined modestly. "I have the good fortune to be the housekeeper here."

"Then you are just the one to direct my wife and me to the room where breakfast is served."

The lady pivoted. "If you would be so good as to follow me, I will show you."

"Despite that dear Miss Darcy led us on a merry tour just yesterday, I find myself quite lost in the vast house," said Mr. Collins. "It is even larger than Rosings, the home owned by the Darcys' aunt, where I have had the pleasure— along with my wife—of being a frequent guest. We often partake of dinner there—and very fine dinners they are! Have you had the honor of meeting Lady Catherine de Bourgh?"

"Oh, yes, many times." The lady offered no further comment upon Lady Catherine's many sterling merits.

"I do not suppose you have had the honor of visiting Rosings yourself?" asked he.

"Oh, no. I seldom get away—though I am aware of my good fortune to be able to call so lovely a place as Pemberley my home."

They came to the first floor, and the lady led the way down a long marble corridor to the dinner room where a large silver urn reposed on the gleaming mahogany sideboard along with fine porcelain cups and plates bearing the Darcy coat of arms. Mr. Collins' eyes widened and a smile climbed up his rotund face when he saw the plentiful amounts of toast and kippers that were offered on the sideboard.

"Mr. Darcy prefers coffee, so that is what you will find in the urn," she told them.

"It will gratify you to know," Mr. Collins told the housekeeper, "that Lady Catherine will not be the Darcys' only connection to the nobility." The manner in which Mr. Collins stood there with such an air of importance could rival that of the Regent himself.

"The Darcy family has many common ancestors with the nobility, I am sure," she replied.

Mr. Collins's eyes sparkled. "Alas, not so great a connection as Miss Darcy winning a proposal of marriage from an earl."

The lady's eyes rounded. "Do you mean to tell me that Lord Fane has offered for our dear Miss Georgiana?"

He nodded. "He indicated as much to me last night—and in Miss Darcy's presence—"

"Dearest," Mrs. Collins interjected, "That is not exactly what Lord Fane said—"

Mr. Collins's brows lowered, his eyes narrowed, and he held up a flattened palm to silence his wife. "My dear, when you have had as much experience as I in dealing with people you will know these things I have come to know so instinctively." He looked up in time to see the housekeeper scurrying from the chamber, no doubt to tell the others of Miss Darcy's betrothal.

Mr. Collins was well aware that there wasn't a servant in all of Great Britain who did not aspire to be in service to the nobility, and he was rather proud of himself for being the bearer of such stupendous news.

* * *

Since Lucy had determined to continue feigning her illness, she planned to keep to her bed. The first thing she did that morning was to write a letter to Mary Ann to beg that her sister switch places with her. Lest Mary Ann think the position as Miss Darcy's companion undesirable, Lucy wrote,

"Miss Darcy is a perfect angel, and Pemberley is one of England's greatest houses. In every aspect, my position here is one to be envied. In strictest confidence," Lucy wrote to the sister to whom she was closest, *"I will confess to you, my dear Mary Ann, what I will tell no one else: I have the misfortune of having fallen rather stupidly in love with a man who is most ineligible, and I must remove myself from the painful necessity of seeing him regularly."*

When the maid brought a pot of hot chocolate to her chamber, Lucy asked her to post the letter.

"Oh, Miss Wetherspoon," the exuberant maid said, "the whole house is in a dither with our wondrous news. You'd think the queen 'erself was coming to Pemberley!"

Lucy fluffed up her bed pillows and settled back so the young woman could tuck the tray on either side of her. "Whatever has incited such happiness?"

"Our Miss Darcy is to become a countess!"

How could this be? Less than a full day ago, Georgiana had no prospects of matrimony, and the only nobleman . . . Lucy's heart constricted. Surely Lord Fane had not offered for Georgiana on the very same day as . . . The Kiss.

Lucy's pulses hammered, her breath became labored, her stomach felt like it did at the sight of maggots gnawing at spoiled gray-green vegetables. The only time Lucy had heretofore felt so wretched was the day she lost her dear Mama.

Grief. That's what she was experiencing! Grave, senses-numbing, tear-inducing, soul-destroying grief.

For even though Lucy suspected Lord Fane may have had designs on making her his mistress—certainly never his wife—something deep within her told her that she had in some small way captured his affections.

But she had clearly deluded herself. Because she was so besottedly attracted to him, she had mistakenly thought he might return her regard.

She need not ask the maid to whom Miss Darcy was betrothed. Lucy instinctively knew the dreaded answer. "On second thought, I think I shall wait to send that letter," she told the maid. If Miss Darcy would soon be marrying, she would have no further need for another companion when Lucy left. And leave, Lucy must.

The maid took Mary Ann's letter from her apron pocket and placed it upon Lucy's tray.

Lucy's voice shook when she spoke. "To whom has Miss Darcy become betrothed?" One miniscule particle of childish hope strummed in her breast. *Perhaps it's not he. . .*

"Lord Fane of Bodworth House!" The maid placed the tray on Lucy's bed, then stepped back and regarded her. "Are you sure I can't post yer letter?"

Lucy dare not try her voice for she was on the precipice of tears. She attempted a smile while nodding. Once the door closed behind the maid, Lucy wept.

She knew she should go congratulate Georgiana on her forthcoming nuptials, but she also knew she was incapable of doing so without completely breaking down. And that would never do. While Lucy was incapable of feeling malice toward sweet Georgiana, she lacked the magnanimousness needed to look upon her friend without jealousy.

How could such a transformation have come over that young lady in less than a day? Lucy was certain that Georgiana had not been in love with Lord Fane on the previous day. (Of course, Lucy also would have said she was certain yesterday that Lord Fane was *not* in love with Georgiana, but she had obviously been mistaken.)

Now Lucy bitterly regretted that she had not gone to Bodworth House the night before. Would Lord Fane still have offered for Georgiana if Lucy had been there?

What did it really matter *when* he offered for Miss Darcy? Such a proposal was inevitable. The sad reality was that he felt compelled to marry an heiress. That he was so mercenary in the selection of a wife tarnished Lord Fane in Lucy's eyes—but not tarnished enough to eradicate her profound feelings for him!

In her whole life Lucy had never been capable of jealousy. She had not coveted the lovely dresses other ladies wore. She had never unfavorably compared the Wetherspoons' modest house on Milsop Street to the fine mansions in Mayfair. She had never even wished she had been born blonde like Mary Ann—even though Lucy preferred blonde hair. It had always been Lucy's lot to happily accept what she had for there were so many others who were less fortunate.

Yet today, she was prostrate with jealousy of Miss Georgiana Darcy.

* * *

Fane had encouraged Hugh to see to electioneering in Halifax today. He wanted him out the way. His brother need not know his intentions toward Lucy Wetherspoon. (Truth be told, he feared that both of them had romantic designs upon the same lady.) For today Fane planned to drop to his knees and beg that lovely creature to become his countess. And if that most perfect being did him the goodness of accepting his suit, *then* he would tell Hugh.

For when it came to Lucy Wetherspoon, Fane did not want an even playing field. He intended to do whatever he could to increase the probability of garnering an affirmative answer from her. *Probability.* The very word reminded him of her: clever, amiable, bewitchingly beautiful Lucy Wetherspoon.

It seemed almost inconceivable that it had only been one day since he'd last seen her. The deprivation of not seeing her at that interminable dinner the previous night must account for his current thirst to behold her.

With a quickening in his heart and a smile upon his face, he rapped upon the front door of Pemberley. The butler himself opened it and begged Fane to enter. On previous occasions, that man had exuded a most somber countenance, but not today. On this day his face brightened upon seeing who was calling. Before Fane could even tell him he desired to call upon Miss Wetherspoon, that most capable of servants smiled at him. A smile, for pity's sake! He'd never before seen a butler smile. Had it been part of a butler's training to appear as one would at the wake of a beloved friend?

As if the smile were not shocking enough, that servant reversed their roles and greeted Fane with astonishing courtliness. "Lord Fane, allow me to say what felicity has come to all of us at Pemberley over the announcement of your nuptials."

How in the bloody hell had all these people learned he planned to marry Lucy Wetherspoon? He had not told a single soul. And he was quite certain she would not have. He wasn't even certain she would have him. He regarded the upper servant from beneath lowered brows. Why in the bloody hell did it matter to Pemberley's servants that he wished to marry Lucy?

"That is very kind of you," Fane said, "though I daresay nothing has yet been acknowledged." It was not as if Lucy had ever indicated a preference for him. Quite the contrary. She had repeatedly tried to impress upon him the many worthy merits of Miss Georgiana Darcy.

"Yes, quite. I do understand—especially since the lady's brother is out of the country."

But Lucy's father was still alive! Would it not be him—and not a brother—who would have to give Fane consent to wed his daughter? Of course, she *was* of age to marry without a parent's permission.

Then he experienced the sluggish feeling that something was amiss. Was it not Miss Darcy whose brother was away from the country? Good lord, could the source of this man's felicity be because he thought Fane was going to make Miss Darcy his countess?

Surely not! He'd not told anyone he was considering courting The Heiress. Except for Hugh. Had Hugh thought to ensure a clear path to Miss Wetherspoon's heart by entrapping Fane in a loveless marriage with another woman?

He had never been more out of charity with his back-stabbing brother. Hugh was sure to know that Fane, as a man of honor, would feel obliged to actually offer for The Heiress rather than to publicly humiliate her. Especially since Fane was so close to Darcy, who was exceedingly attached to his sister. He would never again be able to face Darcy were he to make his sister a pitiable laughing stock.

But what of his own needs? God, but he'd never needed anything like he needed Lucy Wetherspoon.

Sunk in melancholy, he wondered if fate was trying to shake sense into him. It must be fate that was pulling him toward matrimony with Miss Darcy, fate that lie in the restoration of Bodworth to honor the past and preserve the future.

As if the weight of every single stone and brick in Bodworth were upon his back, Fane knew where his duty lay.

He cleared his throat. "Is Miss Darcy available to callers?"

"I am sure she will be to *you*, my lord. Allow me to announce your lordship. Won't you come wait in the morning room?"

Fane was grateful he would not have to climb that huge, open staircase to the floor where the drawing room was located. The sooner he was shown into the nearby morning room, the less likely he was to have to face that annoying Mr. Collins. *One more day.* And the Collinses would return to their parsonage. Fane would prefer to break his leg than have to sit through another dinner with that man.

While Fane had never admired the arrogant Lady Catherine de Bourgh, that woman now earned his sympathy for her considerable civility to The Soliloquist.

As he awaited Miss Darcy, he sunk even lower with the weight of all Bodworth's rocks and mortar.

When Miss Darcy finally entered the chamber, her downcast eyes avoided his. She looked as low as he felt. She finally lifted her gaze ever so slightly and spoke in an equally slight voice. "Won't you be seated, my lord?"

"You first."

Despite all the sofas and settees in the chamber, she determined on a single chair. Was that so she would avoid having to sit near him? He had to own she had never given him the slightest indication that she would favor his suit.

He remained standing, moving closer to her. The sooner he did his duty, the sooner he could leave. He did not know where he wanted to be, but he wanted to be alone with his morose thoughts.

He forced himself to clear his throat. "Miss Darcy, I would like to ask if I might seek your brother's permission to woo you." It was a very bad effort, but he was inexperienced in such matters.

Her eyes rounded as she looked up at him. "But my brother is in Italy."

Did she think him an idiot? "Perhaps I did not clarify myself properly. I am certainly prepared to wait until his return to speak to Darcy. What I need from you is permission to do so. It is a grave step, an irrevocable step; therefore, I understand if you need time to consider it."

Her gaze was trained upon the pale blue of her frock. Indeed, she did not look up from her lap. She merely nodded. "Yes, my lord. I should like time."

Her response oddly pleased him. At least he was not yet caught in parson's mousetrap.

On his return to Bodworth, the skies became black, then erupted. Nothing could have better suited his bleak mood.

$\mathcal{C}$hapter 8

It was only natural that Miss Darcy would be solicitous of Lucy's welfare. Servants—even ones permitted to dine with their betters—never stayed in their beds unless they were gravely ill.

The door to Lucy's chamber eased open, and Georgiana came strolling into the room, attempting to effect a cheerful countenance. But Lucy understood Miss Darcy well enough to know her cheerfulness was as feigned as Lucy's sickness. "I've brought you flowers in the hopes of brightening your day. I've been ever so worried about you." She came to set the vase of daffodils on the table beside Lucy's bed.

"There is no more cheerful flower than the daffodil. I thank you."

Georgiana scooted a chair across the carpet and sat near Lucy. "Shall I send for the apothecary? I understand you're no better than you were last night."

"Please do not trouble yourself. I have a monumental aversion to both medicinals and to bleeding, but that's enough of me. I must offer felicitations upon your betrothal."

Georgiana's brows lowered. "I do not understand how it is that everyone at Pemberley has heard that his lordship has offered for me."

Even just hearing that dreaded confirmation caused Lucy's stomach to drop and her heartbeat to drum madly.

"As enamored over nobility as is Mr. Collins," Georgiana continued, "I cannot help but to sense his hand in this. Nevertheless, I am not yet officially betrothed to his lordship."

"How is that?"

"He has given me time to consider the proposal before he seeks my brother's permission."

How could any woman need time to accept Lord Fane? Why, there was no finer man in the kingdom. Even if he had stolen a kiss from her. "Just think how happy your brother will be over the match."

"That is at present the single most important inducement for me to agree to the marriage."

"I don't know how it is that you are not in love with him, but I urge you to wait. You must not marry where your heart is not engaged."

"It is not, and I do not believe his is, either." Poor Georgiana's youthful face collapsed with worry. Finally she looked up and addressed Lucy. "Since you are like a sister I should like to ask you a question. If you do not want to answer, I will understand."

"What is it you wish to ask?"

"I know I've not been much in the world, but I am not so stupid that I do not know a woman as beautiful as you has had to have received many proposals of marriage. Have you not?"

Lucy swallowed. "I have."

"Yet you are still unmarried."

Lucy nodded. "I chose to live in my father's house where there was an abundance of love rather to marry a man in the absence of that vital emotion. I did not know Papa would lose our home. . ."

"Then you might have married where there was no love?"

"I doubt that I would."

"Have you ever been in love?"

"I have. I was even betrothed once, a long time ago."

Georgiana's eyes rounded. "Did he die before you could wed?"

Lucy started to chuckle. It was the first time in all these years she could recall that painful time in her life without melancholy. "No, but his love for me did. His mother invited me and Papa to come to their country home, which was nearly as lovely as Pemberley, but once she met us, she convinced Lawrence of how ineligible I was. He broke the betrothal and offered me an annuity for the breech. I was too proud to accept it. Which was very foolish of me." She looked up at Georgiana and shrugged.

"And you've never wanted to marry since then?"

Lucy hesitated before answering. "I think most women want to marry. It is just that the men to whom I am attracted will always find me ineligible."

"I do not believe that. It is inconceivable to me that someone with your beauty could not marry any man in the kingdom. Even a duke!"

"Now I will say you do need more experience in the world, my dear Georgiana!"

After Georgiana left, Lucy should have reflected on the good tidings that Georgiana was not *yet* betrothed to Lord Fane, but even if Miss Darcy told him today that she could not marry him, Lucy knew he would just find another heiress.

She had to leave Pemberley. She had to keep up the pretense that she was in declining health.

* * *

It was just as well that Hugh was away. He knew Fane too well. His brother would have judged his thunderous mood and understood its source. After Fane left Pemberley, he rode his horse as fast and hard as he possibly could. How in the devil could he have so thoroughly destroyed his own happiness? All for honor. And Bodworth.

It mattered not to him that he was wet and cold and physically miserable. What did it matter if he took sick and died? Life without Lucy was just another kind of death. He had knowingly just agreed to sacrifice his life. For honor and Bodworth.

There was no consolation in that knowledge.

* * *

In the next few days, Lord Fane *did* become sick and was forced to his bed. Hugh returned from electioneering and grew alarmed over his brother's grave condition. He stood helplessly by Fane's bed as fever ravaged his brother's body.

In his delirium, Fane kept calling for Lucy. Not once did her utter Miss Darcy's name. Hugh sent for the apothecary. He summoned a physician. Yet still, Fane's condition did not improve.

On the second week, the physician began to prepare Hugh for the worst. Though he had not left his brother's sick room since returning from his electioneering, Hugh thought of something. Perhaps there was one more thing he could do to restore his brother's health.

* * *

Lucy was sick of pretending to be sick, sick of the bedchamber which once had given her so much joy. She was even sick of reading— something she would never have dreamed possible even a week earlier.

While she was stretched out on her bed—wearing her old blue bombazine—there was a knock upon her chamber door. The butler announced himself, and she permitted him to open the door. "Miss Wetherspoon, I know you're ill, but Mr. Hugh Farrington is begging to see you. He says it is an urgent matter, a matter of life and death."

She had heard that Lord Fane had been suffering with fever, but would not allow herself to think . . . the worst. She leapt from her bed. "I shall come right down."

The dread that had filled her when she learned his lordship had offered for Georgiana was nothing compared to the dread that filled her at that moment. She was far too upset as she raced down the staircase to even consider why Mr. Farrington was seeking her.

When she beheld that young man, the morose look on his face confirmed her worst fears. "My brother. . . " his voice cracked, "is dying, and I cannot deny him the only thing that he asks for."

She only barely summoned her shaky voice. "What does he ask for?"

"You. He keeps calling your name."

"I must go to him." Now her voice, too, cracked.

* * *

Fane was dreaming. He felt as if he were in a long tunnel. He kept calling Lucy's name. Then she asked, "Why does he call for me?"

"My brother's in love with you." Fane was vaguely aware that was his brother's voice. And Lucy's.

"You are mistaken," said she.

"Nooooooo," Fane cried out.

"I knew it would be good for him if you came!" Hugh said. "That was the first time he's been even slightly coherent since the day his fever commenced."

Fane felt bad that he'd thought his brother a back stabber. Hugh was attempting to advance Fane's suit with Lucy. Suddenly, Fane realized this was no dream.

He was gravely ill, and Lucy had come to him. His eyes opened. When he beheld her standing there, her eyes swollen and red, his heart swelled. Then he realized it was she who clasped his hand, and he felt almost as if he could do a Highland fling.

"I must tell you. . ." Fane said to her, "I came to Pemberley to beg your hand, but . . ." He grew breathless and was unable to continue.

"I believe Mr. Collins might have inadvertently announced to some servants what he *thought* your intentions were. . ." she faltered.

His gaze swept tenderly over her. "You're beautiful. Even in that hideous dress."

A smile transformed his brother's face. "I believe Fane *is* on the road to recovery."

* * *

That afternoon Georgiana Darcy came to the sick room. She stood silently at the door for a moment, then spoke. "I believe I knew before either of you knew that you were made for other. I felt sure Lord Fane was in love with you, my dear Lucy." Then her soft gaze fell on the sick lord. "That is why I could never consent to marry you."

Lucy could have swooned with relief.

"In fact, I traced the rumor of my supposed betrothal among the servants until I reached the source. Mrs. Reynolds said that the morning after

I dined at Bodworth that Mr. Collins told her I was to wed Lord Fane." Georgiana's gaze returned to Lord Fane. "It appears then that when you came to call that morning, dear Tibbs congratulated you; therefore, your sense of honor compelled you to offer for me. It's all been a big muddle, the blame for which squarely rests on Mr. Collins' meddling shoulders. I will own, I was not sorry to see them leave Pemberley, though Mrs. Collins was exceedingly gracious."

Fane still was very weak, but he managed to respond in short bursts. "Miss Darcy is far wiser that her tender years would indicate."

* * *

Lucy refused to leave his side the next few days. She understood now that he loved her, though his brother's words were the only ones to confirm it. She did not need to hear dear Lord Fane's words to know that he was in love with her. Knowing that in his darkest hour he had called for her, seeing the look of love flicker in his gentle gaze, feeling his hand firmly clasping hers spoke more eloquently than any words ever could.

She swelled with love when Hugh Farrington attributed his brother's recovery to her. On the third day, Lord Fane insisted he was strong enough for a walk with Lucy in Bodworth's parterre garden, which was sheltered from the north winds.

It was cool but sunny, and she continued in that same serviceable bombazine dress as they strolled hand in hand.

"That night you failed to come for dinner," he began, "I had planned to try to entice you into marrying me by showing you Bodworth's finer features. I even hoped to get you alone that night and bring you here so that I could beg for your hand."

Her eyes moistened. "I feigned sickness that night because it was too painful to be with you and know that for Bodworth's sake you must wed another. I . . . planned to leave Pemberley." It was the boldest statement she had ever uttered to a man. For once, she had tossed her pride to the wind to express her love.

He stopped and faced her, two masculine hands tilting her face toward him. "You are my Bodworth. You are my reason to live. You are the only one with whom I've ever wanted to spend the rest of my life." Then, shaking from weakness, he lowered himself to his knees and peered up at her, love sparkling in those beloved eyes. "I beg you to accept the heart I give you. I beg that you will do me the goodness of becoming my countess."

At first she was frozen to the spot. She knew that until she breathed her last breath on earth she would remember this moment. Then she realized her dearest Lord Fane was awaiting her response.

"Oh, yes, Lord Fane! Yes!" She threw herself on the gravel path beside him, her arms coming around him, glorying in the feel of being encircled within his sturdy arms. Then their lips met for a tender, powerful kiss.

After they managed to return to a standing position, she grew solemn. "Do you not need to marry an heiress?"

"All that I need is you, Lucy. I could be happy in a crofter's hut with you beside me every night."

They continued along the gravel path. "And now that we are betrothed, my dearest, you must call me Alex," he said.

"Do you know, my lord, I mean my dearest Alex, that throughout my life our family fortunes have had pendulous swings, and because of the many times when funds were low, I have learned a great deal about economizing. I assure you I will not need fancy things."

"You will have the Fane jewels—and you *will* have new dresses. I shan't want you to wear that blue dress again—even if I did fall in love with you in it. And there is one other thing I must insist upon."

She arched a brow.

"You are not to ride a horse unless I am there to keep you safe."

Epilogue

Six months later. . .

"Oh, Alex, wait until you see Elizabeth Darcy! I have never seen a woman look so happy with her wedded state." Lucy lacked only her jewels to be dressed to greet the Darcys for dinner. She handed off the ruby necklace for her husband to clasp at her throat.

He moved to her and lowered his head to drop a nibbling kiss on her neck. "I am offended."

She peered at him through her looking glass. "Why, my dearest?"

"Because I had hoped it was *my* bride, not Darcy's, who was the loveliest, happiest."

Lucy whirled around. "Oh, my dear, dear Alex, there is not a happier woman in the world than I."

Just as he went to kiss her, there was a knock upon her chamber door, and her husband bid the butler to enter.

"Lady Fane," the butler said, "you've received a post that's marked urgent. I thought to bring it to you right away." He came forward, extending a silver tray upon which the letter rested.

"Thank you, Stevens." She glanced at it. "It's from Papa!" Her face crumbled. Her head shook. Her voice cracked. "I cannot open it. It must be something terrible."

Alex took the letter and opened it. She watched

him through her looking glass, her heart drumming madly. Then she saw that her husband was smiling, and relief flooded her. She whirled to face him. "What is it?"

"It's exceedingly good news. It appears I've wed an heiress."

"Whatever are you talking about?"

"Your father's plantation in the West Indies has had an unprecedented sugar crop, and each of Mr. Wetherspoon's eleven children is to receive twenty-five thousand pounds."

Papa had always told his laddies and lasses that his ship was going to come in one day. After a stunned silence, she finally spoke. "I am happy for Papa, but I'm happiest for you. You loved me when I had nothing but an ugly dress. You were willing to put all the needs of Bodworth aside in order to marry a penniless woman who loved you with all her heart." She came to her feet, and her most beloved husband drew her into his arms.

"No man has ever been richer than I. Now let us go greet the Darcys. I must find out all about their journey for I fancy taking my own bride on a trip to Italy—now that we are wealthy."

The End

Miss Darcy's Secret Love

(Jane Austen Sequels, Book 2)

CHERYL BOLEN

Copyright © 2016 by Cheryl Bolen

$\mathcal{C}$hapter 1

Miss Georgiana Darcy's debut into Society—if judged by proposals of marriage—should have been considered a spectacular success. Eleven men had offered for the lady, and she had just barely turned seventeen! Those gentlemen included six lords, one up-and-coming Member of Parliament, one poet of moderate success, and three mere misters. These eleven men all had one thing in common: each was in want of a fortune.

And Miss Darcy came with an exceedingly generous dowry of thirty thousand—the same as the enormously rich Duke of Devonshire had settled upon his daughter.

Though Georgiana knew that to return to Pemberley without being betrothed would vastly disappoint her brother, she had been powerless to choose to spend the rest of her life with any of those eleven men. Dearest Fitzwilliam had taken such pains—not to mention considerable expense—to procure for his sister the finest drawing masters, and music teachers, and dancing masters in the kingdom. She truly hated to disappoint him.

She thought perhaps, since she could not win the heart of the only man she had ever wanted to wed, she might accept Lord Hampton. With an eye to appeasing her brother, she had asked that Fitzwilliam invite his lordship to Pemberley, and the earl was due to arrive that afternoon.

Because half the ladies in the *ton* practically swooned whenever the handsome (purportedly reformed) rake was near, she had been flattered by Lord Hampton's attentions.

She must own, he was exceedingly handsome. And his Rafferty Hall was one of the greatest English aristocratic homes. His prowess at sporting pursuits had won the admiration of other men. He was said to be a noted whip. He took fencing from Angelo, and he'd studied pugilism under Jackson. His betting at White's was legendary.

That last, single piece of information about him may have contributed to her reluctance to bestow her dowry upon him. She would not at all approve were Lord Hampton to squander it away on a wager over which raindrop could reach the window sill the fastest. For while the Darcys were possessed of a large fortune, they had never been flamboyant spenders. She knew too many noble families deprived of the homes their ancestors had built because of the frivolous wagering of this last generation.

How she wished there was someone to whom she could confess her apprehensions. Though she adored her brother's wife, dear Lizzy was just as desirous as Fitzwilliam for Georgiana to make a brilliant match. If only Lucy—now Lady Fane— hadn't gone off to Italy. She could ask Lucy anything and be assured of a thoughtful, intelligent response. How she missed Lucy!

Now that her brother had invited Lord Hampton to Pemberley, Lizzy—who truly was wise like Lucy—would have an opportunity to observe his lordship. An excellent judge of character, Lizzy could be depended upon to give Georgiana wise counsel once she was better acquainted with Lord Hampton's attributes.

Georgiana had time enough before Lord Hampton's arrival to indulge in an activity that had always contributed to her felicity. Fitzwilliam had told her that while his lordship was at Pemberley, it might be best if she did not demonstrate her more masculine qualities. Such as angling.

As a young girl she had become nearly obsessed with angling at Pemberley's lovely lake. The obsession had begun when she followed Robert Farrington around like a devoted pup. Wherever Robert went, she had followed. Whatever Robert had done, she did. Vastly kind hearted, he put up with her devotion and allowed her to join him in his endeavors. The inclusion demanded that she emulate a boy. Which she did. Robert thought of her as he would a younger brother. He even shortened her name to George. He could have called her anything as long as he permitted her to shadow his every move.

Though he thought of her as a lad or as a brother, she never thought of him as a brother. To her, Robert Farrington was a demigod. He was the man she dreamed of marrying when she grew up.

Her heart had very nearly broken when he became an officer in the Dragoons and went off to the Peninsula. She prayed often for his safe return, and she vowed she would never fish in the lake until he came home.

And she had not. Until today. Before she united herself to another man, she must resolve to purge Robert from her dreams. She must return to those activities she had previously associated with

Robert, activities that had always brought her great felicity.

When his eldest brother, Lord Fane, had told her that Robert had fallen in love with a Spanish noblewoman, she had only barely been able to conceal her devastation. After many agonizing days, she came to the conclusion she must abandon her dreams of capturing Robert's heart now that she was all grown up. That is when she had decided she would have a Season after all.

When she did marry, her prospective husband must be made to comprehend how important angling was to her. And riding. She loved to ride hard and fast. Her future husband must understand that she would never consent to sitting a horse with her spine stiff as her mount gently cantered across the landscape.

Dressed in her shabbiest dress, she strolled across the park, toting her fishing pole and creel and admiring the varying shades of green in Pemberley's landscape on this fine spring day. As she neared the lake, she saw that someone was already fishing there. It could not be Lord Fane, who regularly fished at Pemberley. Perhaps Lizzy's aunt and uncle had come. Her uncle was fond of fishing. But surely Lizzy would have told her if the Gardners were to be there during Lord Hampton's stay.

As she drew nearer the lake, she thought for a moment the man fishing from the banks was Robert. But it couldn't be. He was standing on the same spot that Robert had always favored. Dear heavens above, could it be Robert? Her heartbeat began to roar.

The fisherman must have caught sight of someone, for he turned toward her.

It was Robert! He was smiling at her. She was powerless to suppress a huge smile.

"George! I thought you were in London."

"I have only just returned." She hurried across the thirty yards that separated them.

He put down his pole and faced her, bowing.

Even if she had lost him to a Spanish noblewoman, she wanted to demonstrate to him that she was now all grown up. She continued to hold the fishing pole in her left hand, but put down the creel, freeing her right hand, and offered it as if they were in a drawing room or ballroom, despite that she wore no gloves.

He stood frozen for a moment. "Good lord, you truly are all grown up!" Then he realized he must kiss the hand, which he barely did.

Her pulse accelerated. Robert Farrington had never before touched her like that. "When did you return?" she managed, her voice surprisingly free from the trembling that seemed to have overtaken her body.

"Only last night. I was disappointed to learn Fane was out of the country." His eyes sparkled with mirth. "I was especially looking forward to meeting the new Lady Fane. I have been apprised of her beauty."

"When you do meet her, you will find reports of her beauty were not exaggerated." Her expression collapsed. "Poor Robert! You must feel exceedingly low to have missed your brother after not seeing him for so long." Then she was unable to prevent herself from gushing, "By all that's holy, it is so very good to see you!"

"I cannot tell you how powerfully I've longed to be home."

"You were greatly missed."

His gaze rolled along her, fastening on the pole she held. "Let us continue our conversation as we fish."

For the next few minutes, they got themselves situated on the banks, she baited her hook with maggots, and tossed in her line.

"Often during these past four years, I recalled those lazy summer days when you and I would never tire of angling."

"Me too." She would not admit she'd no heart to ever fish without him. "Did you have the opportunity to fish in Spain or Portugal?"

"As often as I could, and each time I did, I thought of you."

His comment sent her heart fluttering. In his absence, she could not bear thinking of him. Perhaps that is why she had refused to fish without him. She would have too painfully recalled him, and thinking of him only caused her to worry over his welfare. Scarcely a family she knew had not lost one of their young men to this terrible war. Or they returned with a missing limb. She wanted to remember the cheerful youth Robert had been.

"I daresay you pictured me as twelve," she finally said, squinting at him.

"Of course."

Was he not going to make some sort of comment about her maturity? "Oh, Robert, I am so sorry no one was at Bodworth to welcome you home." Her gaze swung from the lake to peer into his amber eyes. "I assure you, all of us at Pemberley do rejoice in your return."

"I will own, I was disappointed that Bodworth was bereft of my loved ones, but it is entirely my own fault. I should have stopped at Fane House in

London before proceeding. It was my hunger to see Bodworth—and Pemberley—that forced me to come straight from Portsmouth to Derbyshire."

She was pleased that he had such a fond desire to return to Pemberley, that to him it also resonated as home. Of course, this very lake had been built by the Farringtons. Much of the land that was now part of Pemberley had once belonged to the Farringtons. "Whilst you are here, you must think of the Darcys as your family. We shall expect you to dine with us every night. I shan't like to think of you eating alone."

"I shall be most grateful of the opportunity to dine with you. How is your brother? I've heard that he too is now married."

"I've never seen him better. He and his bride fairly glow when in each other's presence." It suddenly occurred to her that Robert may not have come alone. Perhaps he had married that Spanish noblewoman and brought her home to Bodworth. A feeling of dread strummed in Georgiana's breast as she turned to face him. "Have you come alone?"

"Yes."

She exhaled the breath she'd been holding. "I seem to recall Lord Fane telling me something about you fancying yourself in love with a senorita."

"I am in love with her, but I've not wed yet. That is why I've come home. I must procure Fane's permission before I can marry."

Georgiana recalled that he was not yet of age! He would not be one and twenty for another eight months. She was exactly three years younger than he. When he reached his majority, she would turn eighteen. "Have her parents given their consent to the union?"

He shook his head morosely. "Nothing at all has been settled." He frowned. Frowning was most alien to Robert's countenance. He, more than anyone she knew, was forever smiling. "I believe things would be vastly different were I the title holder. Younger sons have it so much more difficult."

"Not necessarily. Before he married, Lord Fane had the burden of rescuing Bodworth from dry rot and leaky roofs. Those worries nearly forced him to marry an heiress." She would not mention that the heiress had been she. It was no source of pride that men wanted her only for her money.

"But I thought his lovely bride was an heiress."

"As it turned out, she did come into a large sum of money—but not until after your brother had fallen in love with her and begged for her hand whilst thinking her penniless."

"I am delighted that love has flourished." He sighed. "I never before minded not being the firstborn. Until Veronica."

So that was her name. Georgiana uncharitably thought of how gratified she would be if Veronica got the pox. Would Robert still love her if her face were disfigured? "I suppose your Veronica is beautiful." Why was Georgiana torturing herself with questions about the lady he loved?

His smiled returned, and he nodded. "Nearly every officer in our regiment fancies himself in love with her."

"How fortunate for you that she favored your suit." And how unfortunate for Georgiana.

He shrugged. "I may have given the wrong impression. Allow me to say I was one of three officers to whom she showed a marked preference."

Georgiana could not help but to wonder if Veronica might be keeping all her options open (as Georgiana secretly prayed the popular senorita would bestow her affections elsewhere, though Georgiana could not fathom anyone *not* falling in love with him).

A powerful tug upon her pole nearly yanked it from her hands. "I've got a bite!" She planted her feet and stood erect as she attempted to reel in her catch. "He's a big one!" Her pole bowed, and she had to grip it with every bit of might her slim body could harness.

It took her a full five minutes before she prevailed over the perch. After she reeled it in, Robert helped remove it from her hook. "This is one of the biggest perch I've seen. He must weigh close to three pounds!"

Had he just told her she was beautiful, she could not have been happier.

While she was tucking the fish into her creel, Robert baited her hook. "I do believe, George, you're the only girl in the kingdom who is not terrified of maggots. Never could see how something so small could produce such agitation in the female gender."

She resumed her command of the pole. "Nor could I, but I daresay it is because I spent too much time with you. Do you know, Robert, I don't believe I ever told you that you were my very dearest friend."

He went solemn for a moment. She saw him swallow, and the expression upon his face softened. "By Jove, George, I believe you were my best friend!"

She frowned. "Why past tense? Have I been

supplanted?"

He gave her an odd look, as if he were pondering a question of great import. "I do not suppose you have. We've been very good friends for a very long time, and it's devilishly good to see you again. I will own, I think of you as a sister."

"That is not what a lady wishes to hear!"

He shrugged. "I cannot think of you as a lady. You're just George to me. Always will be."

"I will have you know there are many others who consider me a lady. Do you know I've just had my first Season?"

"Hugh wrote me that you were a great success. Have you become betrothed?"

She shook her head.

He gave her a pitying glance. "Do not fret. You'll succeed next year."

She whirled to him and glared. "Mr. Robert Farrington, I will have you know that I am not betrothed by my own choice. I had opportunities."

Now he glared. "Opportunities? Plural?"

She did not like to boast. Indeed, she was aware that her great success in London was not owing to either her charms or her beauty but to her fortune. But this once, she felt compelled to flaunt her successes in his doubting face. "Yes. Eleven, actually. And six of them were from title holders."

A smile broke across his face. "Well done, George!"

"Though I haven't yet bestowed my affections upon any of them, I have invited Lord Hampton to Pemberley. He will arrive later today. Do you know him?"

His eyes rounded. "The noted whip?"

She watched the water ripple where she had

cast her line. "I do believe his riding is rather well thought of."

"Then I will have the pleasure of meeting him when I come to dinner tonight?"

His voice showed more animation than it had since they had greeted one another. Would that she could summon a similar exuberance from him. "Yes."

"Capital! Though I've not previously met him, I watched him break the faro bank at White's shortly before I left England."

"Your brother permitted you to accompany him to White's at so tender an age?" She was surprised, since Lord Fane had spent many years avoiding the gaming tables that had almost brought ruin to his family during his father's lifetime.

"Though Fane dislikes gaming, he wanted me to have the opportunity to see White's before I left the country."

She wondered if Lord Fane had feared his brother would die on a foreign battlefield. She had certainly feared as much, though she would not allow Robert to know that, especially with him planning to return to the Peninsula.

Something pulled at her pole, then it went lax. "I am very vexed." She reeled in her line. It was exactly as she had suspected. Her bait had been snatched by a cunning fish.

"Why are you vexed?"

"See for yourself."

His gaze went to her bare hook dangling just above the surface of the water. "They got your maggots!" His brows lowered with concern. "Should you like me to re-bait for you?"

"I am perfectly capable of baiting my own

hook."

He looked admiringly at her. "You fish as well as any man, by Jove!"

She flashed him a defiant look. "And how do I ride?"

"As well as any man?"

"That is the correct answer."

She baited her hook, and they resumed fishing, each of them lost in a comforting silence. Minutes later, Robert started to chuckle, then the chuckle turned into a full-fledged laugh.

"What is so amusing?" she asked.

He turned to her. "Have you dressed as a lad recently to sneak into shooting parties?"

Then she started laughing.

"Do you know how many times in Spain I thought of you when I picked up my musket? It was a great lark, but I'm astonished no one recognized you that day."

"I couldn't believe my own brother did not realize it was me beneath your cast-off clothing!"

"You did have your hair beneath your hat."

"And my figure at the time was that of a lad." She was aware that his gaze darted to her chest, likely trying to determine if that area of her figure had developed in his absence. What a pity that she possessed so little there!

"You've not opened a grouse season since then?"

"Of course not. My brother keeps stressing that I must act like a lady."

"My sisters wrote me of how accomplished you are in music."

"I shall have to express my gratitude to them when we meet."

"So you don't fancy shooting as you used to?"

She shrugged. "I couldn't without you."

"It was just as good that my influence upon you was removed. No proper lady should do something of that sort."

"But did you not just say you could never think of me as a lady?"

"I did not mean it that way! Your brother's right. You can't go around acting like a lad anymore."

"In your absence, I will own that I have not. But now that you have returned, I may very well revert to my deplorable ways. Witness the maggots."

His flashing eyes connected with hers, and they both broke out laughing.

In spite of the years he had been gone and the hardships he must have endured, Robert seemed little changed. In some ways, she felt almost as if the two of them had settled right back into their familiar ways, comfortable in each other's presence.

"By Jove, George, I am happy to be home."

Not as happy as she was to have him home.

She hated to leave him, but as the afternoon wore on, she knew she had to return to the house and make herself—with the help of her French maid—presentable for Lord Hampton's arrival. She reluctantly bid Robert good-bye. "Do not forget you are in the country, and we eat dinner early. We shall expect you at Pemberley at dusk."

He gave her a mock salute. "Captain Farrington shall present himself at that hour."

Her eyes brightened. "You will wear your regimentals?" She could swoon with the anticipation of seeing him in his smart uniform.

"I will."

"One more thing, Robert. You are not to call me

George in front of Lord Hampton."

* * *

Marie was just putting the finishing touches on Georgiana's hair when Tibbs knocked upon her chamber door to announce that Lord Hampton had arrived. Her brother had earlier suggested that she personally greet him upon his arrival.

She leapt up and started for the door.

"Mademoiselle! Are you not going to peer into your looking glass?"

Georgiana shrugged. What did she care how she looked? It was not as if she was eagerly trying to snare the earl's affections. She shook her head and went into the corridor.

Before she reached the drawing room, she heard the male voices. Lord Hampton's and her brother's. They both stood and bowed when she entered the chamber.

"How very good of you to come all this way, my lord," she said to him, offering her hand for him to air kiss. She took the opportunity to give him a long look. Why could she not fall in love with him? He was uncommonly handsome. In many ways, he physically resembled her brother, though they were opposite in personality. Fitzwilliam was quiet, retrospective, and conservative. Lord Hampton was gregarious, conceited, and extravagant.

The two were of the same age—ten years older than she. His lordship's height was as great as Fitzwilliam's—which was above normal—and he was well formed with perfectly tailored clothing. He still wore tea-coloured traveling clothes with soft brown leather boots. Like everything about him, they were of excellent quality.

When she connected with his amber eyes, she

hoped for a wild flurry in her pulse like what occurred when she had beheld Robert. But no such occurrence happened. He smiled to reveal perfect teeth that were abnormally white. His hair looked as if he had been a blond child, but it was now light brown and cut stylishly.

"I confess there were two very strong attractions here," said he.

She was utterly sick of hearing false praises of her person from every man who sought her fortune. Before he could launch into a testament of her purported beauty, she would cut him off. "Allow me to guess. You have no doubt heard how excellent is the fishing in Pemberley's lake."

He regarded her with an amused expression. "For many years now I have heard reports of how grand is Pemberley, and I'm gratified to finally be able to see it and validate the claims that it is truly one of the finest country houses in England."

Fitzwilliam smiled at the comment, and though he was not a stout talker, he took the liberty of suggesting that Georgiana give his lordship a tour of Pemberley on the following day. She knew her brother well enough to know that he, too, was clever enough to see the direction of Lord Hampton's false praise of her and determined to avert it.

"I shall be most happy to. I know you are tired and need to change for dinner, my lord, so I'll have Tibbs show you to your chamber. Dinner is a mere hour from now." Her gaze flicked to her brother. "We have one more guest for dinner, and you will never guess who it is."

Fitzwilliam lifted a brow.

"Robert Farrington has come home!"

Her brother's face softened. "What a pity none

of his family were here to welcome the poor lad home."

"Yes, it is a pity, but I told him the Darcys would be most happy to do so."

Fitzwilliam smiled. "Good."

She fled from the chamber, repenting that she'd had to cut short fishing with Robert in order to greet Lord Hampton, but at least she'd have the pleasure of seeing him in an hour.

$\mathcal{C}$hapter 2

Pemberley seemed like home this evening. Perhaps that was because his own Bodworth was bereft of family members. Whilst Pemberley's butler showed him to the drawing room, Robert took note of the riches which accounted for Pemberley's place as one of the finest houses in England. There were paintings by Van Dyke and portraits by Gainsborough and fine French furnishings and sparkling chandeliers. After his years in tents and tawdry inns in port cities, Pemberley seemed like a magnificent palace.

Robert had forgotten how soaring some of these ceilings were. In the opulent drawing room, the ceiling reached up at least thirty feet. The hand-painted ceiling looked as if it had come from the brush of an old Italian master.

When he entered the room, Darcy leapt up, a broad smile on his congenial face, his hand outstretched. "Welcome home, Robert!"

The two men shook hands, then Lord Hampton also got to his feet. Darcy addressed him. "Your lordship, may I present to you Captain Robert Farrington."

"Ah! Fane's young brother." His gaze raked over Robert's uniform. Robert thought—but it may have been only in his imagination or his exaggerated sense of self-worth—that the earl's gaze paused, with something of jealousy. Robert had known men who wished to emulate soldiers without having to endure their hardships.

The Regent himself fancied dressing in his regimentals even though he would have been useless commanding soldiers. He merely liked the military trappings. Robert would wager Lord Hampton would not hesitate to swap clothing with Robert tonight, given the opportunity. The two shook hands.

Next Darcy said, "I should like to make you known to my wife." Smiling, Darcy looked at a dark-haired woman seated near him. There had been an unmistakable ring of pride in Darcy's voice and a felicity upon his normally grave face.

Robert had been told that Mrs. Darcy was neither a beauty nor an heiress but that she and Darcy had suited wonderfully. Robert's quick gaze brushed over her. His sisters' description of Darcy's bride was correct. Yet, there was something rather attractive about the lady. She was in possession of a good figure and tolerably pleasant face, but her eyes were exceedingly fine.

After bowing before Darcy's wife and saying all that was agreeable, he moved to George. She looked . . . different. Not at all like the girl who had pretended to be a lad in order to go shooting with him. She looked wholly feminine now. Not in the same way as delicate Veronica, of course. And George was no beauty like Veronica, but he must own George looked very handsome tonight in a pale blue dress of some sheer fabric that clung to the smooth, straight lines of her figure. It was not a terribly feminine body. Certainly not like buxom Veronica, but George did possess a certain elegance now that she had become a lady.

He was no authority on women's fashion—

especially after having been away from the country for so long—but he thought her eye for what was fashionable exceptional. By Jove, a princess could not dress in finer taste than did his George!

Good lord, why had he thought of her as his? True, they were great friends. He warmed at the memory of her telling him he was her dearest friend.

"How lovely you look tonight," he blurted out. Then, recalling that she had warned him not to call her by the name he had always used, he added, "Miss Darcy."

Her lively eyes danced. "Thank you. Do you know, Robert, this is the first time I've ever seen you in your regimentals, and I must say you look amazingly well."

He wished she would not call him Robert in front of Lord Hampton. The earl might mistakenly take sweet George for a hoyden. Which in many ways she was. But only with him and only when they were children. He wouldn't want Hampton or anyone to get the wrong idea about her.

Even before he had the opportunity to sit, the Darcy butler returned to announce that dinner was served.

Robert's gaze shot to George, who smiled at him as she rose from the sofa. He was just about to go offer his arm to escort his dear friend into dinner when Lord Hampton cut off his progress, and proffered her his arm. "It will be my honor to escort the lovely Miss Darcy to dinner," the earl said.

Lovely Miss Darcy? As exceedingly fond as Robert was of George, to say she was lovely would be a lie.

As the son of an earl and the brother of an earl, Robert was familiar with the practice of the highest ranking peer escorting the hostess into the dinner room, but he had almost forgotten. *I have been away for too long.* Was he going to have to relearn good manners?

He trailed behind his lordship, trailed behind Mr. and Mrs. Darcy, and suddenly found himself glaring. Robert seldom glared, seldom frowned. What was coming over him? He had always been happy with his lot in life. Until Veronica's father greeted his proposal with a cold shoulder.

That was the first time Robert had ever wished he had been the firstborn.

The second time was now. He wanted to be the one leading George into the dinner room. He was the one who had been from his home for four long years. Did he not deserve to have preferential access to his best friend on the day of his return? Were he the firstborn, the title holder, he might have supplanted Lord Hampton. What a pity.

His place at the table was across from George, who had the earl at her right. Any attempt to converse was held in check until the footman had progressed around the table, spooning soup. Darcy poured wine into glasses for each of them.

Robert was familiar enough with Darcy to know of his deficit of banter. Would his wife step in and keep up a dinner table conversation? He also knew that comments would likely be addressed to the visitor of the highest rank, not to a youngest son like him.

Mrs. Darcy did speak first, but to his surprise, she spoke to him. "Captain Farrington, I do hope you are home for good. Your return has been a great source of felicity to my husband and

Georgiana."

He set down his spoon. "Alas, Mrs. Darcy, I shall have to return to the Peninsula."

George sighed. "I must own that I have been envious of the officers' wives who are permitted to travel to foreign places with their husbands."

"I assure you, the living conditions are not to be desired," he said.

"But," George remarked, "think how much happier is the officer to know the one he loves most is with him."

Truth be told, there had been times during these past four years, he had enviously longed for a wife like some of his fellow officers. Then when he became acquainted with Veronica, he was certain she was the woman who could bring him perfect felicity. He had even fancied the two of them sharing a tent. As man and wife, of course.

"I should think," George went on, "that four years of one's young life is enough to devote to king and country. I do wish you would stay in Derbyshire."

"Returning home—even without yet being able to see my family—has brought unimaginable satisfaction."

Smiling, George nodded in agreement—and he thought perhaps her eyes were tearing. She confirmed it when she silently wiped at the corner of each eye. How very touching. It was as gratifying as seeing one of his beloved sisters. He wondered if Isabella, or Mary, or Harriet, or Susan would weep with happiness when they beheld him.

George was embarrassed over the emotional display she did her best to hide. He therefore determined to draw the attention away from her.

"Do you know, Lord Hampton, that I was one of the gentlemen at White's four years when you broke the faro bank."

The peer's eyes brightened. "What a night that was! When I left, I believed myself richer than the king himself." Lord Hampton shrugged. "But how quickly fortunes are won and lost."

Robert was too much the gentleman to ask outright if Lord Hampton had lost all of it. It had come close to a hundred thousand quid. Robert could not imagine what he would do with a fortune like that. Between his meager funds from the army and the annuity from his brother, Robert got along tolerably on four hundred a year.

Which explained why Veronica's father did not advance Robert's interest in his daughter—even though the man first demanded Lord Fane's consent before he would consider the marriage of his daughter to the captain.

Robert shrugged. "It's rather a case of living by the sword and dying by the sword."

"Ah, so it is," Lord Hampton replied. Then he directed his attention to Darcy. "Though I have learned the error of my former ways."

Darcy merely nodded.

Obviously, the earl was acquainted with Darcy's aversion to high-stakes play. And obviously, he was attempting to ingratiate himself with George's brother. For the purpose of getting his hands on George's fortune.

Robert felt as if he'd been whacked in the chest. George deserved a man who was marrying her for all her fine qualities, not a man who greedily sought her dowry. He was seized with a dislike of the Earl of Hampton.

"I have missed so many things during my

absence," Robert said, "but one of the things I miss the most is the races at Newmarket." He was baiting the reformed gamester.

Another smile crossed the earl's rather good-looking face. "You should have been there last week when Lord Egremont's filly won the sweepstakes by four lengths! I've never seen a more magnificent beast!"

Robert's gaze flicked to Darcy to gauge a reaction, but Darcy's face was inscrutable. Then Robert peered at the earl. "My brother had the good fortune to see Lord Egremont's stables. Have you?"

"Oh, yes!" He turned to address George. "There are three hundred beasts in his impressive stables."

"I cannot understand why anyone would need three hundred horses," said she.

Darcy finally spoke. "Lord Egremont's lavish spending remains unchecked. I believe his Petworth has several hundred paintings and statues that are nearly priceless."

"Were I as rich as Egremont, I too would have a fine stable," Hampton said.

"You already have one of the great country homes, do you not?" Mrs. Darcy asked.

The liveried footmen removed the first course, and turbot, vegetables in every colour, and savory meat pies were laid.

Lord Hampton graciously inclined his head. "Thank you. Rafferty Hall is a grand old pile of which I am exceedingly proud. A pity it's so far from London for I am happiest when in the lively Capital."

"I do believe, my lord," George said, "your ideas are in complete opposition to my brother's."

Lord Hampton's gaze went to Darcy, who nodded in confirmation. "I not only do not wager, I am also happiest when I am at Pemberley." His gaze went to his wife at the opposite end of the table for only a few seconds. "Especially now that I have married. Everything I could ever want is here."

"How fortunate you are," Lord Hampton said. "I have come to that point in life when I find my interests vastly changing, my fondest desire being to wed. I long for the domestic felicity you have found, Darcy." Then he quickly looked at George, his face gentling.

Robert's hands fisted. Lord Hampton was not the right man for George!

"We must ride tomorrow," Darcy said to his houseguest.

"I hope I do not flatter myself when I tell you that riding is my greatest passion." Hampton looked again at George. "My friends have done me the goodness of attributing accolades to my skills as a whip." He shrugged. "I think of my riding as tolerable; but others tell me that no one in the kingdom rides as well as I." His shrug sadly fell short of validating his modesty.

While Robert normally considered himself adept at polite conversation, he could no longer sit there and indulge the man's inordinate vanity. "George is the best rider I know."

Lord Hampton lifted a haughty brow and glared at Robert. "Pray, who is George?"

"Forgive me, Miss Darcy," Robert said, then redirected his comments to the man who sat across the table from him. "George is what I called Miss Darcy when we were playmates. You see, we are lifelong friends."

Lord Hampton faced George. "You permit him to call you that name?"

"It was a name given in affection whilst we were children, so, yes, I do permit it. Captain Farrington has not seen me since I was the age of twelve."

Robert remembered very well that she had actually been thirteen when he had left England, though at the time she looked more like eleven. He thought she must have shaved off a year to make Robert's familiarity less offensive. Certainly, it was not good form to address a young lady by so masculine a name, and thirteen was an age when most young ladies began to transition into young women.

Lord Hampton's expression softened as he turned to George. "So, do you ride as well as Mr. Farrington says?"

"You will have to judge for yourself tomorrow."

"I must prepare you, my lord," Darcy said, "My sister rides rather like a man."

"But I do use a side saddle!"

"I shall very much look forward to seeing you ride. How fortuitous that you and I have so much in common, my dear Miss Darcy."

Robert would bloody well like to know why that was fortuitous.

After dinner and after the gentlemen stayed behind for their port, the three of them rejoined Mrs. Darcy and Miss Darcy in the drawing room.

"I thought perhaps my sister could sing for us. It is my sincere hope that her singing brings to you gentlemen the felicity it does to me."

"While my husband is unaccustomed to boasting," Mrs. Darcy said, "I can tell you with perfect honesty that my dear sister—" she flicked a quick glance at her sister-in-law, "—is blessed with the loveliest singing voice it has ever been my pleasure to hear."

Why did Robert not know that about George?

"You shall put me to the blush," George said without exaggerating. Colour climbed up her slender cheeks.

He felt compelled to lessen her embarrassment. He rose and came toward her. "Would you do me the goodness of allowing me to play for you? I will own, I am rusty but I believe my knowledge of the pianoforte will come back to me."

She smiled up at him. "It will. You used to play as naturally as breathing."

"It was what my mother expected of all her children. I suppose that is why she started our musical instruction when we were but four years of age."

George stood, strode to the pianoforte, and began rifling through a stack of music. Then, finding something agreeable, she handed it to him.

Bough of Love was a selection he and she used to whistle while they fished. He had all but forgotten about it until he sat in front of the instrument and began to play. Then he realized that even though he had not played in four years, he remembered every note of this familiar tune and had no need to consult the pages set before him.

Years and years of practice ensured he could never lose his ability to play, yet his fingers had become stiff from lack of practice, and a few stumbles marred George's performance. Neither Darcy nor his wife had exaggerated her talent. No nightingale could sing with such perfection as

George. He found himself watching her, mesmerized. When she sang in that pleasant trill, standing there in that lovely dress, she looked elegant. Even pretty.

He thought he would be delighted to play all night in order to continue listening to the perfection of her voice. Had she always been possessed of such a talent? He did recall his sisters writing him about the many masters Darcy had gathered around his sister during the years she prepared for her launch into Society.

No wonder she had received eleven proposals of marriage! He found himself at odds with those eleven men. He was sure none of them deserved someone as fine as George. He was sure he valued her more than any of those fortune seekers.

Would that he could enlighten them about all her admirable qualities. Where would he begin? Most of those eleven men were bound to already have discovered her incomparable musical talent, but did they know what a jolly good sport she was?

She not only rode as well as any man he had ever known, but she enjoyed all the things that males enjoyed. She could shoot with great accuracy and never flinched over the tragedy of a fallen beast, as did his sisters. She could fish beside him all day and never become bored, never squirm and squeal at the sight of maggots. She and he had spent many an hour facing one another across a chess board, and her moves were as wise and calculated as any man's.

A pity he had realized only that day that she had been his best friend. For all of their lives. He would jolly well miss her when she did wed. Even if he were back in Spain.

He did not want her song to end, and without communicating a single word to her, when it did end, his fingers raced ahead to another song he knew she would know.

She barely stopped, then continued on with the second song, shooting him an amused smile. Such a perfection of voice he had never before heard. How fortunate was the man who married her and could beg her to sing to him every night!

He did not want the night to end. He knew when the music stopped, good manners would demand that he take his leave and return to Bodworth. He made the numbers odd. With him removed, the four others would be free to play whist.

After five songs, Darcy applauded. It was effectively their cue to stop the musical entertainment. "Though I could listen to the two of you until dawn with much felicity, I am sure this must be taxing my sister's lovely voice." He peered at Lord Hampton. "And I expect his lordship must be eager for a game of whist. I perceive you're exceedingly fond of any kind of gaming."

Lord Hampton shrugged. Though it was difficult for Robert to judge, he thought women would consider the earl a handsome man. He did recall his sisters once saying Lord Hampton was the most handsome man in London. Robert found himself regretful that the man had lost his fortune—not because he cared a fig about the arrogant peer but because Robert did not want him courting George.

"Ah, I shall have to return to Bodworth. There are a great many letters I must write to my sisters and brothers tonight so I can dispatch them tomorrow."

"You must come ride with us in the morning," Darcy said.

Robert nodded. "It will be a great pleasure. I have most grievously missed riding over these green Derbyshire hills."

He stood and faced George, bowing. "I say with complete honesty that your singing is perfection. I could have listened to you all night."

She curtseyed, and the heightened colour returned to her fair cheeks. "Thank you, R-r-r, er, Captain Farrington."

* * *

When they retired that night to Elizabeth's bed chamber, Darcy stood beside his wife's dressing table and watched as she brushed her hair. Elizabeth peered at the reflection of his most beloved face in her looking glass. "Do you know, my dearest, I believe Captain Farrington is the perfect mate for Georgiana. It must be Divine intervention that stopped her from accepting one of those many proposals she received."

Darcy started to chuckle.

"What do you find so humorous, my love?"

"I was thinking the very same thoughts as you—except perhaps the bit about Divine intervention, though I will own the timing of Robert's return could not have been more fortuitous. Robert Farrington is a very fine young man, and there's no question that Georgiana and Robert are exceedingly fond of one another."

"Do you mean to tell me you would rather your sister wed a fourth son over the Earl of Hampton?"

Her husband's eyes narrowed. "While I will own the idea of my sister being the Countess of Hampton sounded very good, the reality is that I find I cannot admire the earl."

"Nor can I. And I don't think Georgiana does, either. It's my belief she invited him here because marriage to him would bring consequence to the family and would make you proud."

"I care not about rank and consequence!"

"I know, my beloved. If you did, you would have taken Anne de Bourgh for your wife instead of me." She laid down her brush, got to her feet, and fitted herself to him, lifting her head.

"Understand this, my love. I never wished to unite myself with Anne. From the first time I actually spoke to you, you became my obsession." His voice lowered to a manly rasp. "You still are."

His lips came down on hers, and she was once again drowning in a fog of sensuousness.

$\mathcal{C}$hapter 3

"Miss Darcy!" said Lord Hampton, his eyes running over the lady who stood before him in a fetching green velvet riding habit the following morning. "Your loveliness positively robs me of breath."

Robert glared at the arrogant earl, who certainly had not been robbed of breath, or else he would have been incapable of such insincere flattery.

The fortune hunter waved off George's groom, insisting he would assist the lady in mounting. The man settled his hands about George's slender waist and hoisted her upon a very fine gray while Robert continued watching, his eyes narrowed.

Robert found himself wondering what it would be like to lift an all-grown-up George. She could not weigh very much. She was far too delicate, despite her height. It was funny that he'd never before thought of her as delicate, though there had been many a time he'd had to offer a strong hand when her strength was not up to a task. There was the time he had helped reel in a massive bream after it left her slim body shaking and weak with the valiant effort. Or the many times she'd been incapable of removing a newly fallen log from one of their bridal paths. He recalled, too, the expressive look of gratitude on her face when he'd carried her to shore after their boat had capsized. For George had never learned to swim.

The very memory of carrying her in his arms suffused him with longing. No doubt, he greatly regretted Veronica's absence—not that he had ever carried her in his arms.

Perhaps it was because he had for so long been removed from those who loved him, he had become eager for a woman to call his own. A wife. For the past several months, his desire to marry had strengthened. He might be young, but he knew himself well enough to know that most bachelors' pleasures held no appeal to him. What he wanted was one woman, a wife with whom to share his life, to build a home together—even if it were only a tent—and later, to begin a nursery.

He mounted his horse and eyed George as she rode off with Hampton. Very soon she could be Lady Hampton. Very soon she could be partaking of the domestic felicity Robert so hungrily craved.

Gathering his forgotten manners, he addressed Darcy. "Mrs. Darcy does not join us?"

At even the mention of his wife, Darcy smiled (a heretofore rare occurrence). "My Lizzy does not share our enthusiasm for riding."

As they continued on, he knew he was poor company to his host, but he kept attempting to eavesdrop on George and Hampton, who rode side by side some distance ahead of them.

At first the four of them only cantered, but when they had put Pemberley's gracious parkland behind them, they began to gallop. Robert could not remove his gaze from George. Just as with her singing the previous night, he thought he could never tire of watching her ride. The way she sat a horse! It was almost like reading a perfectly metered love poem. While she rode as well and as accomplished as any whip, there was still an elegance about her.

Fancy that! His George had become elegant!

Why did he keep thinking of her as his George? Clearly, she would belong to Hampton in the very near future. The earl was so unfit to be her husband that it pained Robert to contemplate it.

There must be something he could do to ensure that she marry a man worthy of her. Perhaps he should speak to Darcy, expressing his doubts about Hampton's desirability. With frustration, he realized the strictures of good breeding prevented him from doing anything so audacious.

As they all galloped, Hampton bolted on ahead of the others—even George—at a break-neck pace. Then he did a most peculiar thing. Feet firm in his stirrups, he lowered the upper portion of his torso toward the ground that was rapidly flashing by. What was the man doing? Was he contemplating suicide? Hampton reached down and snapped the sturdy stalk of a bright yellow daffodil, uprighted himself in his saddle, and with an air of gallantry, handed the daffodil to George. Hampton looked as if his self consequence had added still another foot to his height.

She favored him with a smile. "Oh, my lord! I do thank you, but you gave me a such a fright. I thought you were going to fall to your death!"

"I can think of no more noble way to die than in the service of a fair maiden."

Uncharitably, Robert thought it might not have been so grave a loss if Hampton had spilled from his horse and suffered that noble demise.

If the vexatious earl knew George half as well as Robert knew her, he would have known that hollyhocks, not daffodils, were her favorite flowers! Had Robert's thoughts conjured up the stalky bloom? For some fifty feet ahead, the purple-hued flowers grew wild. He began to race his horse toward them.

As he came near, he straightened his legs, feet gripped in the stirrups, and leaned down with the intention of scooping up the noble hollyhock for his friend. He—not Hampton—would present the lady with her favorite flower.

Just as he went to snap the stalk, he lost his balance. His left foot disengaged, and he went smacking into the hard dirt beneath him.

George screamed.

He had enough presence of mind to block the fall with his right shoulder rather than his head. Once he recovered the breath that had been knocked from him, he cried out in pain. His shoulder was definitely dislocated. Had he broken something? He was vaguely aware of the others rushing toward him. He peered up. Tears streaked George's face.

Once the shock and initial pain of the fall passed, he realized the only thing seriously wounded was his pride. He managed to pull himself up by bracing his left arm. That was when he saw his fingers still coiling around the stalk. Recovering his composure, he handed it to her. "Your favorite flower, I believe, Miss Darcy."

She took it, smiling. "Oh, I do most sincerely thank you, but I beg that you never again give me such a fright!"

Darcy's face, too, was collapsed with concern. "I believe you've dislocated your shoulder."

Just beyond Darcy, Hampton stared down at Robert, attempting to appear concerned, but

Robert detected a smirk.

In the Peninsula, Robert had witnessed dozens of similar dislocations and knew what had to be done. Beastly painful business. And it was impossible to do to himself.

"I think I can restore your shoulder," Darcy said. "What about your leg? Do you think it broke when you fell?"

Robert shook his head. "Pop the shoulder back, and I'll be as fit as a fighting Dragoon." He had to say something that might resuscitate his mangled manliness, to remind them of his military prowess.

"Oh, Robert," George said, "How gratified we are that you did not tumble onto your head! You could have been killed."

Flashing a quick glance at the glaring Hampton, Robert mocked. "I can think of no more noble way to die than in the service of a fair maiden."

Darcy burst into almost uncontrollable laughter.

Several moments and several painful tries later, Darcy succeeded in restoring Robert's shoulder to its socket. During the past four years, Robert's body had been pierced by a bayonet, grazed by a musket ball, and a hot cannon had burnt away a large portion of the skin on his hands, but he was certain nothing he'd ever experienced had bruised so many parts of his body in a single occurrence.

He was also certain he had never been more miserable.

But he forced himself to soldier on and not give away a hint of his suffering.

"We need to take you back," Darcy said. "You're in no condition to even sit a horse."

Robert shook his head. "You misjudge a Dragoon, sir." Nothing sounded more welcome than his bed at present, but he would never own up to it.

"Are you sure?" George asked. She had been so distressed whilst her brother was tinkering with Robert's shoulder that she had turned her back and refused to look. In all her seventeen years, Robert had never seen her squeamish in the least.

With Darcy assisting, he managed to get to his feet and mount his horse.

As they rode along, the cooling wind to their backs, he could not free his mind from attempting to devise ways in which he could demonstrate Hampton's unworthiness to marry George. Everything he thought of succeeded only in making himself a very great meddler.

When they came to a narrow ravine, George leapt from her horse and led it to a swiftly flowing brook in order for it to drink. She looked up at Robert. "Do you know why I chose this place to stop?"

"Because your gray was thirsty?"

She giggled. "Well, that too." Her gaze went to a cluster of brush twenty feet away. "Do you remember that spot?"

He followed her gaze. "Indeed I do!"

She then directed her attention to Lord Hampton to explain. "This is where Rob—Captain Farrington and I once found an injured rabbit and kept him in a little pen of our making beneath those brambles while we nursed him back to good health."

Robert shrugged. "I don't know how adept we were at nursing, but since his mobility had been impaired- - -"

"We think a poacher must have shot him," she added, peering at the earl.

"He needed us primarily to see that he was fed until his leg was sufficiently healed."

"And our pen did keep him from being set upon by predators. Oh, Robert, let's see if any signs of the pen remain."

"It's not likely after all these years," he said, dismounting, tethering his horse, and following after her. It only then occurred to him she had called him by his Christian name. It was so natural an occurrence, he would have thought nothing of it, but Hampton's presence magnified every sense of propriety.

He and she spent several minutes looking for the makeshift pen they had made from twigs bound together with twine, but they found not a single sign of it. "Perhaps it's the wrong spot," he finally said.

She shook her head. "No! I am certain it was here. I know this land as well as I know my alphabet. I have, after all, spent nearly each day of my life exploring every square centimeter."

Lord Hampton approached. "Oh come now, Miss Darcy, I cannot credit what you say. Surely a lady in possession of such vast feminine charms spends more time flipping through the pages of Ackermann than riding across so lonely a landscape."

She stiffened and met his lordship's gaze. "It is not lonely to me, my lord—even when I am alone. How can it be when I've a fleet filly beneath me and so many creatures of the wood to delight?"

"I beg your pardon," Hampton said, his voice as icy as his eyes. "I thought perhaps after your good friend Captain Farrington left England, you might have been lonely." There was an edge to Hampton's voice when he had said *good friend Captain Farrington.* It displayed the same hint of jealousy as Robert had observed in him the previous night when his gaze raked over Robert's uniform.

Robert's anger at the earl increased in direct proportion to his dislike. Was he intimating that sweet George was in an improper relationship with him? Could he not understand that the two of them were like brother and sister?

"With my brother being a decade older," she said to Hampton, "I have been raised as an only child. I am content with my own company."

Hampton forced a smile. "I hope you are not so content that you deny a fortunate man your hand in marriage."

"I believe every woman wishes to be wed." She spun around and hurried back to her horse.

"Allow me to help you, my dear Miss Darcy," Hampton said as he came and cinched his hands about her waist, lifting her as easily as a loaf of bread.

The four of them began to ride again, this time ascending the hill so that Lord Hampton would be afforded an excellent view of Pemberley and all its surrounding land. The higher they rode, the stronger the winds became and the more difficult was conversation. Oddly, when they reached the summit some half an hour later, the wind's force waned, and a stillness settled about them. Not even a bird's trill broke the immediate silence for there were no trees at this elevation.

"If you look off to the west, my lord," George said to her suitor, "you will see Bodworth House, too."

He glared for a moment, then gathered his manners. "Two very impressive estates, side by side. I do believe the two put together would be comparable in size to Rafferty Hall, though I daresay as illustrious as their histories are, they are not as old as ours."

Robert could remain silent no longer. "How remarkable! I did not know your ancestors were Celts."

Hampton regarded Robert as one would a bold child who'd interrupted his elders. "They were not. We came over with the Conqueror."

"As did the Farringtons, but I thought you said yours were here earlier."

"I had not realized the Farringtons went back so far." Hampton offered a tight smile. "Perhaps we are distant cousins or something of the sort."

Robert eyed George. "Do you see a resemblance?"

She looked from one to the other with great contemplation. "I cannot say that I do. Lord Hampton is taller and leaner than you, and his lordship is more fair."

While he could wish for Hampton's height, he believed Hampton would yearn for Robert's well-muscled form. "But you must own, I've been in sunny Spain these four years past. Do you not think that might account for the darkness of my skin?"

"You were never fair. I remember very well how you looked the day you—" She stopped for only a second, then continued. "Oh, what does it signify?" She redirected her attention to her silent brother. "I have a surprise for us."

"What is that?" Darcy asked.

"By the time we reach the temple, Cook will

have sent us a picnic, and we will have the pleasure of Lizzy's company."

* * *

At the temple, Elizabeth waited, the picnic offerings in a hamper on the table which had been covered with a starched cloth. Georgiana came to sit next to Elizabeth. She still had not recovered from the terrible shock of Robert's fall. It was only with the greatest effort she had kept from fainting over his injury, only with the greatest effort had she not blurted out her adoration of him.

As soon as she had sat down on the folding chair, Robert moved to sit on the chair at her other side. To her consternation, Lord Hampton raced ahead of the slowly moving injured officer, nearly knocking poor, dearest Robert to the ground, and slapped himself down next to her. It was all she could do to keep from giving the earl a tongue lashing.

As they ate the cold meat and freshly baked bread, Robert was silent and . . . was he glowering? The always-congenial Robert never glowered. His pain must be unimaginably intense.

"Mrs. Darcy?" inquired Lord Hampton, "Have you had the pleasure of seeing how well Miss Darcy rides?"

"I have been told, but I fear I have such a deficit of knowledge of riding that I shouldn't recognize a good rider from bad."

"Now that you've mentioned bad riding," his lordship said, "Did you know that Captain Farrington took a very bad spill from his horse? Fearing he'd gone head first, we all were vexed with worry."

Elizabeth's concerned gaze rocketed to Robert. "Should I call for the apothecary? Or perhaps the physician over in Derby?"

Robert's face softened. "I am merely bruised. Especially my Dragoon pride."

"Your husband put his shoulder back," Lord Hampton said.

Elizabeth's mouth formed a perfect oval, her brows lowered. "I am gratified that you were not more seriously injured, and I am gratified that I had not the necessity of witnessing so distressing an accident." Her gaze went to Georgiana. "Did you faint?"

"For the first time in my life, I nearly did."

"Delicate Miss Darcy could not bear to watch," Lord Hampton said.

Delicate? No one had ever called Georgiana Darcy delicate. She had lamentably inherited the Darcy family height. She shuddered to think of marrying Lord Hampton, who was as tall as her brother, and bearing a bevy of Amazon daughters.

Her appetite had been lost as soon as Robert had lost his position in the saddle. For one moment, she had feared the worst.

What a touching gesture he had made, nearly killing himself in order to present her with her favorite flower! She was astonished he had even remembered her love of hollyhocks. How fortunate was his Veronica—and how excessively Georgiana envied the Spanish beauty.

Her resolve to pledge herself to Lord Hampton was slowly being unraveled by the dashing officer whose comforting friendship had won her heart many years earlier. What was she to do?

* * *

Much later, after they had returned to Pemberley and Captain Farrington had returned to Bodworth, Elizabeth found her husband in the library. He was already dressed for dinner, which was still an hour off. He was so carefully examining his ledgers that he had not heard her enter. She strolled across the rich red Turkey carpet and came to press her lips to his temple.

He stopped what he was doing, met her gaze with a smile, and secured her hand. His lids lifted, only to quickly lower as he took in her soft dove-coloured dress. "You're already dressed for dinner? Is it not early?"

"It is, but I wished to discuss something with you before dinner."

"You thought I would permit my wife to dine with Lord Hampton without me personally fastening the Darcy jewels about her. . ." He stretched out his own neck in order to nibble at the smooth ivory column of hers. "Throat?"

"It matters not what I thought. I merely wish to ensure that you and I are in agreement about Georgiana and the captain."

Unbeknownst to Mr. and Mrs. Darcy, Miss Darcy was nearly to the library's threshold when she heard her sister say, "I believe that we should strive to do whatever is necessary to see that Georgiana comes to realize how perfectly suited she is to him. And it's not as if he's not from a very fine old family."

They are anxious for me to marry Lord Hampton. Those comments from the two people who loved her most sank her. How could she even think of disappointing Fitzwilliam after his tender care of her for all these years?

$\mathcal{C}$hapter 4

Georgiana had not expected Robert to dine at Pemberley that night. Regardless of his bravado, she knew his gallant tumble must have left him in agonies of pain and discomfort. What he needed was bed rest, though it broke her heart to think of him alone in that big, rambling house with not a single loved one to see to his comforts.

She had implored him to stay at Pemberley until they could proclaim his recovery complete, but he had insisted there was nothing from which he needed to recover. Ever since he was a lad, he had been possessed of the most vexatious resolve to never own a physical weakness.

To her very great surprise, he presented himself at Pemberley at the dinner hour. When they moved from the drawing room to the dinner room—she on Lord Hampton's arm—she stole a glance at Robert and saw that when he thought no one watching, he allowed himself to limp.

More than once during the dinner, she wondered why he had come. He spoke so little, it was obvious his mind was elsewhere. His thoughts must be on Veronica. As melancholy as it made Georgiana to close the book on her dreams of capturing Robert's heart, she told herself it was for the best that his affections had previously been engaged.

She must close the last page on that book, the

book of Captain Robert Farrington. Now, she must direct her attentions toward the man her brother wished her to wed. She watched as Lord Hampton cut his buttered lobster and as he spooned the French sauce onto his plate. His table manners were as perfect as his distinguished appearance.

A pity she could not say the same for his personality. He was not an admirable man. That he felt the necessity to display himself to superior advantage was understandable, given his desire to win out over a deep field of competitors. While she did not like a man who boasted, she understood his perceived need to do so. His excessive flattery of her (which she knew to be untrue in most cases) she could also excuse because he felt it a necessary step on his path to achieve his goal of marrying an heiress. Even his rudeness in almost toppling poor, injured Robert in order to sit next to her, she could excuse for the same reasons.

But, try as she might, it was impossible for her to admire Lord Hampton.

Perhaps some of his disfavor was a result of his propensity to lie. His lies about Georgiana's beauty, elegance (that description had almost sent her into peels of hysterical laughter) and accomplishments she could overlook. But what truly rankled her was when he said he was a reformed gamester when she knew he would continue gambling the minute he got his greedy hands on her fortune.

The man's substitution of false flattery for meaningful conversation demonstrated his disinterest in anyone but himself. While he could praise dear Lizzy as a hostess, he never thought to ask how she might compare Derbyshire to the place of her birth. Or he might have inquired about her wedding trip to Italy.

The only time he spoke in multiple sentences was when he was speaking of himself, and then his determination knew no limits.

I must think only of his good qualities. "Lord Hampton," she began, favoring him with a smile. It only then occurred to her the seating arrangement was different tonight than it had been on the previous night. Now, he was across from her. Taking his former place beside her was solemn Robert. "When we were on the hill today, you intimated that Rafferty was larger than Pemberley and Bodworth together." If Rafferty was to be her new home she needed to learn about it.

Lizzy's eyes widened. "Dear me, it must account for a quarter of England!"

Lord Hampton chuckled. "No. It's just over thirty thousand acres—far more than we need." He shrugged, frowning. "My efforts to sell off a portion of it failed. Because of the entail." He eyed Darcy. "That's where you non-aristocrats are far better off than we nobles."

"Not always," Elizabeth said. "My father is neither a peer nor a baronet, yet all of his lands are entailed to a distant male successor." She grimaced, her gaze darting to Georgiana. "Did I tell you my dear friend Charlotte Collins arrives tomorrow? We have not seen one another since the day I married your brother."

Georgiana sincerely hoped the source of Lizzy's grimace was not what she feared. She eyed her sister. "How lovely! Does Mr. Collins come with her?"

Elizabeth nodded, then explained to his lordship. "Mr. Collins is the distant cousin who will succeed my father. He is presently the vicar at

Hunsford under the patronage of Lady Catherine de Bourgh."

"While I do not know her, I have had the pleasure of meeting Miss Anne de Bourgh," his lordship said.

"She is our cousin," Fitzwilliam said.

Her quiet brother had now made his conversational contribution for the night.

Georgiana sighed. Over the next few days she knew she would grow exceedingly tired of hearing Lady Catherine's name flow from the tongue of the irritating Mr. Collins.

Lizzy faced Georgiana. "I received the news of the Collins' arrival a few days after your brother invited Lord Hampton, and I am ashamed to say I was so absorbed over his lordship's visit to Pemberley I quite forgot to tell you about Charlotte."

"I daresay it was because you knew Mrs. Collins had been to Pemberley before, but Lord Hampton had not," Georgiana said.

"I cannot possibly convey to you, Darcy, and to you, Mrs. Darcy, how violent was my curiosity to see this place," Lord Hampton said. "Many a person of exalted rank had so favorably compared it to Rafferty."

"You must tell me in what ways they are similar," Georgiana said.

He thought for a moment before responding. "I will own that Pemberley's interior is more elegant. More marble and gilt and classical-looking furniture. Ours is. . . well, allow me to say that having been built over the course of several centuries, Rafferty reflects many medieval features, like a central courtyard and fireplaces large enough to roast an ox, and it also has many

Tudor aspects."

"So it's an old pile with a lot of gray stone and cold floors?" Robert said.

Lord Hampton glared at Robert. "Have you not just described your own Bodworth?"

Robert shrugged. "Perhaps. But Bodworth is not mine. My eldest brother is now master there."

His lordship's lip twitched as he regarded Robert. "Then you have no property?"

"A small house in Chelsea has been left to me by my grandmother, but my home is not presently in England."

Georgiana wondered if Veronica had property. Her stomach lurched. Would Robert marry her and make his home in Spain? Dear God, what if she never saw him again? She must divert her thoughts away from Captain Farrington. Her gaze returned to Lord Hampton. "Are the furnishings at Rafferty also in the Tudor mode?"

His gaze went to the classical lines of the mahogany chairs Mr. Chippendale had designed for Pemberley and to the chinoiserie style of the elegant sideboard. "Oh, yes. No graceful chairs there. Ours are big chairs that look as if they could have been suitable for a throne in the days when knighthood was in flower. We have huge tapestries with scenes depicting medieval huntsmen, and there are many dark rooms with tiny windows. Visitors are always enchanted with Rafferty. It's so refreshing for them to find a family that embraces its past and isn't rushing to change things with each new trend every generation."

"It does seem the families that embrace antiquity are those without fortunes to adapt to new trends," Robert said.

Oh, dear, she had never in her seventeen years

witnessed Robert being so ill mannered. What had come over him? She was vastly afraid that Lord Hampton might challenge him to a duel or something equally dreadful if he did not mind his tongue.

She had never seen anyone look angrier than did Lord Hampton at that moment.

"That is not the case with the Earls of Hampton," said he, his eyes flashing with defiance. "It is well known that my grandfather— the one who engaged Capability Brown to do our landscape—was one of the wealthiest men in all of Great Britain."

Fitzwilliam cleared his throat. "My father always had a rule that a man's worth was not to be discussed over dinner, and I daresay it's an embargo I should like to continue."

To their credit, the two male visitors effected remorseful looks while solemnly nodding.

The remainder of the dinner, dear Lizzy smoothly orchestrated the talk to pleasant topics of broad appeal.

Though Robert was still quiet, his behavior displayed more congeniality, mostly toward Georgiana. Whenever her wine glass was low, he refilled it, and he frequently offered to pass her various covered dishes.

And whenever Robert did her some small service, Lord Hampton glared.

At the conclusion of the meal, Lizzy turned her attention to Robert. "Captain Farrington, I beg that you not run off as you did after dinner last night. It would give me great pleasure to hear you play. Your family must be musical prodigies."

"Actually," Georgiana said, "when they were young, the Farringtons were often compared to the Linley family."

"But we never played in public," Robert added. "My father did not think it dignified." Smiling at Lizzy, he continued. "I shall be honored to stay and play tonight. I had not realized how acutely I had missed the pianoforte."

                              * * *

As soon as the men entered the drawing room following dinner, Darcy addressed Lord Hampton. "Pray, Hampton, could you oblige me by giving me an opinion about a book in my library?"

Hampton's brow quirked, then he offered his host a tight smile. "I shall be honored to do so, though libraries are not my area of expertise."

Robert did not have to hear those words to know their veracity. Hampton's expertise would run in the direction of the race meetings at Newmarket.

In the drawing room, Robert went straight to the pianoforte and was touched to see George's single hollyhock standing in a tall vase on top of the instrument. He sat down before the pianoforte. George moved toward him. "Should you like to request a particular song?"

She shook her head. "It matters not, but I should prefer something without a fast tempo, something with a sweet melody."

He started to play, and to his surprise, she continued standing beside the pianoforte. "I know you will not own to any weakness, my dear Captain Farrington, but I know you must be suffering from today's injury."

"Would I not be home in my bed if that were the case?"

"Then what else could account for your uncharacteristic silence at dinner—save for the comments you made—the inexcusable remarks you addressed to poor Lord Hampton?"

"Forgive me. I shall also need to apologize to Darcy for being the cause of such uneasiness at the dinner table, but I will not apologize to Hampton."

"I understand that you two have no love for one another, but I do not understand why you could not be more agreeable at dinner, unless you were in great pain."

"I am not in great pain." Though he was in pain.

"I must warn you that you will not even be given the opportunity to speak at tomorrow night's dinner table."

His brows hiked. "You are treating me as if I were a disobedient child?"

She started to laugh. "Oh, no! I am merely giving you warning of what to expect from Mr. Collins."

"The vicar who will succeed Mrs. Darcy's father?"

"Indeed. A more foolish man you have never had the misfortune to meet. I daresay by the end of the evening you will be wishing that Lady Catherine de Bourgh had met the same end as her late husband."

"Is Lady Catherine coming?"

"No, but Mr. Collins believes he was put on earth in order to expound on that lady's multitude of perceived merits."

Robert smiled. "And is the lady deserving of such accolades?"

"She is my aunt, so I dare not speak ill of her, but it is my belief no one could possibly be deserving of the many accolades Mr. Collins attributes to my aunt—and his good opinion also extends to her exceedingly plain daughter, Anne."

"I do remember Anne. Sickly, was she not?"

"She has never been robust." George paused. "I should also prepare you for Mr. Collins' extreme reverence for the aristocracy. Even though you're from an aristocratic family, I daresay Mr. Collins will ignore you and address all his comments tomorrow night to Lord Hampton."

Robert tossed his head back and chuckled. "That will be jolly good!"

"It was really shameful how wretchedly Mr. Collins snubbed your brother's wife—before she became Lady Fane—all because she was my companion."

"While not likeable, he does sound like a thoroughly entertaining fellow."

"You will have to judge for yourself."

"Why do you think he worships Lady Catherine so?"

"Though I know not the history, it is my assumption that she may be the first person of the nobility he ever had the opportunity to address. I would also assume that for the duration of his life, he has placed aristocrats in some exalted realm above the rest of us commoners. And, of course, Lady Catherine has the living at Hunsford, so he does owe his livelihood to her."

"Will you favor me with a song?" he asked. Why had he done that?

"If you'd like."

Once more he began to play their old favorite, and once more she sang with perfection. It was good that he knew how to play it by heart, for he could not remove his gaze from her. What pleasure her voice gave!

It was too shabby that it would be Hampton who would have the pleasure of hearing her for the rest of his life. The man was so unworthy.

* * *

An idea had come to Robert that brought him great satisfaction. He was anxious to be at Pemberley, anxious to meet this annoying Mr. Collins. He thought perhaps the peer worshipper could be useful.

So, in spite of aches in every quadrant of his sore body, Robert hauled himself to the neighboring property the following afternoon for the purpose of calling on the ladies. The previous night he had declined Darcy's invitation to go shooting with him and Hampton today. Had Darcy no knowledge of how keenly his sister would love to have been included in the shooting party?

Sadly, Robert supposed her shooting days were behind her. If she had married Robert, he would not have objected to having a wife who adored shooting.

Now why had such a silly notion popped into his head? Him married to George! His thoughts naturally transferred to Veronica. Without having ever asked, he was almost certain Veronica did not shoot. Or fish.

He was gratified when Pemberley's butler confirmed that the Collinses had arrived and were presently in the drawing room with Mrs. and Miss Darcy.

In the drawing room, the Collinses were presented to Robert. "You will recall Lord Fane," George said.

The portly Mr. Collins grinned insipidly, nodded enthusiastically, and began his recitation. "A very great man—and so solicitous of me and Mrs.

Collins."

George cut him off. "Captain Farrington is Lord Fane's youngest brother."

"So," Mr. Collins said to him, smiling rapturously, "you had the honor of growing up at Bodworth? It is one of the finest country homes in the kingdom. I am sure it may even be larger than Rosings. Know you Rosings?"

"I know it belongs to the de Bourgh family, but I have not seen it."

"It is my good fortune to be permitted to spend a great deal of time at that magnificent home. How many chimneys does it have, Mrs. Collins?"

"I do not remember."

Mr. Collins' expression became so celestial that Robert wondered if the man had been administered large doses of laudanum. "Suffice it to say, there are at least thirty chimneys at that wonderful, aristocratic house. Sometimes as often as twice a week Mrs. Collins and I are invited to dine there, and after dinner we retire to her ladyship's opulent drawing room—a very great Italian painter did its ceiling—and there we have the honor of playing whist at the good lady's table." He shrugged and attempted to effect a modest look. "I must own that those in my calling have many similarities with the nobility."

"To be sure," Robert said with not the least conviction.

Though George avoided conversing with Mr. Collins, Mrs. Darcy was all that was most gracious. The woman was a saint.

An even greater saint was the woman who suffered the calamity of being united to the obnoxious vicar.

When he was quite certain he could not tolerate

but one more moment in the presence of the determined talker or bear hearing one more word in praise of Lady Catherine de Bourgh, Robert stood and addressed Mrs. Darcy. "If I'm to return for dinner at Pemberley, I must go to Bodworth for the purpose of making myself presentable tonight." Then he eyed Mr. Collins. "Will you oblige me, Mr. Collins, by walking to the door with me? There is a minor point upon which I wish to get your opinion."

A smug smile lighted Mr. Collins' face. "Oh, my lord captain, it will be my humble honor!" He stood, then spoke to his wife. "You know I am accounted to be useful in ecclesiastical matters."

"Indeed, Mr. Collins," his unfortunate wife said.

Once they were in the corridor, Robert said, "You have been informed that Lord Hampton is also a guest at Pemberley?"

"I just learned today that we will share our residency with so illustrious a guest, but I have not yet met him."

"The earl is far too humble to admit this to you, but I thought it would gratify you to know that his lordship is most anxious for a connection with Miss Anne de Bourgh. You are just the man to forward such a unification."

Mr. Collins' eyes widened and his smile broadened. "You may depend upon it."

$\mathcal{C}$hapter 5

Before he returned to Pemberley, Robert laid upon his bed. It hurt so bloody badly each time he moved one of his bruised extremities, he needed to lie perfectly still. The result was that he fell promptly to sleep.

As the light in his room grew more faint, something alerted him to awaken. Even though he had gone to sleep, his subconscious was strong enough to intrude into his dreams and remind him he was due at Pemberley for dinner.

He reluctantly came awake, not wishing to terminate his pleasant dream but knowing that he must. He lay there in the semidarkness, telling himself he needed to rise and dress for dinner, but fighting to remember the dream that had filled him with such felicity.

When he did recall it, he shot up in bed, shocked. *Good Lord, I dreamed that I was going to wed George!*

He must forget the foolish dream and get dressed. He rang for his man.

* * *

When Robert entered Pemberley's drawing room, Hampton was stuck in the room's corner whilst Mr. Collins spoke to him without pause. Hampton regarded the clergyman with impatience.

Robert smiled. He had a very good notion what

topic Mr. Collins was expounding upon at that moment. After Robert greeted those assembled on the sofas, the butler announced that dinner was served. On this night, Robert, as the second highest in rank, offered to escort Mrs. Darcy into the dinner room, and Darcy did the same to the unfortunate Mrs. Collins.

To Robert's chagrin, Hampton once against led George into the lofty chamber lighted with hundreds of candles. Robert was pleased that he would again have the good fortune to be seated beside George.

From the chair directly across from her, Lord Hampton said, "Have I told you tonight how lovely you look in yellow, Miss Darcy?"

She offered him a faint smile. "Actually you have, my lord, and I do thank you."

Robert turned to her, his eye moving along the very slight curve of her slender body. He had to own she did exude a certain elegance. It was really shocking to him that his George had turned into an apparent magnet for young men. A pity she most attracted young men in want of fortune. She had so much more to offer. He prayed she would not accept the vane Lord Hampton.

Unaccountably, his thoughts revisited that blissful dream from which he had not wanted to awaken. In the dream he and George were walking hand in hand in Pemberley's parterre garden. Before he knew what he was doing, his hand reached beneath the table, touching hers, clasping it, then lacing his fingers with hers. No woman's touch had ever before rocketed his pulse in such a manner.

To his astonishment, she did not withdraw her hand from his. He waited a moment (all the while trying to avoid making eye contact with the rapidly talking clergyman), then slowly turned to George. Their solemn eyes met.

At that moment, he thought her exceedingly pretty.

Then the corners of her pretty mouth lifted ever so slowly. She was not offended that he had taken possession of her hand! He felt a thousand times happier than when his horse had won the sweepstakes.

His insides were trembling like a callow schoolboy's. How silly for him to act this way. This was George, for pity's sake! They were merely friends. She was like a sis- - - No, he realized, she was not like a sister to him. He had not laced his fingers with his sisters since he'd thrown off leading strings. And his sisters had never elicited in him such profound feelings of . . . what was he feeling right now?

He must own he was feeling as he felt toward Veronica, but multiplied by many times. It was true, he and Veronica had not progressed to holding hands. Had they, he was sure he would have experienced something similar to what he was feeling now.

As lovely as it felt to secure George's dainty hand in his, he owed her the same respect he had paid to Veronica. Sending her a soft look of affection, he disengaged his hand from hers.

"Is that not right, Miss Darcy?" Mr. Collins inquired.

A shocked look came over her face, and she stammered a moment. "Forgive me, Mr. Collins, my mind was wool gathering."

"I was just telling his lordship about your cousin, Anne de Bourgh. Such delicacy I have never beheld. Do you not agree?"

"Indeed I do."

Were he a cat, Mr. Collins would be purring right now.

"I suppose," Lord Hampton said to Mr. Collins, "that a great many men must be seeking her hand."

Mr. Collins sighed. "Alas, owing to her delicacy, she was never presented."

"But I would think men would seek out one with a large dowry. She is in possession of one, is she not?"

The despicable earl was hedging his bets. If George turned him down, he just might present himself at Rosings.

"Lady Catherine has oft remarked to me that the man who chooses her only offspring will be very well fixed indeed," the clergyman said, "but that dear lady is loathe to lose her dear child to matrimony."

"While I am very fond of my cousin Anne—though we are vastly different," Georgiana said, "I have never believed her nearly so delicate as her mother makes her out to be."

"Our cousin is lazy," Darcy said. "When she wishes not to apply diligence to a task, she declares herself infirm."

"Dearest!" Mrs. Darcy chided, "You must not speak so bluntly!"

Darcy shrugged. "My propensity to speak bluntly is a lamentable fault my dear wife has been powerless to curb in me."

Mr. Collins' eyes rounded. Had Darcy just proclaimed himself a loathsome atheist, the clergyman could not have appeared more dismayed. "It pains me to disagree with my illustrious host, but you, sir, are mistaken about dear Miss de Bourgh. She's as delicate as a petal lashed in the wind."

"There is truth in both of your descriptions of my cousin," George said. "Now let us move this conversation to more agreeable subjects."

The short lull was just long enough to enable Mr. Collins to wedge in what to him was the most agreeable subject imaginable: the virtues of the benevolent Lady Catherine de Bourgh.

Robert found himself wishing for a very large handkerchief to stuff down the determined speaker's throat.

Just as Robert went to refill George's glass, Hampton snatched the wine bottle from his reach. The earl offered George a broad smile, then proceeded to refill her glass, even though it meant the sleeve of his fine velvet coat dipped into the bowl of buttered French sauce as he reached across the table.

"What a shame, Hampton," Robert said without sincerity, "that you've dirtied you excellent coat with cream sauce."

Hampton's frantic gaze darted to the large white blotch on his expensive black dinner coat, and he almost dropped the bottle of wine.

"Oh, your lordship," said George with great sympathy, "I am so sorry. Why do you not let Captain Farrington do that?"

The earl recovered with so smooth a transition it would have rivaled Edmund Kean. "You cannot know, my dear Miss Darcy, what pleasure it gives me to do you the most insignificant service. There is no undertaking I would reject if it could contribute to your felicity."

Now Robert wished for two very large

handkerchiefs.

"You are too kind," she shyly replied, taking up her wine glass.

Hampton shrugged, then stood. "Mr. and Mrs. Darcy, you will, I pray, understand my need to have my valet attend to my coat. I shall rejoin you in the drawing room later."

As the earl was leaving the chamber with the look of an embarrassed schoolboy summoned to the headmaster, Robert caught the slight look of amusement which Mr. and Mrs. Darcy exchanged with one another. So Lord Hampton's discomfort also amused them!

Robert had not been much in their company, but he had seen enough to know the two were very close. And very much in love. How fortunate they were.

As gratified as Robert was to have Hampton out of the way, he knew that Mr. Collins would be seeking a new victim. Robert therefore vowed to avoid any visual connection with the clergyman, and he turned toward George and spoke in a low voice so the others would understand that what he was saying was of no consequence to any of them. "Were you too disappointed to be excused from the shooting party today? I know how strongly it absorbs your interest."

"Of course I was, but Fitzwilliam says I must now comport myself as a lady."

"If I were your elder brother, I would always include you. And I would wager your skill with a musket is superior to that of your illustrious visitor."

"Hear, hear!" said Mr. Collins, directing his attentions at the pair. "Were you speaking of Lady Catherine de Bourgh? I heard you say illustrious, and quite naturally, I realized you must be speaking of that great lady with whom it is my good fortune to be so closely associated."

Robert drew in his breath. He would be forced to make visual contact with Collins. "We were not. I was speaking to my oldest friend about a mutual interest that would be sure to bore the rest of you."

Collins' brows elevated. "Oh, so you and Miss Darcy are merely friends? I had thought . . . oh, it does not signify."

Mrs. Collins quickly changed the subject. "When will you have to return to the Peninsula, Captain Farrington?"

"I am incapable of answering your question for I do not know when my brother comes home to England. There is a matter of grave importance I must discuss with him before I return to Spain."

"You have not met your brother's bride?" Mrs. Collins asked.

How could so normal, so congenial a woman have chosen to unite herself with Collins? It was true that she was very plain, but would not spinsterhood be preferable than having to live with that irritating man? "I have not had that pleasure. Have you?"

Mrs. Collins smiled. "I have, and I believe he made an excellent choice. She is not only beautiful, but she is also intelligent and possessed of a sweet nature."

"She speaks six languages!" George said.

Robert was duly impressed.

"What is more," Mrs. Collins said, "I had the pleasure of observing her at the time your brother was falling in love with her. The love between the two of them was palpable, though I believe they both attempted to deny it initially."

"I am very happy for my brother. He deserves a domestic felicity like Mr. Darcy has found with his lovely wife."

After witnessing the Darcys' happy marriage, Robert was distressed that such felicity would be denied dear George were she to unite herself with Hampton. No one of Robert's acquaintance deserved happiness more than she.

What could he do to prevent such a disastrous alliance? He was already glorying in pointing out Hampton's shortcomings. But there had to be something else. As much as he wanted to impart his objections to Darcy, he knew it was not his place to do so.

Unsuccessful in devising a scheme to discourage Hampton from seeking Georgiana's hand, Robert determined to be so much a thorn in Hampton's side that it would be impossible for the earl to ever be alone with Miss Darcy. Were they not alone, he would be prohibited from offering for her.

And of course, Robert would continue to praise Miss de Bourgh's merits (with Mr. Collins' assistance). If only Hampton would choose to seek another heiress and leave George alone! Pemberley could not be rid of the Earl of Hampton soon enough to please Robert.

Throughout the remainder of the dinner, there was never a lull in Mr. Collins' speech. And never had Robert seen Darcy appear more bored.

* * *

When he entered the drawing room after dinner, Robert was vastly disappointed that Lord Hampton—dressed in blue coat of inferior quality to the one he'd ruined with French sauce—

awaited them. He stood when they entered and sketched a bow in front of George first, then Mrs. Darcy, and finally to Mrs. Collins.

Before Mrs. Darcy took her customary place on the sofa, she cast a glance at George. "I beg, dearest, that you and Captain Farrington entertain us with your incomparable musical talent."

"Before they do," Hampton said, "I beg a word with the Captain."

Robert's brows lifted in the most haughty manner he could impart. He felt as if he were about to be scolded, but it was not his fault the fortune hunter had ruined his coat. "You shall have it, my lord."

"Over here, if you please." Hampton moved to the same corner where Mr. Collins had steered the earl earlier.

They crossed the long Aubusson carpet to their destination, and Hampton faced Robert, his back to the others, his face distorted with anger. "I am sick of your efforts to steal Miss Darcy from me. A woman with her fortune cannot throw herself away on a fourth son—especially when she can have the great honor of becoming the Countess of Hampton. There's not a woman in the kingdom whose heart I cannot capture."

"Yet I believe Miss Darcy has already rejected you once, has she not?"

Hampton's squinted eyes looked like sizzling coals, and his mouth was fixed in an ugly sneer. "It was very clear to me when I was invited to Pemberley it was for the purpose of furthering my intimacy with Miss Darcy. I. Will. Have. Her." His lordship then spun around and stormed across the chamber.

Had anyone else spoken to Robert with such rage, it would most decidedly have upset him. But not Hampton. All Robert felt was amusement over the man's discomfort. As he returned to the pianoforte, where George awaited him with a gentle smile, he kept thinking about Hampton's accusation. How preposterous! He had never tried to steal away the object of Hampton's intentions. Robert and George were merely friends.

His heartbeat roared at the very memory of taking her slender hand within his. What kind of friends held hands in such a fashion? Dear lord! Could he be falling in love with George?

Of course he loved her. But being in love was something altogether different. His sincere affection for her accounted for his continued sparring with the earl who was so exceedingly unworthy of her.

Robert's fingers danced over the keys. It was a wonder he could play as well as he did after so long an absence. When he went back to Spain he would have to make the effort to find an instrument and play more often for it brought him much satisfaction.

A pity he could not take George with him. Few things in life could equal the satisfaction of hearing her sing, as she was now. His gaze flicked away from her sweet face to observe Hampton. Surely the earl would fall violently in love with George when hearing the perfection of her singing voice. But to Robert's dismay, Hampton's bored gaze was trained not on George but on a painting above the chimneypiece!

At that very moment Robert thought he should like to hurl a fist into the man's handsome face. Robert would marry her himself before he would allow her to marry the Earl of Hampton!

* * *

Georgiana would have been consumed by curiosity to learn what Lord Hampton had said to Robert were it not for the greater emotion consuming her: the touch of Robert's hand clasping hers. Even though no one had ever so intimately touched her, because it was Robert holding her hand, it had felt perfectly acceptable. It brought a satisfaction such as she had never experienced. She had felt as exuberant as one did from drinking an entire bottle of champagne.

A cursory mental survey of those other eleven men who had professed to love her revealed not a single gesture as indicative of genuine affection as the many gestures she had received from Robert. She knew that he was not in love with her, but she also understood how deeply he loved her.

And no other man would ever regard her as did dear Robert. A pity she could never compete with his Veronica. The very thought elicited tears.

None of those in the room seemed to notice how moist her eyes had become. Except Robert. His brows dipped in solicitous query, and she silently responded by giving him a broad smile to indicate that nothing was wrong.

His answering smile gladdened her heart.

She sang on, all the while pondering her dilemma. When she had asked her brother to invite his lordship to Pemberley, it was with the intention of revisiting his offer. Robert had been hundreds of miles away and had made it clear he intended to marry another.

But he was no longer hundreds of miles away. And he was not yet married!

She should regard his arrival during Lord

Hampton's visit as a gift from the gods. Almost like Divine intervention to prevent her from marrying the wrong man.

But how could she disappoint Fitzwilliam? There was no finer brother. She had always strived to do what gave him pleasure. That is why she had spent so many repetitious hours toiling away at the pianoforte and the harp to learn difficult songs and make her brother proud of her.

She must put aside her personal gratification. How proud Darcy would be to have the Countess of Hampton as his sister.

* * *

After all the guests had retired for the night, Mr. and Mrs. Darcy sat on a settee before the fire in Mrs. Darcy's bedchamber, their hands clasped affectionately.

"I believe, whether he knows it or not, Captain Farrington is falling in love with Georgiana," Elizabeth said.

"That is more than you can say for Hampton! I don't think he cares a fig for her."

"He is a self-absorbed man who will be the worst sort of husband to the unfortunate woman who marries him."

"All I've ever wanted for my sister is for her to be happy."

"Then we must do everything in our power to advance the romance between her and the captain."

"Perhaps I should send Hampton away."

Elizabeth's eyes narrowed. "I cannot allow you to be so ill mannered, my dearest, even though that man rates such treatment."

"What can I do, then?"

"Continue doing what you did last night when

you stole his lordship away to your library to keep him away from Georgiana."

Darcy smiled. "You believe if Robert and Georgiana are thrown together a bit more, neither of them will be able to deny their affection?"

"I do." Her hand came to stroke her husband's lean cheek. "Credit me with knowing about love."

He lowered his head to kiss his wife most tenderly.

Chapter 6

Georgiana had a wretched night's sleep. Or lack of sleep, to be completely accurate. She kept remembering how it felt to have Robert's big, strong hand clasping hers. Nothing had ever given her a more comforting feeling. It recalled the time their boat had capsized, and Robert carried her to shore—after saving her from drowning.

For as long as she could remember, she had adored him. For as long as she could remember, she had known she could depend upon him to see to her welfare. For as long as she could remember, she had desired to spend all the days of her life with him.

How could she ever consider Lord Hampton's offer while Robert was in England and still without a wife? That he was in England just as she was on the precipice of becoming the Countess of Hampton seemed to her as if it truly were Divine intervention! Were the angels in heaven sending her a message?

The message, she feared, was only to prohibit her from making a misalliance with Lord Hampton. Surely the heavens would not also be directing dear Robert to her. Would it even be possible to divert his plans with Veronica? Oh, how Georgiana hated that Spanish beauty! She could not possibly love Robert as Georgiana did.

When she entered the breakfast room, Lord

Hampton stood to greet her. She saw that he had no plate of food, only a half-drunk cup of coffee. "Have you already eaten, my lord?"

"No, I was waiting for you, my dear Miss Darcy."

Oh, dear. She did not want to be alone in this chamber with him. He might make his final plea to capture her for his bride.

From some distance down the corridor, she heard Mr. Collin's prattle. She never thought she would be so thrilled to have that man's company forced upon her. He came into the breakfast room with his silent wife beside him. His eyes sparkled when he beheld the noble Lord Hampton.

"Your lordship, allow me to say, if I might be so presumptuous as to infringe upon your conversation with Miss Darcy, that it was only with the greatest effort I could go to sleep last night for my mind was utterly consumed with worries over the repair to your distinguished coat."

"It was but a trifle," Lord Hampton said. "I have many more coats at home equally as fine as that— and besides, my man is a genius at the removal of stains."

"I did read a description in one of the London publications . . . now let me see which it was. . ." Mr. Collins turned to his wife. "Do you recall, my dear, which paper I was reading when I commented upon the fine tailoring of Lord Hampton's clothing?"

"I'm sorry. I must have been engrossed in what I was reading at the time."

Mr. Collins waved a pudgy hand. "It does not signify! The point I was trying to make was that his lordship is well known for his fashionable dress."

Lord Hampton bestowed a positively benevolent look upon the vicar. It may have been the first time Georgiana had ever seen any person regard Mr. Collins with such approval.

"I must admit," said Lord Hampton, "It is an immense burden when one is considered the most handsome and fashionable man in the Capital." He then tossed a self-satisfied smile at Georgiana.

How she wished Robert had been there! He would surely have found a sarcastic retort to knock his lordship down from the pedestal upon which he had placed himself.

Try as she might, she could not remember a time when Robert had ever boasted about himself. Not even when he'd been a lad.

The four of them filled their plates and began to partake of their breakfast. Even Mr. Collins was unusually silent, owing to the vigor with which he ate his heaping portion of hogs pudding.

As they were all finishing, she looked up to see her brother standing silently in the doorway. "Why do you not come and join us, Fitzwilliam?" she said.

"Lizzy and I have already eaten." His gaze went to Lord Hampton. "I came to see if I could persuade his lordship to come with me to the stables. I should like his opinion on my last purchase at Tattersall's."

To her great astonishment, her normally reticent brother continued. "Your knowledge of horseflesh is legendary."

Fitzwilliam was actually praising someone? How very peculiar. Sadly, it was another confirmation of his high regard for Lord Hampton.

His lordship set down his fork. "I should be

honored to share my knowledge with you, my good man." He stood, bid farewell to her and the Collinses, and he left with her brother.

Oh dear. Darcy must excessively favor Lord Hampton. How could she disappoint the brother who had been both mother and father to her these many years?

Right now she needed to make her excuses to the Collinses lest the husband attempt to launch into one of his long-winded soliloquies.

* * *

Once more, Robert had dreamed of George. Again, he and she were walking in Pemberley's parterre garden, only this time they were holding hands. No other woman's touch had ever affected him with so profound a feeling of well-being.

Long after he awakened, he thought of her with great affection.

It suddenly occurred to him that his coming home to England at this precise time was Divine intervention. George was his fate.

All his life, she had been there like an unnoticed rug on the floor. He had taken her for granted. Until another man, a man in no way worthy of her, wished to steal her away. And now it seemed to Robert he had unearthed a buried treasure more precious than all the crown jewels in all the kingdoms on Earth.

Now he was flooded with memories of all that he and George had been to each other. Always. He could look the world over and never find her equal, never find one whose interests so closely mirrored his own, never find one with whom he shared so many of life's events.

He suddenly longed to be with her. He must try to make a claim upon her heart, try to convince her that he would cherish her until his dying day. Was there any hope that she could forget her desire to be a countess in order to follow the drum? Was there any hope that she could love him half as potently as he now knew he loved her?

                              * * *

Georgiana stood at the doorway to the drawing room where Lizzy and Charlotte Collins were having a *tete-a-tete*. "Where is Mr. Collins?" asked she.

"I suggested he go off to the portrait gallery," Mrs. Collins said. "My husband's desire to behold portraits of the de Bourgh ancestors never wanes, and I knew he would be bored listening to Lizzy and I chatter upon topics in which he had no interest."

"I will leave you ladies to your chatter. I merely wanted to tell my sister that I will be in the parterre garden. I should like to get in a walk before rain comes."

Both ladies quickly turned to look out the tall casements. "It doesn't look like it will rain," Lizzy said.

"Not now," Georgiana answered, "But there are some very dark clouds off to the east. I do hope they stay in the east!"

Mrs. Collins raised a brow. "Is that where Captain Farrington's Bodworth House is?"

Why should that signify? "No. He is to the west."

"I do hope we'll see him today," Lizzy said. "He's a very fine young man. Darcy's exceedingly fond of him."

A pity her brother was more fond of the earl.

She put on her pelisse and bonnet and went through the French doors out to the parterre garden which offered rows and rows of boxwood-lined paths in which she could stroll. Why must her life be so complicated? If only she did not always feel so compelled to please her brother. Were it not for worrying that she had disappointed Fitzwilliam in not accepting an offer, she would never have persuaded him to invite Lord Hampton to Pemberley. She wished to make Fitzwilliam proud of her.

Even if Robert had not come home to Derbyshire, even if she never again saw Robert, she would not wish to unite herself with Lord Hampton. But how could she disappoint Fitzwilliam? No one ever had a finer brother.

Gravel crunched beneath someone's feet behind her, and she prayed it would not be Mr. Collins. Would it be possible to ignore him? She had come here to bring focus to her thoughts and had no desire to speak to anyone.

She turned back.

Her gaze connected with Robert's. How handsome he was in his uniform! He moved to her, she to him, their gazes never breaking. Why did he have so solemn an expression upon his (most beloved) face? His face was so grave, she feared he was going to tell her he was about to return to the Peninsula.

Her heartbeat tripped, her stomach dropped. "Pray, do not say that you are returning to Spain." Dread strummed through her.

"No. At least, not for a while."

"I am very happy to learn that." Dare she ask why he looked so troubled?

He fell into step beside her, and she noticed the proffered crook in his arm. He meant for her settle her hand upon his sleeve! Robert had never before treated her with such a gesture! He had finally come to realize she was a grown lady. Ripe for marriage.

She linked her arm to his, and they continued strolling along the gravel path. "Do you think it will rain?" asked she.

His head rose, his gaze shooting to those dark clouds in the east. "I think, because of the wind's direction, those black clouds will stay in the east."

"I hope you're right."

Robert drew a breath. "There's something I've been meaning to ask you."

Her heartbeat stampeded. She knew he was not going to offer for her, but miracles did occur. She tried to sound calm. "What is that?"

"Now that you've grown into an elegant young lady, do you object to me calling you George?"

An elegant young lady! She was incredibly touched that he had noticed. What was even more reassuring, she believed he really meant it when he said she was elegant. Unlike all those suitors who professed her beauty (which she knew to be non-existent), Robert had spoken with honesty. As he always did. He had refrained from telling a falsehood about her loveliness. "I would only object if you did not call me George—at least when it is just the two of us."

"Why is that?"

"Because if you ceased calling me George it would seem as if I'd ceased being your dear friend."

He patted the back of her hand. "Never that."

They came to the huge cone-shaped topiaries at the north end of the walled garden. Primrose in every colour surrounded the cones in perfect circles. They then turned to the next path and continued in silence for a few moments before he eventually cleared his throat. "I must speak to something that has been troubling me."

What could be making him so grave? "Please do."

"I believe you fancy becoming a countess. Don't know why females crave being called Lady This and Lady That and wearing coronets and all that, but I wish you wouldn't marry Hampton."

"You, of all people, should know I am not like other ladies. For example, I do not think being a countess would be nearly as exciting as Veronica's prospects."

His brows lowered. "Who in the devil is Veronica?"

"Your Veronica."

"I . . . have not thought of her since—" He shrugged and looked down at Georgiana. "What did you mean by Veronica's prospects?"

"Being married to a dashing officer, following the drum, visiting foreign lands—not that Spain is foreign to her. I would adore living in a country where the sun shines with great regularity."

"You cannot mean you would prefer being wed to a lowly officer in His Majesty's Dragoons over becoming a countess!"

How could she answer without throwing away her pride? "What I'm saying is that it would be difficult for me to marry Lord Hampton. I do not love him."

"I am very happy to know that."

They continued on, the only noise the ruffle of wind upon the yew hedge.

"Do you really think you would enjoy being a soldier's wife?"

"Oh, yes."

"Why?"

"The excitement, the lure of following the drum, sleeping in a tent with the man you love." The very thought of sleeping in a tent with Robert caused her breath to grow short.

To her astonishment, he suddenly stopped. "Confound it, George! I can't get the notion out of my mind."

"What notion?"

"I have been plagued with thoughts not of Veronica, but of you. I have found that the most perfect of all females has been under my nose for most of my life." He peered at her. "I am in love with you. Deeply. Profoundly. And I cannot bear the thought of returning to the Peninsula without you."

She gasped. Tears began to stream from her eyes. And she launched herself into his arms, weeping with joy. She hugged him tightly. "Oh, Robert! It is you whom I have ever loved. Only you."

* * *

Darcy and Lizzy stood before the French windows peering out upon the parterre gardens, their hands linked. When they saw Georgiana and Captain Farrington embracing so joyously, they, too, embraced.

"I am so happy you got Lord Hampton out of the way so true love could find its path," Lizzy said.

"I couldn't be more pleased. Robert's an excellent fellow." Darcy settled a tender kiss upon his wife's forehead. "Now I shall go dispatch Lord Hampton."

Lizzy giggled. "I suspect before he leaves, he'll encourage Mr. Collins to assist him in furthering a connection with your cousin Anne."

Darcy chuckled as he left the chamber.

* * *

Robert directed his most adored George to the sturdy garden bench, set her down, then knelt before her with his handkerchief in hand. "It pains me to see you cry." He dabbed at her wet face.

"You mustn't distress yourself. I've never been so happy in my life." Sniff. Sniff. "Is my nose terribly red?"

He guffawed. "I've never seen you more lovely, my dearest, dearest love."

She took the handkerchief from him and after one final sob, completely dried her tear-splattered face. "Am I dreaming, or did you just ask me to marry you?"

"It is I who feel as if I'm in a dream. Did you really agree to make me the happiest soldier in His Majesty's Army by consenting to become my wife?"

She did not answer for a moment. Then she nodded and gave a wistful smile. "How does this sound to you? Mrs. Farrington? I love to hear it. Georgiana Farrington."

"That name is a source of great felicity to me, also."

"What is that noise?" she asked, her gaze moving in the direction of the stable block.

"It sounds like a coach and four." They both came to their feet and climbed atop the bench in order to peer over the garden's brick wall.

"It is Lord Hampton's coach," she said.

"He must be leaving."

"How can that be? I am sure it will vastly disappoint my brother if I do not become a countess."

"You underestimate your brother. He wants only your happiness. He even mentioned to me, when it was just two of us, he did not think Hampton would suit you."

"That is the second best news I have learned today."

Robert grinned. "I suppose the earl must have witnessed us embracing."

She turned to him. "Do you think we could . . . do that again?"

He drew his most cherished George into his arms and settled a gentle kiss on her lips.

* * *

"You are sure my brother will not be disappointed?"

"Shall we go speak to him?"

"Should you not address him first?"

"I want to stack the deck in my favor. I believe if Darcy sees how happy you are, he will be incapable of rejecting me."

She could not dispel the notion that she was in a dream. How could so much happiness be possible? How could her greatest desire have come to such stunning fruition? Robert truly loved her. Of that, she was now certain.

They went for the French doors, and before they could open them, her brother did. Lizzy was beside him, and both of them were smiling.

"I believe felicitations must be in order," Fitzwilliam said.

Georgiana stopped and regarded them with shock. "You do not object?"

"Lizzy and I could not be happier."

"One had only to see you two together to know how perfect you were for each other," Lizzy said.

"I was just hoping," Fitzwilliam said, "that it

would not be too late when the captain came to recognize what we already knew."

"That he loved you as much as you loved him," Lizzy finished.

Fitzwilliam hugged his wife, smiling broadly. "Lizzy said that Robert's coming home at this precise time was Divine intervention."

Georgiana's eyes widened. "I thought the very same thing!"

"Make that three of us," Robert added, shrugging.

She looked up at him, almost fancying there would be a halo about his head.

The End

The Liberation of Miss de Bourgh

(Jane Austen Sequels, Book 3)

CHERYL BOLEN

Copyright © 2016 by Cheryl Bolen

The Liberation of Miss de Bourgh is a work of fiction. Names, characters, places, and incidents are the products of the author's imagination or are used fictitiously. Any resemblance to actual events, locales, or persons, living or dead, is entirely coincidental.

$\mathcal{P}$rologue

Rosings, in Kent

In his eight and twenty years no one had ever had the arrogance of manner to threaten Charles St. John, the Earl of Seaton. Until now. Now he was being subjected to appalling threats—not from a powerful man, but from a woman. Lady Catherine de Bourgh was a thoroughly unpleasant woman, to be sure.

Lord Seaton recalled the time in Bath when his trembling mother, head down to obscure recognition, hurriedly crossed Milsome Street to avoid having to address the woman who considered herself only barely beneath royalty (even though Lady Catherine *had* failed to attract a husband from the ranks of the aristocracy).

As his carriage passed through the gates of Lady Catherine's Rosings, he thought of the woman's abrasive letter to him. Though he had committed it to memory, he remained in the dark about just what it was she wanted from him. Her nasty letter had ensured that he would endeavor to make the half-day journey from London to Kent and present himself before the widow, if for no other reason than to satisfy his curiosity.

His coach drew up in front of Rosings' portico. A cold wind cut into him as he disembarked and climbed up one of a pair of curving steps to reach the home's main floor. Although the late Sir Lewis de Bourgh had not been aristocratic, this exceedingly opulent country house with its vast size and rows of pedimented windows was as fine as that of a duke. But, then, bankers as successful as Sir Lewis sometimes *were* as rich as dukes. Clearly, the de Bourghs were more rich than mere earls like he, whose losses on the exchange coupled with his late father's gaming debts had rather decimated the Seaton fortunes.

The wide door swung open before Seaton reached the top step, and a footman dressed in scarlet livery greeted him. "Lord Seaton?"

The earl nodded.

"Lady Catherine has instructed me to show yer lordship to the library."

They passed through the main hall—a huge chamber with soaring ceilings—continued down a marble corridor, and came to a walnut-paneled library. Even though he had never been introduced to the woman, he immediately recognized the tall, formidable looking woman who stood warming herself near the fire as Lady Catherine de Bourgh. She was possessed of a hawk-like nose that seemed in perfect harmony with what he had learned of her character. Though he knew her to be close to the age of his mother, Lady Catherine appeared older. Silver threaded her dark hair, and the bitterness etched into her face bespoke many years of disappointments.

That her rank was inferior to his in no way lessened the pride emanating from her as she peered at him with dark, menacing eyes. He suddenly understood his mother's desire to steal away from a confrontation with Lady Catherine, for he felt exactly the same at this very moment.

He stood in the doorway, offered a curt nod, and said, "At your service, my lady."

With the stiffness of a queen, she offered her hand to kiss.

Could she not have the courtesy to say something like, *How good of you to come, my lord*? He moved to her and effected an air kiss several inches above the back of her hand, cursing himself for coming.

"You may sit down," she commanded.

Seaton was not accustomed to being commanded, but nevertheless did as she ordered and sat in a high-backed, upholstered arm chair near the fire, grateful for the warmth. It was beastly cold.

His hostess continued to stand, her stern gaze boring down on him like an immovable judge upon King's Bench. "While we may not have formally been introduced, I knew your mother well, and I believe my daughter once saw you at Lady Jersey's."

The woman had a daughter? He had no recollection of ever having met a Miss de Bourgh.

Neither Lady Catherine's purported connection to his mother, nor a supposed fleeting glance between himself and this woman's offspring could explain the vicious summons that had compelled him to come here today.

"Forgive me, my lord, for the ruthless means I employed to ensure that you would heed my call." There was nothing in her stern face that indicated any measure of remorse.

He frowned. "You must know it is impossible for me to buy back the mortgage on Seaton House at this time."

"Of course I know that! Why else would I have procured it from the man to whom your father owed a great deal of money?"

She wanted something from him, and he feared he would be obliged to perform an unsatisfactory service in order to regain ownership of the Cavendish Square house that had been his family's for a hundred years.

What a pity his father had left the estate so vastly in shambles. "Pray, my lady, what is it you wish from me?"

A flicker of softness passed over her craggy face and vanished as swiftly as it had come. "If you will oblige me, I shall *give* the mortgage to you—and, later, a great fortune as well."

It suddenly occurred to him that the woman was going to demand he marry her daughter. Why had he not suspected earlier that the woman had a homely daughter to force upon him? Had not half the mothers in the *ton* tried to foist their plain daughters upon him these past several Seasons? The fathers, too. Seaton had turned down hundreds of thousands of guineas' worth of dowries since the very day he had succeeded.

That this woman had gone to such severe measures to obtain a husband of rank for her daughter indicated desperation. How ugly Miss de Bourgh must be!

He had no intentions of shackling himself to Miss de Bourgh. His seething gaze drilled hers. "Go on."

"My only child is dying." Her voice broke on the words.

Guilt bolted through him. "I am very sorry." He still did not understand what he could do to assuage their suffering.

"I should like for Anne's last few weeks to be happy ones. My girl was never able to have a proper Season, owing to the ill health that has plagued her throughout her life. I believe she always wishcd to wed a peer." A faint smile played at her lips. "It's been said my Anne could adorn the rank of duchess rather than be adorned by it."

Then why in the blazes had she not married a bloody duke? He had a very good idea why such a marriage had not occurred.

"If you will make my Anne your countess for her final weeks on Earth, I will make you my heir. And I will, of course, give you the deed to the Cavendish Square house."

His insides squirmed. "So you want me to wed your daughter before she dies?"

She glared at him. "You have no idea how privileged you are to receive an offer such as mine. As our only child, Anne is. . . " Her breath hitched. "*Was* scheduled to inherit Rosings, all the land that goes with it, as well as our vast banking interests. May I remind you that if you refuse me, I will claim the house on Cavendish Square. How, then, my lord, will you present your unwed sisters? Not to mention how you plan to go about dowering those young sisters."

Were it just himself he had to consider, he likely would have marched away from Rosings right then, but he did have his sisters' futures to provide for. By honor, he was obliged to see to the girls' needs first and foremost. How could he present them without the house on Cavendish Square?

Under normal conditions, he would never have considered marriage to this woman's daughter—or to anyone's daughter for mere money or property.

Where the de Bourgh woman was concerned, he would not have united himself to this woman's family even for the greatest fortune in the kingdom. But, he had to own, this was a most intriguing situation. If Miss de Bourgh was only going to live for a few more weeks, it wasn't as if he were going to be shackled for life to this most unsatisfactory woman's daughter. But for just a few weeks. . .

One had only to look at the opulence surrounding them at Rosings for proof of the de Bourgh fortune. At last—that is, after Miss de Bourgh died and the prescribed mourning period was over—he would be in a position to offer for Lady Harriett Lynnington, the only girl he had ever fancied himself in love with.

The very idea of profiting by this grievous situation made him feel beastly. Good lord! What was the matter with him? Charles St. John, the Earl of Seaton, had never before directed his thoughts on so mercenary a trajectory.

"I should like the inscription on my daughter's tomb to read *Anne, Countess of Seaton, beloved daughter of Lady Catherine de Bourgh and Sir Lewis de Bourgh.* It was always my plan that only a peer would do for one of such distinguished birth."

It struck him as odd the woman should turn her thoughts to so morbid a subject, odd that it was *her* feelings, rather than her daughter's, which were being considered. Uncharitably, when she had alluded to Miss de Bourgh's distinguished birth he found himself trying to recall a de Bourgh ancestor with rank above that of a lowly baronet, but he was unable to do so. He did recall that Lady Catherine's birth was considerably higher than that of the wealthy man she had married.

"Is Miss de Bourgh aware of this scheme?"

"Not yet. You were my first choice, and though I am accustomed to getting what I want, I was not certain of your compliance."

"Does Miss de Bourgh have no say in the selection of her own husband?"

"Why should she? She has never had to tax her strength with thoughts that I could undertake for her. My daughter knows I will always serve her best interests."

He felt even more sorry for the dying young woman. With so overbearing a mother, how wretched her short life must have been.

Seaton was actually disappointed to learn the marriage was not being sought by Miss de Bourgh. It would have been far easier for him to enter into such an alliance by consoling himself that he was making a dying lady's romantic dreams come true.

"Is your daughter sufficiently in command of her faculties?"

Lady Catherine's dark eyes widened. "Of course she is! I will have you know that my daughter is possessed of a well-formed mind that marks those of superior birth."

He held up his hands. "I meant only to inquire if Miss de Bourgh's infirmity has stolen away her ability to communicate."

"She is weak. Very weak. But she manages to speak tolerably well."

"What is the nature of the lady's illness, if I might be so bold as to inquire?"

Lady Catherine effected a dramatic shrug. "She is on the tail of a long decline."

"And a physician has proclaimed her prospects

without hope?"

She nodded solemnly. "I had Fortescue, who you must know is physician to the Duke of Clarence. If at all possible, I always prefer connections with the Royal Family. Only the best for my girl." She effected a grave countenance. "Fortescue said he must prepare me for the worst."

What was he to do? Despite that Lady Catherine was a nasty piece of work, how could he deny her? The poor woman's heart must be in tatters. Miss de Bourgh was, after all, her only child.

One little niggling doubt clung to his befuddled mind. What if this sickness was a sham to secure his title for the lady's perfectly healthy daughter? It was the kind of deceit a woman like Lady Catherine was likely to employ. "I must see Miss de Bourgh before I can give you my answer."

"Allow me to speak to her first."

* * *

Anne smelled her mother's overpowering fragrance, and her eyelids slowly lifted. There stood her mother, peering down at her, a lively expression in her dark gaze. "You have a caller, my dearest."

No one ever called upon her. She could not recall a single time in her five and twenty years when someone had come to see only her. She tried to sit up from her reclining position on the long sofa by the drawing room fire, but she was too weak. "Pray, Mama, who?"

A completely self-satisfied smile covered her mother's face. "It's Lord Seaton. I remember you commenting upon how handsome you thought him when you saw him at Lady Jersey's."

"But I do not know him. We were never introduced."

"Oh, fi! It matters not. The earl must have been satisfied with what he saw of you. Such breeding as you have, my dear, sets one apart. I believe he's quite taken with you for he's come to beg for your hand in marriage."

That her mother's comment did not cause a fatal rent to her heart must be proof that she was not as gravely ill as she had been led to believe. For nothing in Anne's life had ever shocked her more. "There must be an error. It has been six years or more since I glimpsed his lordship. He surely has mistaken me for another lady."

That stern look that always frightened Anne appeared on her mother's face. "There has been no mistake. Lord Seaton wishes to pay his addresses to *you*."

It's not me he wants but my fortune. Her pale eyes widened. She drew her shawl more tightly about her, but her shivering would not abate. "Today?"

"Yes, of course! He's come all the way from London."

"Should I not contrive to—" She started coughing. When she finally stopped, she finished. "Make myself more presentable?"

"You are lovely just as you are. His lordship is aware that your health is not robust. I'll go and invite him to address you." Her mother spun on her heel and stormed to the door.

Anne wanted to ask if she might be permitted to refuse his lordship, but her desires had never been either consulted or encouraged. She was accustomed to doing exactly what Mama wanted her to do. Clearly, Mama wished for Anne to become a countess.

It would take someone with a much stronger backbone than Anne to stand up to the formidable woman who was her mother.

As she awaited the handsome earl, her teeth began to chatter.

* * *

He looked up as Lady Catherine returned to the library, a smug look on her narrow face. "If you will come this way, my lord, I shall introduce you to my daughter."

He stood and strolled to the door.

"I ask that you not mention the short time she has left. I could not bring myself to tell her. I want her to know only happiness until she succumbs to her suffering."

He nodded gravely.

In the drawing room, Miss de Bourgh lay on a floral sofa near the fire. He had no recollection of ever before seeing her, but perhaps her illness had greatly changed her appearance. To be sure, this young woman looked almost childlike in her emaciated state. She was as pale as she was thin, and her skin was snowy white, deeply veined with blue. In fact, there was a blue cast to her exceedingly pale skin.

As soon as he saw her, he knew the mother was not trying to deceive. Miss Anne de Bourgh would not be long for this world. His heart went out to the frail creature.

Lady Catherine said, "My lord, may I present my daughter Anne."

He moved to the sofa and sketched a bow. "We have not previously been introduced, Miss de Bourgh, but I seem to recall having seen you before." What could it hurt to tell a lie to a pitiable, dying girl?

She attempted to clear her throat. "I believe we were both at Lady Jersey's a few years back."

He forced a smile. "Indeed!"

An awkward silence followed.

Lady Catherine, who had remained standing beside them, broke the chill. "His lordship wishes to see you in private. I shall take my leave." She tossed a glance at Seaton. "You do not have to stand there. You may sit."

He dragged a chair to sit beside the slightly built wisp of a girl. "I say, Miss de Bourgh, you must not respond to me in a manner calculated to please your mother. I am going to ask you something, and I desire you to give me an honest response."

"Yes, my lord," she whispered.

"I have come today to beg that you make me the happiest man in kingdom by consenting to become my wife, but you must only accept me if it is a connection that can bring *you* happiness. Do not accept me because you want to make your mother happy."

She did not respond for a moment. Unaccountably, his insides churned. Was she going to reject him?

"I will accept you, my lord," she finally said in a quivering voice.

He felt as if he had turned into molten butter. He took her slender, bluish hand within his.

The door to the chamber burst open. "I was listening at the door," Lady Catherine said as she came striding into the room. "I could not be happier over the match. I must send for Collins at once and have him see to getting the special license." Lady Catherine sighed. "Were my dear

Anne in better health, I'd wait until such time as we could procure the Archbishop of Canterbury himself to perform the ceremony, but since Anne's so weak, a quiet wedding at Rosings will answer our needs adequately."

Were it not for the grievous circumstances, he would have lost patience with Lady Catherine a half hour earlier. He kept telling himself he had to suffer the loathsome woman's company for only a few weeks.

$\mathcal{C}$hapter 1

Two weeks later

Anne de Bourgh's mother had insisted she have a new gown for her wedding. In a rare show of democracy, Lady Catherine de Bourgh had even consulted Anne regarding its colour. "What do you think, my dearest, about chalk white? I believe it conveys an innocence that brides are expected to bring to their marriage."

"I, too, thought a snowy white would be just the thing." White suited the colorless woman Anne was. It would not do for someone as frail and pale as she to attempt to wear cheerful colours.

Her mother's unexpected democracy ended with that single concession. She immediately rejected Anne's plea to be allowed to stand during her wedding ceremony. "I will not have your strength taxed. Lord Seaton perfectly understands your need to be seated during the service."

Every time his lordship's name was mentioned, Anne's pulses pounded. After two weeks of becoming accustomed to the idea of wedding him, she should be comfortable with the notion. But she was not.

She was cognizant that almost any other unmarried young lady in the kingdom would enthusiastically exchange places with her. Were she six years younger and full of romantic expectations as she had been at nineteen, she too would have been thrilled to have caught Lord Seaton's attention.

Even if his only interest in her was for her fortune.

But in these past six years as her health continued its long, sad, debilitating decline, she had come to understand how hopeless were her prospects of living one of those happy, normal lives. Lives in which a woman fell in love, married, and bore a brood of children.

Every time she thought of his lordship, she recalled that first night she had seen him from the top floor of Lady Jersey's house on Berkeley Square. She and several other gawking debutantes peered down the stairwell as he had mounted the stairs beneath the brightness of hundreds of candles. She had thought surely someone as handsome as he had to be some deity. In her idealistic youth she had still hungered to be swept from her feet by a lord as dashing as the Earl of Seaton. For months after that night she had dreamed of him.

Such dreams had disappeared as the last vestiges of her strength had slipped away.

But why did her heartbeat accelerate every time she heard his name?

As her maid was assisting her in dressing for her wedding, with Mama lending a hand, their butler knocked upon Anne's chamber door.

"Pray, what is it?" Mama stormed to the door, her blackening mood matching the tone of her voice. She yanked the door open, careful to preserve her daughter's privacy.

"Your nephew, Mr. Darcy, his wife, and his sister, who is now Mrs. Farrington, have arrived,

and Mr. Darcy asked that I present this to you."
He held out a silver tray upon which a letter
rested.

With a huge sigh, she mumbled something
under her breath, took the letter, and began to
tear it open.

"Oh, Mama, I shall be the happiest of brides
now that my cousins have come to share my
special day. Please say you'll allow them to stay."

Her mother, in one of her frequent fits of ill
temper, attempted to dissolve all ties to Anne's
cousin, Fitzwilliam Darcy, because he wed a
woman of whom Mama did not approve.

Though it embarrassed Anne to admit it, she
knew Mama had been in a temper because she
had always fancied a union between Fitzwilliam
and her own daughter. It mattered not to her that
such a union had never been the object of either
Fitzwilliam or Anne.

Mama's face softened as she read. Once
finished, she carefully folded the letter and shoved
it into her pocket, then turned to face Anne, a stiff
smile upon her face. "It seems Mrs. Collins has
written to her friend—" She grimaced. "Darcy's
bride, to inform her of your nuptials, and Darcy
said his regard for you outweighs any differences
there are between him and me. He wished to be
here for your wedding."

Anne's eyes grew moist over her cousins'
affection toward her. She had always admired
Darcy, even more since the burdens of owning
Pemberley and being both mother and father to
his much-younger sister had been thrust upon
him at a young age. No one could have been a
more considerate brother to Georgiana, a sweet
girl whose companionship Anne enjoyed

exceedingly. Were the Darcy parents alive, they would have been very proud of the young adults their offspring had become.

Lady Catherine squared her shoulders and effected a haughty air. "I can be magnanimous. I shall forgive my nephew for his rash behavior and allow him to attend your wedding." A wicked smile transformed her stern face. "We will show him! Nothing less than an earl for my daughter!"

After five and twenty years, Anne had come to accept her dominating mother's fixation on rank, but she was most sincerely determined not to follow her mother's lamentable practices. "I do hope Captain Farrington came. I should ever so much like to see dear Georgiana's new husband."

"Yes, he has. Darcy said the four of them had come."

* * *

As Darcy sat in the drawing room where poor Anne's wedding would take place, he regretted that he had never been more sympathetic to his cousin, who was just three years younger than he. He had never truly believed her the invalid her mother made her out to be. When Charlotte Collins' letter imparted the news that Anne had but a few weeks left on earth, he had been filled with remorse. Why had he always thought her illnesses feigned? He had believed Anne merely lazy, using her purported inclement health as an excuse to prevent her from doing things she found unpleasant. Things like practicing at the pianoforte or translating foolish French passages.

And now she was dying. Why had he not been more solicitous of her? He loved her. Enough to come to Rosings despite his aunt's wicked treatment of the most perfect of beings: his most beloved Lizzy. He had once vowed that he would never forgive his aunt. To speak ill of Lizzy was to sever all ties to Fitzwilliam Darcy.

But for dear Anne's sake, he would be civil to his abrasive aunt. Unless she slighted Lizzy. He had wanted to come without his wife for fear of Lady Catherine abusing her, but Lizzy said she could not bear to be separated from him. In the year they had been wed, they had not spent a single night apart. Though he hated to admit any weakness, Darcy had no wish to ever spend a night without Lizzy in his arms, either.

His gaze lifted once more to Seaton, who stood next to that annoying vicar, Mr. Collins, whose tongue had not stilled during this half hour they had been waiting for Anne. Darcy's sympathies would have been more with the earl (who appeared to be bored beyond tolerance) were it not for the fact the earl must be taking advantage of his cousin's grave a situation.

Darcy and Seaton had been at Oxford together, and Darcy knew nothing about the earl that would in any way disparage him. Yet the notion of taking advantage of a situation of a dying young woman rather rankled the young lady's cousin.

He sincerely hoped Seaton could make Anne happy her last days on earth.

* * *

How in the blazes could Lady Catherine tolerate this long-winded, self-important, rank-worshipping clergyman, Seaton wondered. The sooner his bride entered the chamber, the better. His glance flicked to the empty silken chair beside him. Poor Miss de Bourgh was not deemed strong enough to stand throughout the ceremony.

He attempted to stifle thoughts of Lady Harriett

Lynnington. How melancholy it was to be marrying another woman when all he his life he'd loved only Lady Harriett.

When the chamber's door opened and Miss de Bourgh slowly glided into the room with only her mother to assist, his heart constricted. A more delicate girl he had never seen. Even her dress— soft and white and without structure—conveyed the very delicacy that defined the dying young woman. He took a long look upon her pale face and realized she was actually pretty. Not beautiful like Lady Harriett Lynnington, but pretty.

How heart wrenching that she would not see the next Christmas.

She did not look at him but offered a smile to Darcy. It seemed almost inconceivable to Seaton that Darcy, who was one of the most solid fellows Seaton had ever known, could be so close a relation to Lady Catherine, who was one of the most obnoxious persons he had ever known.

He prayed Miss de Bourgh resembled the Darcys more than she resembled her trying mother. But what would it matter? He had only a few weeks to spend with her. One could tolerate anything for a short time. Even an ill-tempered mother-in-law.

Or an irritating wife.

Yet gazing at Miss de Bourgh as she gracefully lowered herself into the chair beside him, he doubted she could ever be an irritation.

It was only then that she looked up into his eyes.

He smiled at her, and without being aware of what he was doing, he took her fragile hand into his own and continued to clasp it as he turned to the exasperating vicar.

That she had not returned his smile troubled him. He hoped to God she was not being forced into this marriage by her overbearing mother. Was her failure to smile the consequence of a natural shyness not unlike her quiet cousin Darcy? Or was she upset over the marriage?

The blithering clergyman commenced with the ceremony. When the word *vow* was uttered, Seaton silently vowed that he would do everything in his power to make Anne de Bourgh's last days on earth happy ones.

Throughout the ceremony, he continued holding her hand, and when the time came to speak his vow, he did so in a determined voice. When she spoke hers, her voice trembled.

At the completion of the service, the vicar said, "Your lordship, you may kiss Lady Seaton."

For a fraction of a second, he thought Lady Seaton was his mother; then, he realized Anne de Bourgh was now Lady Seaton. His heart hammering, he bent down, swept Anne into his arms, and settled a gentle kiss on her bluish lips. Shyly, tentatively, her arms came around him.

Then she offered him a smile.

Darcy stood and clapped.

* * *

There was to be a wedding breakfast, after which she would accompany Lord Seaton to his Margrove Manor. She felt rather like a fairy princess as his lordship carried her to the table and set her down, then took his place beside her and tucked her hand into his as the footmen offered a vast array of delicacies.

Oddly, she no longer felt uncomfortable in his lordship's presence. By his tender attentions, he had lubricated an easy camaraderie between them. More than that, because of his concern for her, she felt unaccountably happy. That Darcy and Georgiana had come to share this day added even more to her felicity. Were she any happier, she thought she might burst with these excessive emotions to which she was not accustomed.

She looked around the table and beamed. She had met Miss Bennett—who was now Mrs. Darcy—before and found nothing at all offensive in her. Now that Anne had the opportunity to see the newlyweds together, she realized it was a true love match on both sides.

Regarding Georgiana and Captain Farrington's match, she was greatly surprised over the captain's youth. He could not be more than one and twenty. She had thought a great heiress like Georgiana would have snared a peer of the realm. She doubted, though, that Georgiana could have found another man who would be a better match for her, judging from the frequent displays of affection she had witnessed between the two of them. "I declare, there are six of us all wed within the last year. Tell me, Georgiana, had you know the captain long before you wed?" Anne seemed to recall a Farrington family living near Pemberley.

Georgiana giggled, and she and her husband exchanged amused glances. "Indeed. We've known each other all our lives."

Because Anne had never been much in Society, she often asked questions that more polite people would not. "Had you always been in love?" The way their eyes sparkled when they looked at each other convinced Anne they were deeply in love. What a silly question for her to ask! She had not had romantic notions in many years, and now she could not free her thoughts from questions and observations about love.

Georgiana giggled again. This was really quite remarkable. Georgiana Darcy had always been reticent like her brother. What a transformation her marriage had wrought! "Always on my part, but my darling Robert took much longer to realize we truly belonged together."

Robert Farrington sent a loving smile to his wife.

Anne wistfully wished her marriage could be a true love match like Georgiana's. And Darcy's. Even though Lord Seaton could not have been any kinder to her, she was well aware he had married her for her fortune.

"So," Darcy said, eying Lord Seaton, "My aunt tells me you go to Margrove Manor today."

"Indeed we do," her husband answered. "Despite that Lady Catherine was loathe to let Miss. . . I mean Anne, leave Rosings, I am persuaded that a change of locale may do her good."

"One cannot blame her ladyship," Mr. Collins defended, "for not wanting to spend her daughter's last days with her."

Anne was aware that both her mother and her new husband glared at the vicar with anger flashing in their eyes.

Good lord, did all these assembled people believe her to be dying? Her levity sunk, replaced by a sickening thud in the cavity of her chest. She saw everything so clearly now. No doubt Mr. Collins had told his wife Anne was dying, and she in turn had written to her dear friend, Mrs. Darcy. Anne's cousins had come not because they wished to be at her wedding; they had come to say their farewells.

What had a few minutes earlier been the happiest day of her life now became the most melancholy.

"What Mr. Collins obviously means," Lord Seaton said, his solemn gaze on hers, "was that your mother would have enjoyed sharing your *first* days as a new bride in order to impart to you the many things she has learned about being mistress of a fine country home."

Her mother's icy glare still on the clergyman, he quickly nodded in agreement. "You may be assured that is exactly what I meant, your lordship." His apprehensive stare moved to her. "And your ladyship."

Anne was not convinced. She was convinced that everyone here believed she was dying. Is that why Mama had paid so exorbitant a sum to bring Fortescue all the way from London? Was there nothing that could be done to extend Anne's time left on Earth?

Her appetite vanished.

"I am still vexed with Lord Seaton," Lady Catherine said. "I have never been separated from my only child. Not for a single day."

"It's good for one's child to fly away from the nest, Aunt," Darcy said. "I am confident that whenever Anne needs you, Lord Seaton will welcome you at Margrove Manor. It's not even a full day's drive away, is it?"

"You're correct," Anne's husband said. "I believe another advantage of being at Margrove is that it is farther south, so I am in hopes the warmer weather there will be more healthful for my dear countess."

His dear countess! It was hard to credit he was speaking of her. Skinny, sickly Anne de Bourgh was now countess to this handsome lord! She considered his words about the warmer climate. Dare she hope her health would improve were she to live further south?

She had not been privy to the discussions between his lordship and her mother. Mama seldom consulted Anne for her opinions. Anne had known that Mama had originally insisted that Lord and Lady Seaton reside at Rosings, but the earl refused to do so. How he had persuaded her normally inflexible mother to consent to the separation, Anne did not know.

Though she had never been away from her mother, she rather liked the notion of being independent from the domineering woman. Of course she loved her mother, but there had been too many clashes of their wills over the years. How wonderful it would be to be her own mistress. To be liberated.

Even if she might be dying.

* * *

Seaton had heard that Darcy married a penniless woman, but now that he had the opportunity to observe her, he thought Darcy had done very well for himself. And no question about it, the two were completely devoted to one another.

"Do eat your parsley potatoes, my lady," Lady Catherine said to her daughter. "Parsley is said to be uncommonly good for the lungs."

He had wondered how long Lady Catherine would wait before she bandied about her daughter's new title. It had taken less than five minutes. He was coming to read the woman like a Minerva Press novel. It was she—with little help from her solicitor—who he dealt with in the settlements. She was shrewd, but as good as her word.

No other mother of his acquaintance had ever attempted to tell her adult child what to eat, but he believed Lady Catherine ordered the daughter about as if she were the lowliest of servants. The sooner he got Anne away from that woman, the better. In that, his firm insistence during the negotiations had prevailed. He had conceded that when Anne's time drew near, he would send for the mother.

He had very nearly not been able to remove his wife from Rosings. Lady Catherine, after all, was accustomed to getting her way. It had taken a gamble to secure his victory over the headstrong woman. He'd curtly told Lady Catherine that he must insist on a private honeymoon—a honeymoon in which he would be especially mindful of Miss de Bourgh's frail state of health— or else she could seek another peer of the realm to marry her daughter. Looking at him with hatred in her dark eyes, she acquiesced.

"I don't like parsley potatoes," Anne said in a wispy voice.

"And, my love," said he, "you shall not have to eat anything you don't want." He lifted the hand that had rested in her lap and kissed it. How could this be? He had been married scarcely more than five minutes and he was referring to his sickly wife as *my love*. A fleeting memory of the affection he held for Lady Harriett stung. He had always thought she would be the one he married.

Anne's face gentled as she peered up at him and smiled.

"If I might be so bold as to interject my humble opinion, your lordship," Mr. Collins said, "it gratifies me to know that Lady Seaton's care will be entrusted into your capable, aristocratic hands. I have always said no one would ever do for Miss de Bourgh but a man of noble birth. Yes, indeed. Did I not always say so, Mrs. Collins?"

"Indeed you did," his unfortunate wife answered.

So Collins, too, wasted no time in referring to his benefactor's daughter as *Lady Seaton*.

Not content to be silent, Mr. Collins continued. "Indeed, I've always said that because of Miss de Bourgh's—Lady Seaton's—sickly constitution, the British court has been deprived of its brightest ornament. Have I not always said that, Mrs. Collins?"

His wife spoke in a monotone. "Yes, Mr. Collins, you have always said that with great regularity."

Unlike Collins, Anne had given Seaton no evidence that she held matters of privilege and rank to be of great import. But what did he really know about her? They had scarcely exchanged more than a dozen words.

He was exceedingly anxious to get her away from Rosings and that wretched mother. He had assured Lady Catherine that a more southern climate might improve Anne's health.

He could tell that Anne was wearying, and he was determined to sweep her off to Margrove Manor. His gaze sifted to her. "I think this momentous occasion has taken its toll on Lady Seaton. Are you finished eating, my dear?"

She looked up and nodded.

He stood and scooped her into his arms. "My carriage awaits." With an almost imperceptible bow, he nodded to Darcy and the captain. "Thank you, all of you, for sharing this wondrous event."

The entire group followed the newlyweds to his coach, and all of Anne's relations, including her for-once condescending mother, kissed her, said sweet things, and wished her well.

As the coach rolled away, his bride astonished him by sitting up as straight as a poker, even though he had begged her to recline. She still looked very weak, but her eyes were lively.

"Pray, my lord, tell me about Margrove."

$\mathcal{C}$hapter 2

What the devil? When his bride had projected an almost-normal energy, his first thoughts were that Lady Catherine and her daughter had duped him into this marriage. But as his gaze settled on his wife, her extreme frailty and the shaky rasp in her voice only served to reaffirm the weak state of her health. He realized the poor lady was merely excited at the prospect of having her own home and her own husband. She was still in a very bad way, and it was up to him to see that her last weeks were full of happiness.

"If you have no plans to recline, Lady Seaton," said he, "may I suggest you come and sit next to your husband." It was quite incredible to think of himself as anyone's husband. Other than Lady Harriet's, he thought with a gnawing remorse.

Anne's pale blue eyes were still lively as she moved to get up.

"Allow me to help, dearest." He had not meant for her to have make the physical effort.

"I am capable of such a small movement, my lord." She plopped beside him.

"You are not to refer to me as *my lord*."

"Then what shall I call you?"

His thoughts flitted to his parents. His mother had always referred to his father as Seaton, when they were not using endearments. But Seaton sounded much too stuffy to him. He thought of what his sisters had called him before he succeeded and they too had adopted the practice of referring to him as Seaton. They had called him Charles. "I wish you'd refer to me by my Christian name."

"Charles?"

"Yes, and I will call you Anne."

"Darcy's the only other man who's ever addressed me by my Christian name. I do hope you and I shall get along as well as I always have with my cousin."

That was the most words he had ever heard her string together. Surprisingly, she had not sputtered for breath as did those in the final stages of consumption. Which pleased him very much.

He found himself wondering if there had ever been an informal agreement that the cousins would one day marry. Had Anne ever been in love with Darcy? He was certain many other girls had wished to capture Darcy's affections these past few years.

"Now, about Margrove," he began. "What should you like to know?"

"I suppose first I should like to know who will be there."

"At present, just the staff. Do not forget, dearest, this is our honeymoon. It is a time for us to further our acquaintance without distractions from my incessantly babbling sisters."

"Did I not read in Debrett's that you have several younger sisters?"

"Indeed I do, and you will meet all of them in good time." How he wished she would have more time. "They are now at our aunt's in Middlesex."

She sighed. "I always wished for sisters."

"You vex me, woman."

"Why?" Her eyes widened as if she were frightened.

"Because I'd rather you had said you always wished for a husband, a husband exactly like the one you've now got!"

She did not respond for a moment. Then her solemn expression brightened. "You tease me."

"Of course I do."

A silence fell between them. His thoughts were on her comment about always wanting sisters. "By the way, dearest, you will have sisters. Four of them. All in good time." *Time.* He was growing to hate the word, for with each passing tick of a clock, her life grew shorter.

"I suppose your sisters are accomplished. I am not, you know."

"Your mother told me. It matters not. I understand the limitations imposed on you by your illness." He still was not precisely sure what that illness was.

"Do you not think it vastly unfair that it was my mother—and not me—with whom you made all the arrangements about our wedding?"

She *did* resent her mother's constant interferences in her life! Thank God. He had feared she would be like an abandoned infant without the mother who had orchestrated every move of her entire five and twenty years. "I most certainly did think it unfair. That was one of the reasons I insisted on removing you from Rosings. I should like for you to learn to speak for yourself." His face went solemn. "You even have the right, now that you are away from your mother, to tell me I am not the man for you, and I will understand."

A mournful expression crossed her pallid face. "You don't want to be a husband to me."

"That is not what I said, Anne. I most certainly do want to be married to you."

"And I have come to realize marriage to you is precisely what will make me happy."

He peered down at her face, at the way her light brown lashes shaded those incredibly blue eyes of hers. "Your comment has made me very happy." He clutched her slender hand and lifted it to settle his lips upon on her fine white gloves.

A long silence fell. They were some distance away from Rosings now, and the land on both sides of the country lane was cultivated with a barley crop. The only sound to be heard was the rattle of the carriage wheels.

"I am dying, am I not? That is the real reason why my cousins came, the reason you consented to marry a drab thing like me." No voice could have sounded more forlorn than Anne's at that moment.

How could he answer? He had always been severely averse to lying. This once, he would respect Lady Catherine's request that Anne not be told how grave her condition was. How could anyone be expected to reap any measure of happiness with so gruesome a fate looming over them? And he meant for Anne's final weeks to be as happy as he could make them. "You say that because of the words spoken by that fool Collins! Pray, do not listen to the man. I will own, you've been very ill, but I am certain the change of environment will speed your recovery. When your mother comes for Christmas, I vow, she will not recognize you."

How painful it was to know that when

Christmas came, Anne would likely be lying in her grave.

"I pray you're right, my lord."

He lifted her chin with a knuckle and spoke softly. "My lady, what are you to call me?"

She offered him a whimsical smile. "Charles."

On her lips, his name sounded almost like an endearment. He absently dropped a soft kiss into her flaxen hair, put his arm around her, and eased her into his chest. "You must try to rest. You'll need your strength for when we reach Margrove. I mean to give you a tour of your new domain."

She nodded. "Have you an invalid's chair for me?"

He had not thought of it. "Blast it! I should have brought the one from Rosings, and even though you are as light as you are, I fear I will not be able to carry you from one side of Margrove to the other. There are four stories and more than two hundred chambers."

Her eyes widened. "Then it's much larger than Rosings."

"And not nearly as well maintained as Rosings. It will need the mistress's touch."

"If I rest now, perhaps I can walk for a while when we get to Rosings."

He nodded. "We can divide the tour across several days so as not to rob your strength."

* * *

To her disappointment, night had fallen when they reached Margrove Manor, and owing to the lack of moon, she could see very little of the mansion as the carriage approached it. She did realize it was a massive structure.

Just thinking about being its mistress was

overwhelming. What did she know about running a household? What did she really know about anything? She wished she could be normal. She wished she were not so sickly. She wished like the devil she could be a good wife to Charles.

Once the coach drew up in front of the massive door and footmen swung open the carriage door, her husband moved from the vehicle, then reached back to lift her into his arms. It rather amazed her that he did so with no more effort than if he were lifting a sofa cushion.

How embarrassed she was to make her entrance into her new home being carried like a baby. Once he crossed the threshold, she whispered in his ear. "I beg that you put me down. I believe I'm capable of standing."

"Are you sure?" he asked, concern in his voice.

"I'm only sure of my determination to do so."

He did as she bid but pressed a hand to her waist. "Lean on my strength if you need to."

After being alone with Lord Seaton these past few hours she had come to a stunning realization. The romantic notions she had directed at this paragon of a man six years previously had come to fulfillment. She believed she was falling in love with her husband.

Never had she thought to be able to call this handsome lord her husband. Never had she thought a man with so many fine physical attributes could possibly be possessed of so caring a nature. Every minute with him was like a precious gift.

If Mama had done anything to push forward this marriage, she vowed to never again be out of charity with her.

A pity her husband merely wanted her for his

wife because of her fortune.

Was there anything she could do to make him fall in love with a skinny, plain woman past the first flush of youth? A pity that was the one thing her money could not purchase.

In the home's huge foyer at least five and twenty servants had assembled to greet their new mistress. She felt rather like a general inspecting his stiff-backed soldiers and prayed she could remember the names of the upper servants to whom she was being introduced.

The housekeeper was likely the age of Anne's mother but was possessed of a far more congenial countenance than her authoritative parent.

"My darling," Charles had said, turning to her, "may I present Mrs. Borden, who is the most capable housekeeper in England, I am sure."

Mrs. Borden dipped Anne a curtsy. "We are very pleased to meet you, Lady Seaton, and look forward to a long association. I do hope you are satisfied with your chambers. Even though there was no time for painting, his lordship insisted upon new draperies and bed coverings for his new countess."

How incredibly thoughtful of her husband. What had she ever done to merit such a great mate? She never would have credited that she could ever be Lady Seaton.

Then she realized with melancholy that Charles had likely wed her because he'd been told she was dying. How much had Mama settled upon him to marry her? He could be compensated most handsomely for a few weeks or months with a dying *nothing*. For *nothing* is how she thought of herself. She had no accomplishment. No beauty. Until today, she had not even been possessed of an aristocratic name.

She found that she did not want to know her price.

"Your dinner is ready at your convenience, my lord," Mrs. Borden said. "I thought you would be hungry after the journey."

"It's very kind of you," said he, "but we had a large basket of food for the journey, and I am completely without appetite." He turned to Anne. "What about you, love? You didn't eat much in the coach. Are you hungry?"

She shook her head. "Not in the least, but we do appreciate your efforts, Mrs. Borden." Long ago Anne had vowed that if she ever became mistress of her own house, she would treat her servants with a compassion her mother had seldom demonstrated.

Next, the butler, Tubbs, was introduced. She hated to admit that the name suited the tall, portly man.

After Tubbs moved on, Charles bent to speak to her in a low voice. "You are expected to stroll along the row of servants and smile agreeably. Do you think you can manage—with me to lean upon, of course?"

"As long as I have you, I feel anything is possible." It embarrassed her that she was gushing so frankly to him. He was apt to think her indistinguishable from the gaggle of girls at Almack's who worshipped him.

I am one of them!

They began to stroll the twenty-five feet along the corridor, with her leaning heavily on his solid arm. She was determined to go the length with the appearance of being on her own. Her breath was coming only with the greatest labor, but she would conceal that from these most obliging servants. And hopefully from her husband. When she finished smiling and nodding agreeably to each of them, Charles said, "Come, love. Allow me to show you our private chambers."

He moved to the stairs.

She knew it would be impossible for her to mount them, but hated to appear such an invalid in front of his servants.

He spared her from having to protest by dismissing the servants, and when the corridor was empty of all but a pair of magenta-liveried footmen, he scooped her into his arms and began to mount the broad stone stairway.

A sense of great well-being filled her, and she linked her arms around him. Why had she never before realized how big he was? There was nothing fat about him. He was just big and tall and solid.

He set her down in front of the closed door to her bedchamber. "I hope you approve of my choice of color. I asked your mother's guidance."

Why had he not asked her? Why had no one in her five and twenty years ever deferred to Anne de Bourgh? Because she was a *nothing*.

When he opened the door, she saw that crisp new silk in vivid turquoise covered her large, postered bed as well as the chamber's three tall windows. How stunning the turquoise looked against the stark white backdrop of the walls. An elegant Carrera marble fireplace took up the greater part of one wall, and on its chimneypiece stood a beautiful, gilt-handled Sevres vase of the same shade of turquoise.

He had done all this for her, a *nothing*? What a thoughtful man he was! She peered up at him. "Oh, my lord, it's beautiful!"

Once again, he lifted her chin with a knuckle and quirked a brow. "My lord?"

"Sorry, Charles."

"I'm happy you approve." He made no move to lift her again but took her hand. "Come, allow me to show you the other chambers of our suite."

Our suite. Hers and his. She really was Lady Seaton! They strolled across the creamy carpet in her chamber to the countess's dressing room, which had been redone in the same color scheme, then to the countess's study. It was an opulent room with heavy French influences, a slender-legged escritoire, and more turquoise Sevres porcelain. Quite lovely.

"No doubt, this is the chamber from which you'll write to your mother every day." His voice rang with levity. Charles was the only man she had ever seen who could stand up to the stern woman who was her mother.

"You mock me. I *did* tell Mama I would write every single day with an update on my health."

"I know you did, my sweet, and I will own that I infinitely prefer that you write daily—even twice daily—than have to live with her."

She rather thought she shared that preference, but she dared not own it. What an ingrate that would be after all Mama had always done for her. Besides, as much as Anne craved the freedom she would now have, with it came responsibilities, and she was not secure in her ability to handle those duties.

Next, they came to his bedchamber. Though it was almost the same floor plan as hers, it looked vastly different. It was all gilt and regal blues, with rich Turkey carpets, and a dark wood chimneypiece that harkened back to Tudor times.

Her gaze went to the room's dominant feature: the huge tester bed that was swathed with rich blue velvet curtains. She found herself wondering what it would be like to lie there with him on a cold winter night with the curtains closed all around them . . .

The very idea sent her trembling, and she collapsed into an upholstered arm chair before his fire.

He rushed to her. "Are you all right?"

She looked up at him, nodding.

"Beastly of me to tax your strength so."

"You did no such thing. It is just that I am so pathetic."

"Never say that," he said in a soft voice. "You will grow stronger now that you are at Margrove."

She wished it were true. She wished that she would one day share his bed. She knew they would not truly become man and wife on this, their wedding night. Mama had already told her that she and his lordship—without consulting her, of course—had agreed to delay . . . the intimacies until her health was improved.

Would it ever improve? Would she ever truly become his wife in every way?

"You are merely tired," said he. "It's been an exhausting day, and if you're like me, you did not sleep well last night, either."

"I hardly slept at all."

He bent to lift her into his arms, then he carried her back to her beautiful bed chamber and set her upon the bed that was high off the floor. Without saying a word, he began to remove her pelisse. She was accustomed to others doing everything for her, but here at Margrove, she must become a woman. "I am not a helpless child."

He straightened. "Sorry. I only wanted to help."

"You may call my maid."

After he left the chamber, she regretted that she had spoken harshly to him, regretted that she had not sat idly whilst he removed her clothing. All of it. Like other men must do on their wedding nights.

$\mathcal{C}$hapter 3

For the first time in the past two weeks, he hadn't thought of Lady Harriett the moment his candle was extinguished for the night. On this, his wedding night, the perplexing woman he had married was on his mind. He thought perhaps she *did* have a backbone after all. Not with her mother, but with him. She had certainly been annoyed when he had innocently tried to remove the heavy pelisse from her upper torso. Had she feared that he was going to try to seduce her? Nothing could have been further from his mind. One did not lust after dying women.

He could not purge from his mind that moment she had told him she was capable of seeing to her own needs. He would vow she had never uttered those words to her mother. At Rosings, Anne's function was to be a helpless ornament that fueled Lady Catherine's slavish devotion to her daughter's infirmities.

Also perplexing him about Anne was the fact Lady Catherine had never been able to put a name to the ailment that was depriving his wife of life. He had studied his bride for signs of the most common diseases and conditions, but she lacked the symptoms of those fatal maladies. He had been able to observe her speaking in long stretches both in the carriage and after they arrived at Margrove, with no ill effects.

While moving about her own three chambers at Margrove and into his bedchamber, she had proven to be capable of walking for at least five minutes without either gasping for air or having to sink into the closest chair. It was his opinion that she could have stood for the entire wedding ceremony.

Away from Rosings, she projected a considerably more healthful countenance. The only symptom that seemed consistent to him was her lack of appetite. And that was concerning, for lack of appetite was the one symptom that always indentified a dying being, whether it be human or a pet, like the many dogs he had lost over the years. Those on the verge of death never wanted to eat.

He vowed to himself to learn what were her favorite foods and try to tempt her with them—if for nothing more than to confirm her imminent death.

Before he went to sleep he also vowed that he would coax her to increase both her activity and her speech a little more each day.

As hopeful as he was that she would improve, he had to remind himself that those measures would be useless if her condition—whatever it was—were, indeed, fatal.

* * *

The following morning, after her maid had assisted her into a new pale blue morning gown and arranged her hair in a most stylish fashion, his lordship called for her. How difficult it was to remember to refer to him as Charles. She was so unfit to be his countess.

"I've come to show you the public rooms of your new home, Lady Seaton," said he.

At first the thought of descending the stairs petrified her, but she must entrust herself into Lord Seaton's care.

"I hoped you would be able to go downstairs on your own legs, provided you are holding on to me, of course."

"Going down does not hurt my lungs as going up does." No one had ever before treated her as if she were *not* infirm! She would do everything in her power to show him that she was capable of doing those things which he thought she could do.

She placed her hand on the crooked arm he proffered. "As long as you are standing beside me, I have a great deal of confidence in my abilities."

He patted her hand. "As your husband, I plan to be at your side whenever you need me. That's what marriages are about."

"I've had little opportunity to observe happily married people," she said as they moved into the corridor. "My Papa died when I was a babe, so I was never able to observe him and Mama together. Since then the only married people I've been in company with are the Collinses, and I've seen no evidence that Mrs. Collins is particularly happy in her marriage."

They had begun to descend the stairway, and she found the air in her lungs did not seem to be deserting her. In fact, she had spoken a rather long time, and still could go on. Would his lordship think her a babbler? Is that not the word he used to refer to his younger sisters? She wouldn't like for him to think her a babbler.

"It pleases me to hear you speaking so well, my dearest."

Her heart fluttered under his compliment, and she felt unfamiliar buoyancy. He did not think her a babbler! She would continue on the same line of conversation. "I do wish I'd had more opportunity to observe my cousins with their new spouses. Did you have the impression both couples—Darcy and his Lizzy and Georgiana with her captain—were extremely happy in the marital state?"

"I did. I've never seen Darcy look better, never seen him talk so much, and never seen him appear so blissfully happy."

She paused upon the step. "I did not know you and my cousin were acquainted."

"Not well, but we were at school together and are of the same age. I will own, I don't see him much in town."

"That is because he prefers being at Pemberley."

"It's said to be one of England's great country houses."

"While it is lovely—especially the grounds—part of the reason everyone praises it so is that is it so very well maintained."

"Like Rosings. I hope I do not flatter myself when I say I believe Margrove superior to Rosings in nearly every way even though there is much here that needs attention. The leaky roof and faded draperies and overgrown parterre garden are the most troublesome."

She realized their marriage and the settlements it brought would enable him to see to all of Margrove's needs. "I daresay the urge to have meticulously maintained properties is a family trait. Our cousin Colonel Fitzwilliam is just as obsessed over his property."

They had come to the home's second floor. "Then I shall count upon Lady Seaton to assist me in seeing to Margrove's needs." Now he placed a hand at her waist. "This way to the drawing room."

He actually had confidence in her ability to be a competent mistress of his ancestral home! No one in her entire life had ever believed her capable of anything but lying upon a sofa or beneath the coverings of her bed. By Jove, she was going to prove to him she was worthy of his trust!

In the drawing room, she immediately saw that the chamber had much potential but needed a woman's caring touch. In size, it was a great deal larger than Rosings' drawing room, but it was darker and drab. She stood there a moment trying to determine just what it was the chamber lacked, what she could recommend for its improvement. "Do you know, my dearest," she said, conscious that for the first time she had referred to him as *my dearest* but hastening to continue with her sentence, "I believe this could be a very fine room—a showplace, even—with a few improvements."

He gave her an amused grin. "Such as?"

"We could start with the windows. They are dirty, and their draperies are so faded the fabric is, I daresay, brittle to the touch. I can imagine this chamber in scarlet."

"I am incapable of imagining altered chambers. I shall have to trust my wife."

How she adored being referred to as his wife! "And we must appreciate the room's finer qualities and accentuate them."

That devilish grin of his returned. "What finer qualities would that be?"

"All this wonderful, dark wood that dates to the Tudor period. I recommend we remove these French pieces and see that the chamber conveys a

Tudor or Elizabethan look with sturdier furnishings."

"Our attics are filled with study old pieces of furniture that are in pitiable need of new fabric."

"Then take me to your attic." She could not remember ever feeling so . . . so adult before. She even had confidence in her suggestions.

It was at the thought of climbing stairs to the attics—a feat she was incapable of completing—that it occurred to her she had walked down a flight of stairs and she was still able to stand upon her own two legs without weakness or the desire to collapse. Had this change in her constitution been the result of being in a more southern climate? She peered up at him. He was only inches away, so close she was aware of his musky scent and aware of how much taller than she he was. "Do you realize I am still standing?"

Grinning, he nodded. "You can do it, Anne!"

"I can," she whispered. Then she thought of climbing stairs. "Though I assure you I cannot climb stairs."

He swept her into his arms and headed for the central stairway. "Once your lungs are stronger from repeated use, I believe you'll be able to climb stairs too."

She thought he sounded much wiser than Fortescue, even if Fortescue *was* physician to a member of the royal family. Her heartbeat accelerated as her hands came around his neck when he began to mount the stairs.

When they reached the top floor, he came to an abrupt halt. "I can't have you in the attics. Breathing all that dust cannot be good for your weak lungs."

"You are right, of course. Attics always make

me cough and sneeze."

"Later, after I've shown you our park—owing to the lovely, mild day we must take advantage of—you will have to draw up a list of the kinds of furnishings you would like to see in the drawing room, and I'll have Mrs. Borden and some footmen go find them in the attic and clean them before presenting them to you for approval."

Her approval. How novel! She was delighted to finally be treated like a normal adult. It was as if warm honey flowed through her veins. Not only was she a normal adult, she was wed to the man who was her heart's desire. Every minute with him was a precious gift.

Now, she must be worthy of his confidence. "I do hope Mrs. Borden will know of a competent upholsterer."

"She will make it her job to find one. A pity she neglected her job regarding clean windows. I never even noticed until you pointed out to me how dirty they were."

She felt a foot taller because of her husband's confidence in her, his compliment to her. She spun back to face her husband, smiling. "Pray, allow me to draw up that list before we go out of doors. That way, I shall be able to see the furnishings when we return." She had not been so exited in a very long while.

"So you are not only a visionary, you are pragmatic, too."

How wonderful it was to be praised by this man!

They started back down the two flights of stairs he had just climbed, but now she was descending on her own power. Two flights! Could she do it? As long as she had his strong arm to cling to she felt as if she could do anything. Soon, she hoped to be climbing stairs. Alongside her husband.

She was successful, and when they reached the home's entry corridor, he showed her to a writing desk in the morning room. "While you are composing your list," said her husband, "I will see to having Cook prepare us picnic fare. What shall I tell her to put into it?"

"Whatever you'd like."

"Cook knows what I like! I should like to ensure that she puts in something to tempt my wife's dainty appetite."

She felt the colour hike into her cheeks. She was keenly embarrassed over her skinniness. No man was ever attracted to a woman who resembled a twig. Yet even while she sunk in her own shortcomings, she was pleased at the delicate manner in which her husband had referred to her diminished appetite. He was not only the most handsome man she had ever known, he was also the kindest.

She was determined to please him in whatever way she could. If that meant eating more, then she would force herself to eat more. Now, to think of what could possibly tempt her. "I am fond of apples, and I believe it's the season for them."

"Apples you shall have. What else?"

Oh, dear. She did not want him to know that one apple to her was equivalent to another's feast. "I am sure I will be pleased with whatever you are having."

In the morning room, she sat and drew up a list of furnishings she should like to inspect when they returned from their outing. The list included as many high-backed arm chairs as could be found, chunky-legged sideboards and candle tables, as well as Turkey carpets.

Her husband had called for Mrs. Borden and explained her attic quest, handing her his wife's list before leading Anne out the door to the waiting curricle.

She paused on the steps, feeling as if something were missing. It took her a moment to realize that this was the first time in years she had been permitted to go out of doors without being forced to swaddle herself in a woolen muffler and ensconce herself in a rug once she got to the *enclosed* vehicle. Why, she had not been permitted to ride in an open vehicle since she was a girl. And that had been a very long time ago.

She did not feel even slightly chilled and rather fancied the idea of being permitted to enjoy so fine an autumn day.

Lord Seaton's large hands spanned her waist, and he swung her up on the seat, then he hopped up to sit beside her and take the ribbons. "A lovely day, is it not?"

"Indeed it is. It reminds me of when I was much younger and was permitted to drive my own pony cart."

His brows lowered. "I perceive that pleasure was taken away because of your ill health?"

She nodded solemnly. "It was a severe deprivation, to be sure."

"I am sorry."

The park around Margrove was not as well tended as the ones at either Rosings or Pemberley, but the terrain here with its rolling hills was lovelier than at Rosings but not as lovely as the peaks and rivers that surrounded Pemberley.

She vastly enjoyed seeing the countryside on so fine a day, but what pleased her even more was having her very own husband sitting beside her. It seemed as if they were the only two beings in the world. She was conscious of how close they were, that his muscular thighs were parallel to her own slender ones. Her gaze went to his aristocratic profile. He had left off a hat, and she surmised that must be a regular practice because his face was burnished from the sun.

Her gaze drifted to his hands. They were strong and capable. Like him. She never wanted the sun to set on this most perfect of days. Never in her life had she known such happiness as she now experienced.

A pity he was not attracted to her in the same way she was to him. She wished to become his countess. In every way. Though she had not been much in the world, she knew enough to know that the only reason he had married her was to gain her large fortune.

She could not fault him. Men did the same every day. Her cousin, Colonel Fitzwilliam, was extremely candid in owning that he had not the luxury of marrying for love. He must marry a woman who was in possession of a generous dowry.

She found herself wondering if Charles had ever fancied himself in love. The woman would have to have been beautiful. With a sickening thud in the pit of her stomach, she recalled Lady Eleanor mentioning that Lord Seaton was smitten with Lady Harriett Lynnington—and she with him. Lady Harriett was considered the most beautiful woman in London.

Since Anne and Mama read several publications cover to cover every day, they stayed well informed about the *on-dits* occurring in

London, which was undisputedly the social hub of the country. She was certain that Lady Harriett remained unwed. Which was most surprising, given that lady's notable beauty.

Had the dark-haired beauty refused all men to keep herself open for a declaration from Lord Seaton? No other man could ever outshine him. True, a duke or a marquess might outrank him, but an earl outranked most men in the kingdom. And no duke or marquess could ever match her husband's uncommonly handsome appearance.

It was difficult to credit that he was her husband. What had she ever done to deserve a man like this? She was quite sure Mama had orchestrated the offer even though it would deprive her mother of her only child. If for nothing else, she owed Mama a mammoth debt of gratitude.

It was likely Mama already felt as if she had been repaid. From now until the day she died, Mama would revel in hearing *my daughter, the Countess of Seaton* roll off her tongue. For no one cared more about rank than did her mother.

Except perhaps for Mr. Collins.

"I beg that you tell me when you're hungry," said her husband.

That was the pity of it. She never got hungry. "Have you determined where we take our repast?"

His dark head nodded. "I thought we'd eat by the banks of our small lake. There's something satisfying about being near water."

"Indeed there is. I once went to Bognor. When I was a child."

His eyes widened. "Your mother permitted you to bathe in the sea?"

She shook her head. "Never that. But I was able

to sit for a spell and watch the sea. I can't remember when I ever experienced anything so peaceful." She looked up at him and smiled. "Until today."

He favored her with a smile. "Should you like to hold the reins?"

"I can try."

He handed them to her, and her heart nearly exploded when she felt his arm come around her. No man save her husband had ever put an arm around her before. She rather thought she liked it. At first she feared he would detect her tremble. But after a moment passed, her shaking subsided and was replaced with a sharp awareness of Charles, the man.

She once again smelled his musky scent and experienced the almost overpowering sense of his height and girth. It struck her that he brought to mind a gallant knight of yore. In such close proximity to him, she felt as if nothing could ever happen to her as long as her husband, her protector, was close.

It was as if none of those tedious, trying years had passed since the days she had happily galloped around Kent on her own pony cart. She easily remembered how to control the horse, how to make it go faster, how to turn. Her broad smile could not be suppressed.

When they reached the top of Margrove's highest hill, she came to a stop whilst they surveyed the unspoiled lands that stretched before them in every direction. "Is all that yours?" she inquired.

"Ours," he said tenderly.

Her heart soared. It was still hard to believe she was actually the Countess of Seaton.

Still keeping his arm around her, he pointed to a meandering brook on the fringe of the orchard. "See that brook?"

She nodded.

"It is difficult to credit now, but when my father was a lad, that stream was filled with fish."

"Your father, I take it, enjoyed catching them."

"Indeed he did."

Did she not have to consider her husband's needs, she could have stayed in the curricle with him until night fell. She loved everything about this from the feel of Charles' arm around her to the gentle wind ruffling her hair, to the feel of the sun's warmth. Most of all, she experienced a feeling of exhilaration.

By mid afternoon, she knew her husband must be famished and their horse thirsty. "You must be hungry," she finally said.

He pointed to the shimmering blue lake to the south and nodded. "Shall we eat there?"

She took up the reins, and they reached the banks in five minutes. Her husband dismounted first, then reached back to lift her down. When her feet were on solid ground, she rose to her tiptoes and kissed his cheek. What in heaven's name had come over her?

$\mathcal{C}$hapter 4

What had come over her? What had possessed her to kiss Charles? She must act as if what she had just done was perfectly natural, though in truth it was the single most embarrassing act she had ever committed.

To her infinite gratitude, he continued on as if nothing had occurred, gathering up the picnic basket, then offering his arm to lead her to the banks of the lake. There, beneath the partial shade of a beech tree, he spread out a blanket—a single blanket for the two of them to share—and bid her to sit.

She chose to sit in the sun, the glorious sun from which she had for too long been deprived. Even as she sat, rust-colored leaves sprinkled upon the blanket. In just a few weeks, she knew the trees would be barren. And the days would be cooler. And Lord Seaton might be averse to taking her out of doors. Such thoughts as these made her melancholy.

I must enjoy every single minute. It seemed her senses had become sharper. She experienced a greater awareness of the gentle sound of water lapping at the shore, the wind scattering the leaves, the warmth of the sun she never wanted to set—all of this making her feel more alive than she had felt in years.

When he came to sit beside her, her heartbeat

accelerated. He began to unpack the basket, and when he reached the apples, he handed one to her. "For you, Lady Seaton."

She offered a smile, took the fruit, and sank her teeth into it. "This is delicious. Did it come from your orchard?"

He nodded, then corrected her. "*Our* orchard."

How touched she was that her husband so easily had accepted her as his wife. He could have married one far more worthy than she, though. *I must banish such melancholy thoughts.*

While he peeled a hard-cooked egg, she continued eating her crunchy apple, studying his firm lips as he bit into the yolk. Then his gaze swung to her and he offered the rest of the egg to her. *Oh dear.* She was already exceedingly full from the apple, but she did not want to disappoint her husband.

And truth be told, she fancied the idea of eating after him. It was just another of those blendings between a married couple that united them. She very much wanted to be united to this man.

Instead of taking the egg in her hand, she opened her mouth, and he placed the half-eaten egg in it. She slowly chewed it, swallowing a bit at a time, then washed it down with a long sip of Bordeaux. How long had it been since she had an egg? She had quite forgotten how well she liked them. "That was good."

His dark eyes sparkled. "You've made me very happy."

He acted as if he truly cared for her. She knew there was no way she could ever measure up to one as beautiful as Lady Harriett Lynnington. Even Lady Harriett's family lineage was superior to Anne's. Lady Harriett was superior in every way.

Except it was Anne whom he had married, Anne who was Lady Seaton. As incredible as it seemed.

He peeled another, ate half, then offered the rest of it to her.

"You spoil me, Charles. No one has ever peeled my food for me." Smiling, she shook her head. "I assure you, I cannot possibly eat another bite."

"I will own, you've eaten more today than I've seen in the short time we've been together. I'm very proud of you."

Under his praise, she once more soared. Reclining on the blanket, she watched him as one studies a great painting. In the sun, his dark hair was tinted auburn. His teeth were very white, and his profile bespoke power and nobility.

Her gaze traveled along the breadth of his shoulders, the cut of his fine chocolate-coloured coat, the cling of the buff breeches that molded to his solid legs. What a splendid dragon slayer her darkly handsome husband would have made!

His appetite was significantly superior to hers. He consumed a big hunk of freshly churned cheese, a slab of bread, and cold meat. She watched in amazement. How she wished her appetite were bigger. If it were, she was confident she could gain a little padding on her bones. Then she would be prettier to her husband. Never as lovely as Lady Harriett, but she hoped someday she could win her husband's love.

"You have yet to show me your stables, and I must tell you I am exceedingly horse mad, even though I've not been permitted to indulge my interest. Mama is not in the least enamored of horses. I daresay I inherited the interest from my papa." She was astonished, really, at how readily she was speaking and at how long she could go without gasping for breath.

"I had heard about Sir Lewis de Bourgh's stables from my father."

She shrugged. "After Papa's death, Mama sold off all the thoroughbreds."

"A pity." His features brightened. "If you must know, I'm saving the best for last."

It suddenly occurred to her that she did know a great deal about his stable. At least, about one horse in particular. "I have just realized you're the Seaton Stables that own Transcendent!"

His mouth opened in shock. "You know of my prized stallion?"

"Indeed I do! I have been following the accounts ever since he won the St. Leger. I cannot believe I did not realize you were the Seaton who is the owner! I must see the magnificent beast!"

* * *

He could not have been more pleased. Women, as a rule, were not in the least interested in thoroughbred race meetings or the magnificent beasts who won them.

And there was nothing in the universe that interested him more.

Watching her eagerly moving through the stables that had been the pride of the Seatons for generations, he could almost believe his wife healthy. It seemed as if she glowed. Certainly, he had not seen so lively an expression on her face since he had known her.

She paused outside Thunderstruck's stall. "Oh my stars! Is this the Thunderstruck who won the Derby?"

Not even his sisters, who had lived all their

lives around the famed Seaton Stables, knew anything about Thunderstruck. Or Transcendent. He spun to face her, a grin spreading across his face as he nodded. "This fine beast has mightily helped the Seaton Family coffers in these lean times we've been experiencing."

Her brows raised. "Stud fees?"

"Indeed. Every stable in England or Ireland wants to try to duplicate what this magnificent horse accomplished."

She came to stroke the horse's muzzle. "How beautiful he is!"

To his amazement, his wife went on to enumerate the many meetings Thunderstruck had won in his glory days.

They moved along until they came to Transcendent's stall. "He's another real beauty," said she. "Was he sired by Thunderstruck? They have the same white markings."

His wife certainly had a good eye for horseflesh. He shrugged. "Actually they are cousins, if horses can be said to be related in such a way."

"You are so fortunate to own these wondrous creatures."

"We own them, dearest." He was pleased that he and his wife would share his love of horses.

"I am beyond thrilled." Her voice sounded stronger than ever. "I should love to observe him training."

"You will tomorrow, my dear."

"Oh, I do hope he can win the triple crown!"

So she was well informed enough to understand that if Transcendent won one more of the prestigious meetings, he would achieve a rarified triple crown. It was a feat that Thunderstruck had previously achieved. "As do I, dearest. As do I."

All the way back to the house she chatted enthusiastically about his stallions. It was the easiest conversation had ever come to them since they had married. No one observing them would suspect this woman was dying.

The very thought made him melancholy.

When they returned to the house, Mrs. Borden had assembled an array of sturdy Tudor furnishings from the attic. "With help from Jeremy and Nathan, we've gotten them all cleaned up," she told them proudly. "A bit of new fabric, and they'll be as good as something from a fine London cabinetmaker."

He watched his wife as she eyed them. "I think they're magnificent!" She faced him, her fair brow lifted in query. "What think you, my dearest?"

Hearing himself addressed as her dearest melted something deep inside of him. "I think that chair," he said, pointing to the one with the highest back, "looks like a throne. I wonder if Henry VIII sat there? You know, do you not, that he visited Margrove?"

Her mouth gaped open, even though she still looked utterly feminine. He supposed it was because of her frail appearance. "I did not! That is exceedingly exciting."

She stood back some distance from the chair and looked. "You know, dearest, it does look like a throne chair! We shall have to call it the Henry VIII chair. What a splendid conversation piece it will make."

Then she addressed the housekeeper. "What do you think about getting it covered in paisley tapestry?"

"That sounds wonderful to me, my lady."

"Lady Seaton thinks red should be the dominant colour in the drawing room," Seaton said.

"I'm afraid I lack her ladyship's vision, but I'm exceedingly fond of red." Mrs. Borden's face brightened. "And I know of an excellent upholsterer."

"Capital!" his wife said. All signs of ill health had disappeared.

For the next two hours she directed the footmen as they changed the furniture in the drawing room. First, they stacked up a sizeable number of French pieces to put in the attics, then she told them where to place the Tudor pieces—frequently shaking her head and mumbling that a certain placement would not do. "I think that lower-standing sideboard would be handsome at the back of the sofa," she suggested. "What do you think, dearest?"

"I am incapable of making decision until I see it there."

After it was moved, Seaton was astonished at how well it did look running along behind the sofa. Where in the devil did she get such ideas? There was nothing at Rosings that in any way resembled the room she was putting together. And putting together with uncommon good taste, he thought. It was a talent he certainly lacked, but he had a discerning enough eye to realize that she excelled at this.

Toward the end of the second hour, she gracefully lowered herself onto the sofa—one of only a few pieces of furniture that had not been moved or changed out.

He was exceedingly proud of her, both the way she was making Margrove better and in the way her health had so dramatically improved. How curious it was that away from her mother, she was much stronger.

Once the servants had settled things to her approval and he and she were alone in the drawing room, he came to sit beside her and took her hand in his. "Thank you. I do believe this room will indeed be a showplace once my wife gets the new draperies and chair fabric. I could not be more proud."

Her pale blue eyes danced. "I am not accustomed to receiving compliments."

"You have earned them." A moment later he said, "You do realize a vast change has come over you?" He eyed her somberly.

Her mouth formed a perfect oval. "I . . . I am no longer terribly sickly, am I?"

"I will own, you appear normal. Except for the stair climbing. And your feeble appetite."

"I promise at dinner tonight I shall try to eat even more than I had at our picnic."

He directed a mock glare at her. "Under no circumstances would I say you ate well at today's picnic."

Her lashes—much longer than he had earlier realized—lowered. "For me, it was a great deal. You must not expect miracles, Charles."

He lifted her hand and kissed the back of her glove. "I believe in miracles. You've shown me they are possible."

* * *

At dinner that night, she ate a bit more than she had that afternoon. Which meant she had one bite of mutton, two bites of buttered lobster, three spoonfuls of lentil soup, and half a bite of plum pudding.

The following day, she made an effort to increase her food intake in small increments over what she had eaten the day before. In addition, she began seeing to ordering new draperies for all of Margrove and sent for the upholsterer and painters.

When afternoon came, she and he drove in his curricle to the paddock to watch the trainer and jockey working with Transcendent. Since it was much cooler than it had been the day before, he had insisted she don a warm woolen pelisse, and when they sat in the curricle watching Transcendent, he pulled her close to him and kept his arm around her slender shoulders.

"Have you ever ridden him?" she asked whimsically, peering up into his eyes.

"Any number of times."

"I wonder if I'll ever be able to?"

"Do you ride?"

"I haven't in years. When I was very young, I had lessons. Mama said the only reason she consented to them was because it was what my father would have wished, but she eventually came to believe that I was not strong enough to ride."

"If your improved health continues, I promise you a ride next week. Provided I can be beside you."

A nervous look crossed her face. "I shouldn't expect to go fast."

"I wouldn't permit you to go fast." He found himself fancying the role of proctor. How curious. He felt toward her much as he did toward his younger sisters. But decidedly different. He had never pulled his sisters to him like this, with his arm around them. Very curious indeed.

"Perhaps you should ride Transcendent, and I'll ride Thunderstruck."

A smug expression crossed his face. "My wife is no fool. You realize Thunderstruck has mellowed considerably since being put to pasture seven years ago."

"For me, mellow is good!" Like her entire countenance, her voice too had become more lively. What a pity she had not gotten away from that overbearing mother of hers years earlier.

The wind grew stronger, and he was fearful of a setback in her health. "Why do we not return to the house? I daresay there's an army of footmen awaiting her ladyship's instructions. What other rooms does my lady wish to rearrange?"

"The library beckons to me. It's such a magnificent chamber, but it has been sadly neglected."

He nodded. "In addition to the faded draperies, I should think you also object to the French pieces my grandfather chose for that chamber."

"You are coming to know me well, Charles. But you must own, the room begs to be done in Tudor style."

"Of course it does. After all, it was built in Tudor times and must originally have been furnished so."

"Would it not be wonderful if the original furnishings are still in the attics?"

He began to share her enthusiasm for the project. "I pray the footmen won't come to hate the new countess. You are, after all, responsible for all those back-breaking trips up and down three flights of stairs carrying exceedingly heavy furniture."

"At least the heaviest furnishings are coming

downstairs whilst the lightest go up. You said yourself, coming down is much easier than going up."

* * *

The following day the linen draper came with a vast array of samples for Anne to peruse. There were brightly coloured silks from China, brocades and Damasks from Arabia, subdued velvets from France. A lifetime of indulgent birthdays was no match for this excitement. She spent almost all the day with them, going from chamber to chamber, agonizing over selections, and writing down notes to help herself remember these selections for the painter was coming on the following day, as was the upholsterer.

When the man left at nightfall, she realized she had stood for most of the day. And she was no worse for the exertion. But she was exceedingly tired.

She went to her husband's library, where he was catching up on writing letters to his various siblings, and she collapsed on the faded velvet sofa before the fire. He stopped what he was doing and came to sit beside her. "You look tired," said he.

"I am. It was a wonderfully exhausting day."

"I should have monitored you more closely, insisted that you force yourself to rest."

She vigorously shook her head. "I shouldn't have listened to you for I was terribly excited over it all. You have never in your life seen so many beautiful fabrics. It was so difficult not to select all of them!"

He rolled his eyes. "I am gratified you spared me from choices I am ashamed to say I would have found tediously dull."

She giggled.

He was not sure, but he thought it the first time he had heard his wife giggle. When she did so, she sounded like a girl. Like one of his young sisters. While being vastly different than a sister.

"If you cannot share my interest in redecorating *our* home, we can at least share our passion for thoroughbreds."

His eyes danced as he watched her sitting so close to him, her gaze fixed on the fire in the hearth. What a feeling of contentment had come over him. He no long relished the bachelor life. How comforting it was to be wed to someone with whom you shared everything. Especially a future, he thought, feeling his chest tighten.

"First, my lovely wife, while I may not share your enthusiasm for decorating, I very much appreciate the changes you are and will continue to make at *our* home. And secondly, I could not be happier that I've married a woman who shares my passion for thoroughbreds."

Dare he hope they would have a future together? Was it possible she was *not* dying? The very notion was cause for rejoicing, but that he could not do. His wife had never been told she was dying, and he had resolved to never tell her.

When they had first come here, he had not been aware of her as a living, breathing, *desirable* woman. With her improved health, all that was changing at an alarming rate. His head bent, and he went to taste her lips.

$\mathcal{C}$hapter 5

He would wager that she had never before been kissed, but nothing about the way she responded to their kiss bespoke a maidenly inexperience. Mutual goals, shared interests, and—he had come to realize—a true affection tied them to one another. Still, he must be mindful that she was in very delicate health.

When he pulled back, he settled an arm about her, coaxing her head to nuzzle into his chest as he continued to stroke her hair and drop the occasional kiss upon her crown. He started to chat about other things, the upcoming Derby, the paint colors she was considering, inquiring about her well-being.

Once they were summoned to dinner, he eyed her skeptically. "Promise me you'll eat better tonight?"

Her eyes full of tenderness, she nodded.

* * *

The next morning as his wife was busy with the painters, he made the trek up to the attics, candle in hand, and began to forage amongst the old furnishings there. There was a lot more than furnishings. Propped against walls were portraits in varying conditions. He paused, hoping there would be information on the backs of the paintings to identify earlier members of the St. John family.

Few of them bore such information. On one painting, which had darkened with many decades of dust, he could barely discern a scrawl that said, "my grandmother, Lady St. Bain." Hmmm. He wasn't aware of being related to the St. Bains. He studied the old portrait and from his limited knowledge of women's fashions, he put the portrait to Elizabethan times. No wonder he did not remember about such a family connection.

A more recent stack of portraits he could identify. His parents had indulged in the practice of exchanging portraits with those with whom they were on friendly terms. He recalled the time Gainsborough had painted his mother—that fine portrait still hung over the chimneypiece in the dinner room—and his Mama had subsequently paid a lesser painter to make a dozen copies of it to give out to family members and other special people.

He flipped through these newer portraits and recognized a handful of men with whom his father had served in Parliament, a German ambassador, and some women whom he could not name. He looked on the backs of these and was pleased to find his mother's familiar hand, labeling each of them.

It seemed such a waste for them to be stuck off in an attic and never be seen, but none of them meant anything to him. Perhaps he should attempt to return them to their families.

He stood back up and, forced to stoop, began to pick his way amongst old portmanteaus in these lower-roofed areas.

Then he found what he had come for. His lips curved into a smile. He could not wait to show it to Anne.

* * *

The rooms most decidedly needed painting. She was anxious to see them all cleaned with new fabrics and pretty colours upon the walls. But when the painter asked if anyone in her family suffered from asthma, she had to own that she did.

"Oh, my lady, you mustn't be at Margrove whilst my workers are painting," said the painter. "'Tis most damaging on the lungs. The lovely thing is, though, that I gives you me word you won't 'av to be out of the house more than a fortnight. We'll get right in and out, and my new colours are noted for drying fast—provided the climate isn't excessively damp."

She sat, frozen for a moment while the impact of what he said sank in. Leave Margrove? She had never known such happiness as she had experienced since coming here. Were it up to her, she would never leave this haven.

Two weeks could pass quickly. She understood that. But she also understood that the main reason why she'd known such happiness here had been because here her husband gave her his exclusive attention.

That would not be the case if they went to London. He would be sure to see his other friends. He might even choose to sit in the House of Lords while they were in the Capital. He would go to his club. She was terrified she would never see him.

All the strides they had made would be wiped out.

"I shall not be able to set a date at this time, Mr. Pennington," said she, her mouth a grim line. "I shall have to pick a time when it is satisfactory to my husband."

She disliked the idea of even bringing up the subject. When it came to Charles St. John, the Earl of Seaton, she wished to keep him to herself. For always.

The door to the drawing room, where she was making plans with the painter, burst open and Charles strolled into the chamber. Seeing that she was occupied, he stood silently behind the sofa where she sat.

The painter bowed to Lord Seaton. "I was just telling her ladyship that ye will have to find other lodgings for just two weeks whilst we paint these rooms. I must tell yer lordship that your wife has a very fine eye for colour. Some of the shades she selected are the very ones the Regent 'imself selected for Carlton House."

She had not realized Mr. Pennington was a painter to the Royal Family! *Oh, how completely thrilled Mama will be when she finds out!*

Her husband, too, seemed suitably impressed.

"If you will give me your direction again, Mr. Pennington," she said, "I shall notify you when to come to paint the chambers here at Margrove."

Once he left, she spun around to face her husband, a broad smile upon her face. "Tell me what has you so excited."

"How did you know?"

She shrugged. "Because I am your wife. We have been married for four days." It sounded so perfectly natural. And it was true. She was coming to read every expression on his face as she had once come to know every page in her favorite children's book.

"Come, I want to show you something." He led her along the broad wooden corridor. At the back of it, he came to a stop, his gaze boring into a splendid old table. Or was it a desk?

She began to circle it, quite certain it dated to the Tudor period and impressed over its excellent condition. "You found this in the attic?"

Unable to suppress a self-satisfied smile, he nodded.

What she at first thought to be a small banqueting table she now realized was a desk because it had drawers with carved wood pulls. Its thick legs appeared to be hand chiseled with some very fine carvings upon them. "It must be original to your library!"

He nodded again. "I must show you what I found at the back of one of the drawers." He held out his hand, slowly opened his fingers, and revealed a small, tarnished piece of metal.

She moved closer, then her eyes alighted. "It's your ancestor's sealing stamp!"

"Not just any ancestor. Because I've seen some of his old letters, I recognize this as being Sir Horace St. John's."

"Have you not mentioned that name to me before?"

"You are possessed of a remarkable memory. Sir Horace is the knight who is credited with building Margrove."

"So this is likely his desk—the original!"

"I believe it is."

"When does Margrove date to?"

"About 1530. That's when the oldest section of Margrove was built."

She launched herself into his arms. "What a wonderful find! Who located it?"

"I did, actually."

She separated from him. "Do not tell me the lord of the manor went hunting in attics!"

"I did, and I found it most interesting."

"Thank you. I am vastly grateful. Do you not agree that it will look very fine in your library?"

"*Our* library."

She favored him with a smile. "Allow me to look at Sir Horace's stamp."

He handed it to her, and she studied it for a moment, attempting to determine what it was. "I declare, it's a fox."

He nodded. "If you'll look at our family's coat of arms, you'll be able to spot a fox."

As she stood there facing this man she had married, it occurred to her she was now a St. John. If she and Charles would ever be blessed with children, they would be the next generation in a long line of St. Johns, dating all the way back to Sir Horace St. John.

Such thoughts caused her insides to feel like the contents of a bog.

It was those very same thoughts and her determined resolve that aided her that night at dinner when she ate twice as much as she had eaten the previous night. She must show Charles that she was getting well.

She wanted him to stop thinking of her as a sickly child and treat her as a wife.

Toward the end of dinner, his face went grim as he turned to speak to her. "I've been thinking of what Pennington said."

It took her a moment to realize Pennington was the painter's name. She hiked a brow in query.

"I think the two weeks you need to be removed during the painting will give us an opportunity to go up to London. I should like you to see our box at Drury Lane—and, of course, Seaton House on Cavendish Square. I fear it is sadly in need of your ladyship's care and ministrations."

As much as she fancied being needed and would adore decorating their home, she was terrified of going to London. It was not that large cities frightened her; quite the contrary. She had always looked upon her infrequent trips to London as happy times.

In the past. Before she married. Now, her happiest times ever had been these past few days at Margrove Manor. Had she her way, she would never leave Margrove. Had she her way, no one would ever intrude upon this special haven she and her husband had created here. Had she her way, she and her husband would never be separated.

"I don't want to leave Margrove," she finally said. It was one of the only times in her five and twenty years she had ever exerted her opinion, and she had done so most forcefully.

"Believe me when I say I do not either. But I left things in rather a muddle once your moth—" He stopped.

It was clear neither he nor Mama wanted her to know what precisely had precipitated this marriage. "The fact is, my dear wife, I have rather urgent matters to attend to in London. I promise they won't take long. We can be back at Margrove in a fortnight."

"I detest sounding selfish, but I know when we get there, I will be forsaken whilst you go off to your club or other things from which I shall be excluded, and I know almost no one in London."

He moved closer to her and took her hand in his. "I give you my word I will not leave you in order to go to my club. Later, when we are not newlyweds, I will probably return to my club, but not this trip. This trip is so I can introduce my bride to what Society there is left in London. And also, I should like you to meet my sister, Susan."

"Your married sister?"

He nodded. "She lives nearly around the corner from us."

"I should like to meet her," she said softly. Once again she had slunk back to the meek, complaisant woman he had married.

"Shall we leave in the morning?"

"I'll send a note around to Mr. Pennington."

$\mathcal{C}$hapter 6

A soft rain fell on their carriage as they rode to London. Charles had insisted she cover up well with the rug because a chill hung in the air. She would have preferred sitting beside him, but he was so preoccupied with his reading that he almost completely ignored her.

At first she had been shocked that someone could actually read in a carriage without becoming dreadfully sick. Neither she nor her mother could, but her husband appeared to suffer no ill effects.

"What are you reading?" asked she.

His dark lashes lifted, and he closed the newspaper. "I have neglected everything—save my wife—since we wed; now, I must brush up on what's been going on in the government since I left town."

"I have learned that about you."

His brows lowered. "Learned what?"

"That you are very proud. You would never like anyone to think you not well informed on all matters pertaining to Parliament." She laughed. "Now, it's an entirely different situation with matters of fashion."

He chuckled at her comment, then eyed her with concern. "How are you feeling? Are you too cold?"

"I am very good."

* * *

For several minutes he sat there facing his wife, building the courage to make his revelation to her and fearing he would completely alienate his wife once he did. He drew in a breath and moved to sit beside her.

"Forgive me if I offend," he started, "but I think your mother unpardonably selfish. Can you not see that it suited her peculiar fancy to think you an invalid and to treat you accordingly, when you are possessed of perfectly normal good health?"

Her eyes rounded. "How can you say such!"

"I'm not saying that she lied. In her perverted way, I believe she coddled you so thoroughly that she came to believe your infirmity was as real as the de Bourgh diamonds."

He drew her hand into his and squeezed, his voice gentling. "You did exhibit symptoms of one gravely ill—as would anyone who had not been permitted to undertake everyday activities for so long. I know of no one who can be deprived of life's movements for a length of time who does not suffer the ill effects of limited activity. But this limitation improves with use until full health is restored."

His heart pounded as he awaited a response. Was she going to be furious with him? Would she deny that her health was normal? Would she defend her annoying mother? Curiously, she did nothing—absolutely nothing but stare at him with hooded eyes.

And then tears seeped from the corners of those incredibly pale blue eyes. "I don't know if I should be happy or sad."

"Be happy, love. Revel in being alive, in enjoying good health."

"It's just that I cannot believe that nothing is wrong with me."

"Right now, you're still very weak. It will take time for a complete restoration of your health. I expect that when your mother comes at Christmas, she will be stunned with your recovery. And she will rejoice."

"I know she loves me."

"I know that too."

Then his wife began to sob. He pulled her to his chest and enclosed her in his embrace, allowing her to cry to her heart's content.

After a good long while the sobs were replaced with whimpers. "I th-th-thought quite p-p-p-possibly I was dying."

He stroked her hair and pressed kisses upon the top of her head. "I did too, love. Your recovery has made me uncommonly happy."

She swiped at her face, then he proffered a handkerchief to blot her tears. "I want to believe you, but it's so difficult. For nearly all my life I've been an invalid. I know of no other existence."

"Just think of the strides you've made in just five days."

"It is not just the more southern climate, is it?"

He shook his head.

While she was in the mode to convey personal feelings, she had one more declaration. "I hated to leave Margrove. I've never been happier than I was there."

"I'm happy to hear that. I vow to make your stay in the Capital enjoyable. I'll take you to the theatre and driving in Hyde Park and perhaps we'll visit the Jerseys on Berkeley Square to commemorate the place where we first saw one another."

She gave him a feeble smile.

"And. . . I assure you, Seaton House is in dire need of your touch."

"You must tell me all about Seaton House," she said brightly.

* * *

A few hours later her husband was showing her around Seaton House. It was narrower than many of the other fine homes on the square, but it offered a fourth floor, which the others lacked.

He terminated the tour in her bedchamber, a lovely room done in floral chintz. "My sister made her home here last week, in this very room, actually," he said, chuckling. "It so happens her house on Curzon Street was being painted!"

Once he had shown her the countess's adjacent sitting room, he faced her and clasped her upper arms. "I know you won't like this, but I will have to leave for a short while. I promised I wouldn't leave you alone. My sister will be here soon to welcome you to the family." His lips brushed across her forehead.

She sank onto the slender chair in front of her bedchamber's desk. As disappointed as she was over him leaving, she was grateful for a few moments to privately consider her husband's stunning revelation.

Could it be that most of her life had been a lie? That there was nothing wrong with her? As she sat there, feeling not a single detriment to her physical well-being, she came to believe her husband must know of what he spoke.

Her thoughts turned to her mother. She understood how abrasive her mother could be. She had even witnessed her mother's authoritarian demeanor with her husband, who outranked Mama considerably. But surely her mother would not so perpetrate such an unfortunate situation for her only child! She knew Mama loved her, knew she was likely the only person on earth whom Mama did truly love.

Then why? The longer Anne sat there thinking about it, the more convinced she became that her husband must be right! Mama had been so excessively overprotective that she had made Anne an invalid. Then Mama truly believed Anne was gravely ill.

As she sat there, she idly opened a drawer on the gilded desk. A sheet of foolscap lay there, and she could tell it was an unfinished letter. Because it was personal correspondence, she knew she should not read it and went to close the drawer.

That's when she saw her mother's name. Curiosity won. The letter addressed to their sister Mary must have been started when Susan was staying at Seaton House last week. As Anne read it, her stomach dropped. The well-being of a minute ago instantly vanished.

Poor Seaton, despite that he's always been in love with Lady Harriett Lynnington, has agreed to wed the dying heiress daughter of Lady Catherine de Bourgh. It is hoped that once our brother has sacrificed himself on the altar of dowries for his sisters, next year, he may finally be able to marry Lady Harriett. Pray, Mary, do not tell anyone of Seaton's arrangement. He specifically asked me not to say anything to anyone. He would not even tell Lady Harriett.

I am dying! A sickness ten times worse than anything she had ever experienced gripped every cell in her body. Her body shook violently, and the tears poured forth like a waterfall.

Then it suddenly occurred to her that when Lord Seaton had consented to wed her, he *had* believed she was dying. Mama must have told him so. Is that what Fortescue had told her mother? Was that idiot physician's visit the precursor to Mama's decision to see Anne nobly wed before they laid her in the ground?

Who to believe? Despite her humiliation and anger at him, she thought perhaps her husband had come to realize that she was not dying after all.

Now the poor man was being prevented from marrying the woman of his heart because he was entrapped in this marriage with a perfectly healthy woman!

Poor Seaton was right! Because he had believed her alarmist mother, he had agreed to wed a woman with whom he was not in love. Now that plain woman was not dying at all. Poor *Seaton.*

There was a knock upon her chamber door. "Lady Susan Madison is calling upon Lady Seaton."

Anne sniffed and walked to the door, cracking it open. "It grieves me to not be able to meet Lady Susan, but I've become suddenly very ill." Lest Lady Susan fear that Anne was about to expire, in which case she would feel bound to summon her brother, Anne added, "I believe it's something I ate."

"I shall convey that information, my lady."

She threw herself on her bed for a good weep. How could the happiest day in her life now be followed by what was doubtless the worst day? Just as she was beginning to believe she and

Charles were making a success of this marriage, her fears that he loved Lady Harriett were confirmed.

To his credit, were it not for him, she likely would have died long before she ever reached thirty. And despite that her present good health would deprive him of eventually marrying the woman he truly loved, he had been genuinely concerned over her well-being.

He was a good man who did not deserve to be forced into marriage with someone as plain as she. Was there anything she could do to secure his happiness?

She thought she knew of something.

The immature woman who had left her mother's home last week was as vanished as the long days of summer. Now Anne was confident she could stand up to her tyrannical mother. She would insist that Lord Seaton—who had staunchly kept his part of the bargain—receive her fortune. She would also inform her mother—who placed a great deal of importance in what those in the *ton* thought—that she was prepared to risk Society's censure in order to allow Lord Seaton to divorce her so that he could marry Lady Harriett.

Such a thought sent a gush of fresh tears. How fortunate Lady Harriett was.

She sat up, dried her tears, and sent for carriage.

Minutes later, the carriage was waiting for Lady Seaton, who was still dressed in her traveling clothes.

Propped up on her husband's desk was the fragment letter his sister had penned, along with Anne's farewell note:

Thank you for releasing me of the bonds which have gripped me for too long. Had I known under what circumstances you wed me, I should have never accepted you, imprisoning you and depriving you of your true love. I will see to it that my mother honors her bargain with you.

Anne

For the past two weeks she had practiced writing her name as Lady Seaton, and now that she had the opportunity to pen a letter, she realized she would never use that title again.

* * *

"Where is my wife?" Seaton asked when he arrived back at the house.

"She has taken the carriage, my lord."

He was surprised. He had expected to come home and find Anne and his sister chattering away. Where could she have gone? He knew his sister's habits. She would have come in her own coach; were the ladies to go somewhere together, there would have been no need to call for Anne's carriage.

Shrugging, he began to mount the stairs. In his bedchamber, he saw the papers propped up against the oil lamp and smiled. Anne must have left him a note.

He strolled across the carpet to read it, and when he did, his heartbeat thundered. He could wring his sister's lovely neck!

As he stood there holding Anne's letter in his trembling hand, he felt as if his dearest friend had just died. Emotions such as he had never experienced stampeded through him.

He rushed down the stairs. "How long ago did

my wife leave?"

The butler shrugged. "About an hour ago, my lord."

"Send around for my horse at once!"

Minutes later, he was atop one of his most fleet stallions. He knew he could make up some time simply because he could leave the environs of London far more quickly than a cumbersome coach and four could navigate the crowded streets of the Capital.

There was no clue in her letter as to what direction she was headed, but he felt with certainty she would return to Rosings.

The soft mist that had continued all through the day soon turned to pounding rain. God, why had he not brought oilskins? But he could not go back. He meant to intercept her before she reached her mother.

Within ten minutes of leaving Cavendish Square, he was soaked as thoroughly as one who'd leaped into a lake fully clothed. His physical misery—which was very great, to be sure—was not nearly as miserable as his inner well-being—which was more painful than anything he'd ever known.

His teeth chattered. His hands trembled from the cold. It seemed even his very bones had turned to ice. Had he not uncharacteristically worn a hat, he would have been blinded by the sheets of rain which kept falling.

As slow as he was being forced to go, he knew the coach, too, had to have been impeded by the foul weather.

Even though the roads were muddy, he started to make more progress once London was behind him. How he longed for a warm bath. A warm room. Dry clothing. But most of all, he longed for Anne.

As his mount raced onward, he thought he saw the Seaton coach. Had his grievously miserable self conjured her? His heartbeat soaring, he spurred the horse forward. It *was* the Seaton coach! Riding like the wind, he came abreast of his very own coachmen and signaled for him to stop.

Seaton dismounted, and as he did he saw that his wife parted the coach's velvet curtains and stared at him. Those blue eyes he had come to love widened as he opened the carriage door. "Will you allow me to enter?"

She nodded solemnly.

He sat across from her and began to divest himself of his wet greatcoat.

Then she began to sob, even as she threw off her own rug and attempted to place it over him.

"Pray, Anne. Why do you weep?"

"You will take lung fever and die, and I shall be the cause of your death." Now she wailed.

Hang it! Even if he was so soaked, he moved to her side of the carriage. "It would not be your fault, love. And I assure you, I am accustomed to a little rain."

"But this is m-m-more than a little rain." She left off, wailing.

"I shouldn't want to live if I could not be wed to you. Can you not see that I want us to . . . well, to be like other married couples."

Her brows lowered. "You mean like in love?"

He swallowed. "Please, give me a chance to show you how very much I care about you. Give me a chance to try to earn your love."

Now she sobbed even harder.

He wanted to put his arm around her, but he couldn't get her all wet. So he reached out to stroke her soft hair. "What it is it, love?"

She hitched her breath. "I do love you! I believe I fell in love with you the first time ever I saw you at Lady Jersey's."

Hang it all! He did not care if he did get her wet! He hauled her into his arms and kissed her thoroughly.

"And I love you," said he after the kiss. Then he tapped at the carriage roof.

The coachman came to ask for instructions.

"Back to London." Seaton turned to his wife. "I, too, have never been happier than I have with you this past week."

Her slender hand came to cup his face and she peered at him with adoration in her eyes. "When. . . when did you know you loved me?"

He frowned. "I knew for certain when I read your letter today. I knew I could never be happy with any other woman." He lifted her hands and pressed kisses upon them. "I had actually come to realize I'd found the perfect wife the day I discovered our shared passion for thoroughbreds."

She giggled. "That's not a very romantic thing to say."

"Then permit me to say that my ardor for you is greater than my ardor for Transcendent."

She giggled again. "Oh, Charles, that is, indeed, romantic."

He hauled her into his arms, confident that even were she to get wet, she was not going to expire. Their marriage had transformed each of them. For that, he owed a very great debt to Lady Catherine de Bourgh.

The End

Author's Biography

A former journalist and English teacher, Cheryl Bolen sold her first book to Harlequin Historical in 1997. That book, *A Duke Deceived*, was a finalist for the Holt Medallion for Best First Book, and it netted her the title Notable New Author. Since then she has published more than 20 books with Kensington/Zebra, Love Inspired Historical and was Montlake launch author for Kindle Serials. As an independent author, she has broken into the top 5 on the *New York Times* and top 20 on the *USA Today* best-seller lists.

Her 2005 book *One Golden Ring* won the Holt Medallion for Best Historical, and her 2011 gothic historical *My Lord Wicked* was awarded Best Historical in the International Digital Awards, the same year one of her Christmas novellas was chosen as Best Historical Novella by Hearts Through History. Her books have been finalists for other awards, including the Daphne du Maurier, and have been translated into eight languages.

She invites readers to www.CherylBolen.com, or her blog, www.cherylsregencyramblings.wordpress.co or Facebook at https://www.facebook.com/pages/Cheryl-Bolen-Books/146842652076424.

Printed in Great Britain
by Amazon